VIRAGO
CRIME CLASSICS
425

Gladys Mitchell

Gladys Mitchell was born in Cowley, Oxfordshire in 1901. In her first novel, *Speedy Death* (1929), she introduced the now infamous Mrs Bradley to the crime-readers of Britain. Mrs Bradley, later Dame Beatrice, would appear in a further thirty novels by Gladys Mitchell. In addition to the Bradley adventures, she wrote under the pseudonyms Stephen Hockaby and Malcolm Torrie between 1930 and 1950. She taught English and History until 1961, was a prominent member of the Detection Club and wrote several children's books. In 1976, she was awarded the Crime Writers' Association Silver Dagger Award. She died in 1983.

Virago Crime Classics

A Death in the Life
The Hours Before Dawn
The Rising of the Moon
Sheep's Clothing

THE RISING OF THE MOON

———

Gladys Mitchell

To

MIZPAH GILBERT, F.L.A.

"Excellent accomplisht Lady . . . Pardon my presumption,
lend patience to my prolixitie, and if any thing in all please,
thinke it was compiled to please you.'
A Dedication—THOMAS·NASH

A *Virago* Book

Published by Virago Press 1996

First published by Michael Joseph Ltd. 1945

Copyright © Gladys Mitchell 1945

The moral right of the author has been asserted

All rights reserved. No part of this publication may be
reproduced, stored in a retrieval system, or transmitted in any
form or by any means, without the prior permission in writing
of the publisher, nor be otherwise circulated in any form of
binding or cover other than that in which it is published and
without a similar condition including this condition being
imposed on the subsequent purchaser.

A CIP catalogue record for this book is available
from the British Library

ISBN 1 86049 074 3

Printed and bound in Great Britain by
Clays Ltd, St Ives plc

Virago
A Division of
Little, Brown and Company (UK)
Brettenham House
Lancaster Place
London WC2E 7EN

CONTENTS

★

" For God's sake, Mrs. Pocock, what do you with this Rubbish ? "

FRANCIS BLANDY

" . . . find out moonshine, find out moonshine ! "

SHAKESPEARE

" But would anyone murder a man without any other occasion than only for the delight he takes in murdering ? It is not credible."

SAINT AUGUSTINE

CHAPTER ONE

The Antique Shop

WE WERE dressed as we wished to be dressed. Keith wore his bathing costume, a pair of linen shorts and his Wellington boots. I had my riding breeches on, and a pair of grey cycling stockings. I wore a short jacket with military, button-over pockets, a pair of leather gauntlets that flared to my elbows, and I carried a lanyard on my belt and a knife in a sheath on my hip.

It was the beginning of the Easter holiday. Keith was too cold to be comfortable in his garb, and I was too warm in mine, but he had a jacket over his arm, and socks on, inside the Wellingtons, and, as for me, at the age of thirteen I would have sweated myself to the bone rather than discard the smallest item of a costume which so well expressed my feeling for romance and my conviction that I was, in the highest sense, a man of destiny.

We were, as usual at that time of year, by the river. In summer, unless we were at the seaside, we went to my aunt's house in the country and took our bicycles; but we were not encouraged to cycle whilst the days were still comparatively short, as there had been difficulties about our arriving home long after lighting-up time. So, at Easter, our excursions were usually made on foot.

Sometimes we explored the south bank of the river, but often we remained on our own north side and lurked at the bottom of Ferry Lane or paddled at the end of the slipway between the gasworks and the police station. Sometimes, when the tide was out, we could get across from the slipway to Osier Island, which lay out in the stream about fifteen yards from the bank. On this particular day Keith wanted to cross to the island, but I was not in favour of this, as I was not dressed for wading. Even if I took off my stockings there seemed no way to avoid getting mud on my riding breeches, and to this I was averse, although I would have plastered my Sunday suit without a thought.

The high street ran parallel with the river, and a dozen alleys led from the road to the docks and the riverside.   Some of them bent to meet others, but for the most part, once past the small, old houses, the stables, the mills, the repair shops, the smithies, or whatever there was tucked away behind the stream of traffic which congested the narrowest bottle-neck out of London, the intrepid explorer found himself on the river front past which sailed the barges drawn by tugs on their way between London and the docks of our little artery of a town.

Further to the west the high street crossed the canal, and here more alleys and a complication of riverside houses which made a town inside our town, and whose inhabitants seemed to have nothing to do with the rest of the population, offered a wide and exciting field for the explorer where the high street, the river and the canal cut off a long narrow triangle of land which once had been virgin swamp and now was called Old England.

It had been said in our hearing at home that strangers, even the townspeople, were not welcome in this quarter, and that those who left the high street at night to traverse this lost settlement did so at the risk of their lives.   There was a legend that one, Moses Arundell, had been stoned to death on the Leys, which was the part of Old England nearest to the high street, but, although we went down there but seldom, the place was always quiet enough, and the inhabitants seemed self-contained, but neither dour nor belligerent.

The fact that remained significant, however, was that Old England, its alleys, its towing path, its locks, its little houses with their high door-sills to keep out the flood tides, its rough dogs, its village of disused barges and ancient decrepit hoppers, was a place apart from all the rest of our town, a place like a foreign country, having its own fascination and danger, its own code of laws and behaviour, even its own strange *patois* of oaths, exclamations and prayers.

Keith soon gave in about the island.   He was far less selfish than I, although, when he was set on a purpose, far more obstinate.   On this occasion he did not care much whether or not we visited the island.   There were other things to do, and he was willing to do them.

So, having climbed the steep little hill and reached the high street, we walked down Ferry Lane, at the end of which Julius Cæsar was said to have landed troops on his first encounters with the Britons. We attempted, unsuccessfully, to persuade the ferryman to give us a free trip across the river and back. Then we walked along the high street to a little junk shop in which there were sometimes displayed such weapons as daggers, swords and old horse-pistols. It was a favourite playground of ours, for the woman who kept it (and disliked and distrusted children as a rule) had no objection to our going into the shop and handling everything which happened to take our fancy.

She was a very queer old lady, tall and Amazonian as Meg Merriles, and one of her peculiarities was always to wear a hat. We never saw her without this rusty and antique headgear, and she had an air of great dignity and distinction.

There was a rumour that she had once been the proprietress of a small travelling circus, but her own conversation, which included anecdotes of her past, gave no colour whatever to this tale.

She addressed us with old-fashioned courtesy, myself always as Mr. Innes, or Mr. Simon Innes, or Mr. Simon, and my brother as Mr. Keith, and in these nominatives there was never the faintest flavour of irony or patronage. She confided to me once that she could not bear girls, but that young men were always assured of her favour and goodwill.

" Girls, Mr. Innes," she pronounced, " are hussies and will-o'-the-wisps. Trust them less than the serpent that bites the dust, or the adder sunning itself on the open heath. Their appearance is deceptive; their beauty a snare. ' Earthlier happy is the rose distilled.' Aye, Mr. Innes, without doubt; but what of the distiller ? Tell me that."

I could not answer her. Distillers, to me, meant gentlemen whose names appeared upon wine and spirit merchants' vans. As there were not fewer than forty public houses in our town, there were plenty of such vans to be seen. I changed the subject to her own stock-in-trade, which always fascinated us, but she returned to her theme time and again. Girls were wicked and worthless; Eve was the temptress who betrayed mankind. Their looks, their clothes, their voices—everything, in fact, which made girls, to my mind, the fascinating if slightly terrifying creatures that they are—came under her ban, and us she liked because, she said, we loved those things which were of good report. I think she referred to her antiques.

Keith's speciality was guns and pieces of armour; my choice was swords. I longed to own one, but feared to ask the price, lest our friend, who was such an oddity, should ask something less than the true value, and something which she guessed was within our reach. However, there was nothing to prevent my disengaging all her swords from their sheaths and lovingly and reverently weighting them in my hand. I must have spent hours in admiring the chasing on the hilts and what I believed to be the runes along the blades. My chief pleasure, however, was in running my thumb along the edges and in dreaming of how I would polish the blades if the swords belonged to me. I thought of the duels in which I should engage had I been born to the sword in one of the duelling periods. There was nothing I did not know at that time, although I have forgotten it since, of the etiquette of fighting to the death.

When we reached the shop, which was on our way home, our friend, Mrs. Cockerton, was standing in her doorway. One story she had told us was that she had been the wife of a writer, but he had left no money when he died, and she had never learned to do anything by which she could earn her living, so she had sold some of the contents of what must have been a beautiful home, and had taken the rest and set up a shop in south-east London as a dealer in antiques. Some of her things were rare and genuine, but she knew, I imagine, too little about the business ever to make it a success. She had sunk, as time went on, to this little shop in this old, low-ceilinged house in our little, dirty, old town, and always said that she would have to be content to end her days with us. How soon that end would come we did not know. She seemed to us incredibly, fantastically old. Actually I think she must have been sixty to sixty-five. She made five shillings a week by subletting the back of her premises, including the shed and the yard, to a rag and bone man. He paid the rent regularly, which was surprising, and was friendly with the police, whom he went out of his way to truckle to and oblige.

We had a special interest in the matter of Mrs. Cockerton's

death, for one day, when it was raining, she had told us that she would leave each of us a present in her will.

We did not believe that she meant it.   She had her own form of humour, as we knew.   But it was interesting to speculate upon the probable nature of the presents, and to try to work out how long it would be before (if we were to get them) they would be ours.   In fact, we looked forward to the day of her death with a lively anticipation, which was intellectual rather than ghoulish in its origins, and yet we dreaded the day, for, as Keith pointed out on more than one occasion—for, with us, repetition, as with savages, was held to strengthen a case—we could hardly expect that the next tenant of the shop would allow us the same free run of it, and the shop itself might be sold to a trader in more mundane, fleshly merchandise.

" It will do away with one of our bases," said Keith.   " It is a great advantage to be able to come here when we like.   We do not come all that often, but, except on early closing day—oh, and, of course, on Sundays and Bank Holidays, when, in any case, we have to go out with the rest—it makes a pretty good hide-out."

I fingered the swords and said nothing.   The guns did not mean to him what the swords could mean to me.   They interested him as weapons, and as examples of the inventiveness of mankind, but they were not the stuff of life and its poetry.

Upstairs was a large front room overlooking the street.   In this place were collected the less saleable portions of the junk, but to our minds this room held matter of such variety and interest that when we had done downstairs, where the shop was neat and not overstocked, considering the kind of merchandise it held, we went up to nourish our imagination and sense of wonder, and spent an hour or two in hunting for buried treasure.

There were chests and cabinets big enough to hide in, and cumbrous books which we always hoped would prove to contain a hidden will, or a spell for raising the devil, or even—glorious thought—both.   There were all kinds of brass trays and vessels, old pictures (worthless from our point of view, for none was in colour and the subjects were either dull or depressingly religious), pieces of furniture neither old enough to be called (even by their owner) antique, nor new enough to be serviceable—most of the

chairs had lost either seats or back, and wash-hand stands were
already out of fashion—and such oddments as velvet-covered
boxes encrusted with shells, moth-eaten mantelpiece covers, glass
paperweights, plates wired to hang upon walls, candle-snuffers
and candlesticks, fire-irons, castors for the legs of beds, bits of
linoleum, stained and ragged rugs, small fireguards, a clothes-
horse, a rusty pickaxe, antimacassars, an old-fashioned, very
much discoloured bed-pan, fern-pots and a *commode*, and various
bits and pieces we neither knew the use of nor could name.

We never tired of playing in this room, and, although we knew
everything in it, we never failed to hope that one day we should
stumble upon something new to us, and preferably something of
value. I think our friend the proprietress hoped this, too, for
she would nod her head, which was always covered by the old
black hat which she tied beneath her chin with a scarf, and
remark, when she came up from time to time to have a chat
with us, that she herself did not know exactly what she had in
the house. Then she sometimes would throw out delicious hints
that she suspected she might have something of very great value,
and said that if we came across anything fresh we were to let her
know at once, and she would give us ten per cent. of the purchase
price for our trouble when she had sold it.

We had not much idea of the value of any of her things. She
told me once that she had had thirty shillings for a sword with a
damascened blade, and that if she could come upon another of
similar pattern she would ask four pounds for it. She also
mentioned a witch-ball which she said her mother had had, and
which, after her mother's death, had never more been found.

" It must be somewhere," she declared. " I could get ten
pounds for such a thing if only I could find it. But, there, I don't
know whether I'd sell it or not, Mr. Innes. There's such a thing
as *Kismet*. One must take care."

We begged her to describe the witch-ball to us, for even Keith,
who was not good at computations, knew that ten per cent. of
ten pounds is one pound, and, as our weekly pocket money was
sixpence, a pound seemed to us a sum of such fabulous pro-
portions that we doubted whether our brother Jack, in whose
house we had lived since the death of both our parents, could
earn much more in a week. As our sixpences were usually

mortgaged at the sweet shop from one week to the next, so that we were chronically in debt and should have been, by Dickensian standards, in a state of misery from one year's end to another, we have very little idea of the value of money. A pound, we fancied, would set us up for life—or, at least, so much of life as would cover the remainder of our childhood and bring us to the threshold of the hateful period of responsibility and dullness which we associated with becoming grown-up.

On this particular Thursday in Holy Week we met, however, the same reward for our labour as theretofore—nothing at all.

" Never mind," said Keith, when we had bidden Mrs. Cockerton good-bye and were on our way home. " To-morrow's Good Friday, anyway, and there will be the buns in the morning, and, if we can crawl in under the flap, the circus in the afternoon. There's always something to look forward to."

" I'm not so sure about the circus," I replied. " Isn't Good Friday rather more so than a Sunday ? "

" Only to Catholics and the Church of England," said Keith with comforting assurance. " We don't have to bother. We're Wesleyans."

I was not as confident about the religious aspect as he was, but the circus only came to us once a year. We had watched the procession that morning. It sometimes came to our town on the Friday before Whitsun, but we had never had it as early in the year as Easter. The day of the procession was also the day for putting up the big marquee. The circus people backed the caravans and the animals' cages into position around the marquee in Mr. Taylor's field, and, late in the afternoon, set up the little booth—much like a Punch and Judy stage—at which people paid their money to see the show.

We went home at half-past four. June, our sister-in-law, was at home with Tom, her three-year-old son, but neither Jack nor Christina, our lodger, had come in from work.

" You can have tea if you like to get it," said June. " Otherwise you'll have to wait for the others."

We weighed up the respective merits of eating and laziness, and decided that we would rather eat; so I got out the loaf and some butter, Keith took down the mugs we used when we had meals on our own, and spread the cloth, and then, with books propped against the mugs which we half-filled with cold water from the tap and then filled up with milk (for we were never allowed to make tea for ourselves, and did not care for it much), we were soon deeply sunk in the twin delights of wolfing our food and our literature, the feast resulting often in mental but never in physical indigestion, otherwise June would not have allowed it. She hated us to be ill.

" If you'd waited," said June, " I was going to fry some fish."

" Hungry," said Keith. " Couldn't wait." This was true as far as it went. There was also the question of spare time. We had not done nearly enough, we felt, to justify the first day of what was, except for its shortness, the finest holiday of the year.

" Just finish my chapter," I said hastily to Keith when the bread and butter I had cut had all disappeared, and he looked up for a moment from his book.

" Right," said he; for the finishing of a chapter was sacred even to our elders, and we never cheated them over it, even if to have done so would have meant staying up longer at bed-time.

I finished my chapter, and, putting the plates together, carried them out to the sink. Keith pushed the mugs towards one another, and said good-bye to June, and we went out quietly before she could suggest that we set the tea for the others. There was seldom time in our day for any refinements. Left to ourselves, we would have used our mugs and plates all over again, and would never have spread a tablecloth—to our minds an abomination which exercised a spell of its own to get things spilt on it.

" The circus," said Keith. " And the sooner the better. The light's not too good as it is." These were superfluous remarks. We both knew whither we were bound. We had to work out the lie of the land for the morrow, and it had to be worked out in daylight.

" We couldn't have gone any earlier," I said. " The marquee wasn't up this afternoon."

CHAPTER TWO

The Rising of the Moon

MR. TAYLOR's field was west of our house and slightly north of it, out on the Manor Road. It was fenced with thick wooden railings on the side which faced the road, was divided from Mr. Hopkinson's house by a high brick wall of mellowed red and yellow, and on the extreme west sloped down to our little River Bregant, which flowed into the Wyden on the south side of the high street.

It was a very large field, and the circus always hired it, sometimes for a night, or a day and a night, sometimes for a full Bank Holiday week-end.

As we had never had the circus upon a Good Friday before, I had not been compelled to make a visit to it a matter of conscience, but as we walked up our road past the baths and the library, and then turned into Manor Road, I began to be seriously troubled. The dishonesty of our practice in crawling in under the tent-flap never bothered me. If I had had to produce an argument in defence of it, I should have said that our keen appreciation of the wonders disclosed to us as a result of our questionable behaviour was in itself the justification of our action. But there was never any argument about it. Those of our contemporaries who got in by the same means could scarcely question our methods; those who did not were envious of our courage and resourcefulness but never set themselves up as critics of our morals. Our elders, forgetful, possibly, of their own youth, seemed not to fathom the depths of our depravity, and those among them who wished to see the show, and who had paid for admission, were content, and even pleased, to allow us to wriggle to the front row, there to squat on the edge of the seat between their knees or kneel on their piled-up overcoats and peer up over the rail that divided us and them from the magic of the sawdust ring. Our town was so small that most people knew us, and we them, and the general feeling was one of indulgence towards the children of the place, no matter what the social standing of the parents. Thus, at the circus, it was into our shrinking but delighted faces that the clown would thrust his own. It was our black but romantic hearts which burned with holy love when the equestrienne blew kisses, or stood on one foot on her galloping Arab steed.

But this particular evening of Holy Thursday was not the appointed time for these more than human joys. It was merely the time when we took stock of the position, made plans for the capture of the citadel next day, and visited the cages of the animals and watched the circus people having their evening meal.

Our depositions made, we dismissed them from our minds and began to prowl round the cages of the beasts. Numbers of the townspeople were similarly amusing themselves, and the deep wheel-tracks at the gate, which had begun as three-inch ruts in the early afternoon, now resembled a quagmire, and muddied us to the ankles. The animals, bored and listless, either stared at us with their golden eyes and twitched their tails in half-unconscious resentment of our proximity, or took no notice of us.

The elephants, tethered to stout pegs hammered by a mallet into the deep, damp turf of Mr. Taylor's field, appeared to be oblivious of us until we looked at their wicked, intelligent little eyes. One, by whom I stood, lifted his foot and stamped it down within six inches of my shoe. I drew back hastily, and the onlookers laughed. Ashamed, I stepped forward again. The elephant, swinging his trunk as though to some far-off music, took no further notice. He was not one to repeat his effects, having intellectual ideas of amusement.

" Come on," said Keith. " Let's go and see the sea-lions."

" We can't. There's a blind down in front of their cage. Let's go and see the chimpanzees instead."

" Too much of a crowd. We can see them better in the show. What about the tiger ? "

" Somebody told me it's only a boy in the skin."

" Well, let's go and see if we can prove it."

" You couldn't prove it. He stays at the back of the cage. Bob Cammond poked at him with a stick last year, and he didn't even growl."

" Well, I expect he *is* a boy, then. Anyway, let's go and see. We needn't go home just yet."

" We mustn't be long. Besides, I believe there are bloaters."

The evening was drawing in. The circus people had already lighted one or two lanterns, and one of the caravans had a fire in an iron bucket standing at the bottom of the steps. At the gate of the field stood two red lamps, similar to those used to mark a hole in the road at night, and a good many of the sightseers were beginning to leave. We had seen and greeted several of our school friends, but the crowd was already thinning. As the elder brother, I was again wondering whether we, also, ought not to be on our way.

However, it would not take long, I reflected, to see the tiger, and we walked round the backs of the cages to where the listless creature lay near the wall of his den.

Only one other person was there—a seedy-looking man with a cloth cap pulled almost on to his nose, a yellowish cigarette hanging from the corner of his mouth, and his hands in the pockets of his overcoat.

This overcoat was long, and the frayed hem almost touched his heels. To our eyes he had a sinister, unpleasant appearance. He took no notice of us, and the three of us stood in silence looking at the tiger, and the tiger, with his great head dropped on his paws, seemed not to know that we were there.

He was a moth-eaten-looking animal, not worth our attentive gaze, except that a tiger was, in itself, irrespective of its beauty, fierceness or pride, a rare and wonderful object romantically connected in our minds with jungle fastnesses, with the heat and cruelty of the wild. We attempted to attract his attention, but he remained entirely oblivious of our blandishments, compliments and insults, and seemed half asleep and unconcerned.

" Ah," said the man in the cap, " wonderful what they think of, them big cats. Murderers, every one of them. Bloody murderers."

He slouched away, his hands still deep in his pockets. Keith stared after him through the thickening haze of the evening.

" Funny sort of bloke. Coming home ? "

" He reminds me of Mrs. Cockerton's lodger, the rag and bone man," said I, also following the movements of the seedy, down-at-heel fellow."

"Can't think why she can't get a respectable lodger," said Keith.

"Most of the lodgers are factory girls. She doesn't like girls," said I.

June looked rather grim when we appeared. Jack said, eyeing our shoes:

"You can clean 'em yourselves in the morning." He usually cleaned all the shoes, including ours, because he said the rest of us cleaned shoes so badly.

"Have your supper and get off to bed," said June. "You'll have to be up at six to get the buns."

"What is it," I asked, "for supper?"

"You can have a bloater, if you promise to hurry up and eat it. That's what we're going to have."

"Christina as well?" I asked.

"I don't know whether she wants one. There's one for her if she does. She's gallivanting, as usual."

"Keep her a soft roe," said I, for I was in love with Christina. We all were, except, perhaps, June. Christina had the front room upstairs as a bed-sitting-room, but she had her meals in the kitchen along with the rest of us.

"She ought to be in," said Jack, with a glance at his watch. As he said it we heard her key in the door, and the next minute she had come in.

"Good evening," she said. Although we had known her for more than a year, she always said good evening when she came in, and good morning when she came downstairs.

"You're late," said Keith. "Time little girls were in bed."

She caught hold of him and pinched and tickled him. Keith yelped, and everyone but June and I began to laugh. June said, rather sharply:

"Don't play about, Keith. Have your supper and go to bed."

I said, "Don't be a fool, Keith," for I was jealous.

It did not take me long to eat my bloater, but Keith was slower, because he always dreaded the thought of swallowing bones. Christina let her own fish get cold and took his neatly to bits for him.   She spoilt him, and so she did me, but we were not, on the whole, in rivalry, for she used to treat me as though I were her own age, and the flattery of this usually had the effect of neutralizing any feeling of jealousy.

" There you are, boy," she said.   Jack had taken her plate and put it on the hob.   He took if off and gave it back to her. " Thank you," she said.   He cut her bread and butter in fingers, the way she liked it, and then put some more butter on the pieces.   June watched and did not look pleased.   I did not blame her, but I wished she were as young and lovely and charming as Christina.   It would have been better all round. I did not altogether dislike June, and I sometimes thought that Jack was offhand with her since Tom had been born, but Christina was adorable.   I thought so then, and I think so now.

Jack waited until all had finished eating before he lit his cigarette.   We learnt our manners from him.   When he had lighted a cigarette for June, too, and one for Christina, they all pushed their chairs back from the table and began to talk about the Easter week-end.   We listened in agony, fearful lest some outing was going to be planned which would mean that we should be unable to go to the circus.

As Jack and June seemed to have forgotten us, we stayed downstairs and listened.   Jack began the discussion by asking Christina what she proposed to do.   She was vague.   It did not seem as though she had made any plans.   She said she had been asked to walk along the river as far as Wellward and then come back on the steamer, but that she did not think she would do it because the steamer would be crowded.

" We ought to go to mother's," said June.   " We haven't been since January, and then the young ones did not go, and she likes to see them."

We had been left in charge of Christina when they had taken that January excursion.   It had been at the end of the Christmas holidays.   We had had the most carefree time.   Christina had taken us to the pantomime and even to the Zoo, a place we never visited in the winter.   She had treated us to the Aquarium, which we had not seen before, and to a proper sit-down lunch inside a building instead of the usual sandwiches and minerals on a seat in the grounds.   We privately thought she must have beggared herself that week-end, but she seemed able to pay for her room and board, as usual.

" I can't go to mother's at Easter. You know that perfectly well," said Jack. " But there's no reason why you shouldn't go, and take one of the kids for company."

Keith and I, who had slid on to the rug and were half-hidden by Jack's armchair, clutched hands in agony. We had never been in different houses, even for the whole of a day and night, and I felt I could not bear the thought of a week-end at home without him, for, without doubt, he was the companion June would choose. Everyone liked him better than me, and no wonder.

" And you can't have Keith, at that," Jack went on firmly. " I want him for the potatoes to-morrow morning. You'd better take Sim. He moons and dreams instead of dropping them in."

We relaxed again. June would hardly take me to be her sole companion on a long and dismal journey across London and into Kent, with a two-mile walk at the other end during which we should most certainly quarrel.

Christina, after June and Jack had argued for a quarter of an hour, said that she was tired and would go to bed, so we were told to go, too.

We went up the stairs with Christina, our arms round her waist and all three of us squeezed together on the staircase, laughing and hardly able to breathe. We let her have the bathroom first, because it was more fun to go in and say good night to her than to have her come in and say it to us. We loved her room. It was fascinating to play about with her pots of stuff on the dressing-table, brush our hair with her silver-handled brushes, stroke her fur coat and look at her books and pictures.

She would not let us stay long that night. She said she was sleepy. I thought she looked tired and not too well, and tried to hold her in my arms longer than she usually let me. She laughed, and put me off, kissed Keith, and turned us both out.

" I say," said Keith, " just in case June *does* make me go with her to-morrow, let's go back to Mr. Taylor's field when Jack's in bed, and enlarge the hole in the marquee a bit to-night. It'll make it easier for you if you're on your own to-morrow."

" I shouldn't go without you."

" Of course you would ! " said he, in an angry whisper. " Why should both of us miss it ? That's merely silly. I shall want to know all about it. The way you tell things, that's almost as good as going. You *will* go, won't you, Sim ? "

" It seems such a rotten thing to do."

" No, it isn't. Come on. They won't be very long now, and the moon will be full."

We seldom broke out of the house at night, and had never done so so early in the year. In one respect we knew we should be lucky. June and Jack scarcely ever came in to look at us before they went to bed. It was one of the things I had missed most after the death of our parents, but I neither expected nor would have welcomed a kindly, tender, nocturnal visit from my brother and his wife. It would not have seemed the right thing. Christina sometimes came, but that was different.

The moon was already up, and the sky was clear of cloud. Without wasting any more time, we opened the window a little wider as soon as we had put on some clothes, crawled out on to the sill and dropped to the scullery roof. We could hear Jack and June still talking together in the kitchen, but it did not seem worth while to wait, as we did not know how long they would be. I peered downward. The rainwater butt had a cover we had often found useful. We climbed down the water-pipe which emptied the rain from the guttering into the butt, landed on the cover of the butt, and jumped down on to the grass.

There was an alley at the bottom of the garden to allow a back entrance to all the houses in our street. We were along this like cats in no time, and emerged, between Mrs. Bowden's garden and Mrs. Swinton's ill-kept, dirty backyard, on to the moonlit street. It was not yet turning-out time for the public houses. The street, except for ourselves, was deserted and silent. We had on our rubber-soled shoes, and broke into a noiseless trot which soon carried us past the Public Baths and the Library, and on to the Manor Road.

Unfortunately for our primary purpose, we discovered, when we came within earshot of the circus people in Mr. Taylor's field, that they had not retired for the night. There were no houses very near, and the men were laughing and talking and somebody was playing on a mouth-organ. There were lights, too—it was not war-time then—and the whole circus seemed to be up and about.

We drew back into the shadow of an elm-tree which grew just inside the fence and shaded the road.

" That's torn it," said Keith. " We can't risk hanging about until they go to bed. We might be here until midnight. I thought gipsies went to bed as soon as it was dark."

We listened. One or two of the circus people sounded excited and drunk, particularly one of the girls. She was talking in a high, excited voice, and repeated, over and over again:

" Don't you be so silly, don't you never ! It don't do to believe all you're told, 'specially not in a pub."

Then a man growled, " Stow it. Here's the boss."

" They aren't gipsies," I pointed out, continuing our own conversation, " and they're going to have trouble with that girl. We'd better not go back until Jack and June are asleep, and, if they're still arguing, that may not be just yet. Let's scout round, and see if the animals are asleep."

" Better not wake them up. We'd be caught for certain if we did."

" They're sure to be awake, I should think."

" All right. Let's go."

But the gate into the field was shut and secured with a padlock. There seemed to be no admittance for us that night. Keith, however, could be obstinate, and I was not usually daunted by immediate difficulties, so we hung about a bit waiting for inspiration.

" Let's climb the fence," he suggested.

" We might get impaled. That would be beastly. Remember Bobby Johnson last year. Besides, in this moonlight we'd be sure to be spotted, with those drunken people still awake. I'll tell you what we can do, if you're game for a walk."

" Round by the canal, you mean ? All right. And get into the circus ground from the back. I'm on. That's not a bad idea."

So, still on the road, we walked blamelessly northwards towards the little halt which served us as a railway station. We passed Mr. Viccary's farm and the fields where we trespassed for mushrooms, mounted the little hill which led up to the station entrance, and, on the other side of the bridge, climbed an easily-scaleable fence and dropped down into the allotments.

Half-way over, as the land sloped away to the river, a hawthorn hedge divided the allotments from a small wood through which ran tracks and paths made by trespassing children, for the land was private property.

We soon reached the river, which, in parts, became the canal, and all at once I began to feel horribly nervous. I set a quicker pace, and the way Keith followed close behind me convinced me that he, too, hardly relished the adventure.

The moonlight fell white on the grass of the open spaces, and in shafts of greenish yellow between the thin-leaved trees. The river gurgled and splashed, and every now and then it was as though furtive little creatures scurried between our feet among the grasses, or rustled in last year's dead leaves. From a distant farm a dog began to howl.

" Get a move on," said Keith. " We'll never get home at this rate."

" Do you want to get home ? " I asked, my own teeth beginning to chatter.

" Yes, I do," he answered. " It's a beastly night to be out."

I felt the same, and, without another word, I broke into a run. Keith stayed just at my heels, like a long-distance runner who intends to let his rival make the pace. But we were not in rivalry. We were merely two children, suddenly stricken with panic, running away from ourselves, and in no danger, so far as we knew, from man or ghost.

At last the path we were following came out into the open, and we dropped into a walk beside the stream. Leaning on a little bridge which carried the canal towing-path across the river from which the canal had been cut, we saw the silhouetted figure of a man. I went to ground like a shadow, and lay half under a bush, my head well down among the grasses so that the moonlight did not strike across my face and give me away. Keith fell flat beside me. We wriggled into the bush, and did not speak.

The man sat down on the iron coping of the bridge and drew something out of his pocket. The moonlight turned it to silver.

It gleamed like the belly of a fish as it leaps at the bottom of a waterfall.

"Knife," breathed Keith, in my ear. Somewhere the dog, or another one, howled again. The man thrust back the knife, and began to walk away. He walked along the towing-path in the direction of the town. We gave him a count of a hundred, and then we followed. We were no longer afraid. A burning curiosity possessed us. Much handling of the weapons in our friend's junk-shop had inured us to the sight of naked steel, and our reading-matter had stiffened our hearts against dread of cuts and wounds. The marquee and the circus forgotten, we became two bloodhounds on the trail of the man with the knife. Moonlight to me was always romantic and sinister. The murderous man fell within my conception of the night.

Disappointment was in store. Although the canal path was straight and the moonlight clear, we could not get a glimpse of the man. He must have left the towing-path almost at once. My fears in some measure returned. I disliked the idea of being leapt upon out of a hedge and disembowelled. There was neither romance nor adventure in such an end.

We never came out unarmed. We were probably nervous children, as children go. I had my sheath-knife in my hand. Keith had a knuckle-duster he had copied from one a policeman had shown him in the summer. Our rubber-soled shoes made almost no sound as we advanced. We began to dislike the towing-path more than a bit, but, not caring to admit to one another that we should be glad to leave it, our original purpose returned to our minds to relieve them.

"Next field, I think," said Keith. It was strange how unreal and unfamiliar things could look under the moon.

"Yes, next field," I agreed, not too certain that we were right. "I say, though, I'd forgotten Dead Man's Oak."

Keith had forgotten it, too. There it stood, a stark old tree not yet in leaf, on which, it was said, a highwayman had been hanged.

"Sometimes they call it Gospel Oak," said Keith. "It's a better name, somehow, I think."

"Yes, much better," I agreed. Gingerly we crawled through the hedge which divided the towing-path from the fields and, giving the tree a wide berth, began to mount the rise towards the thorn hedge which bordered the circus and Mr. Taylor's field.

Just as we gained the thorn hedge we heard the roaring of a lion and then the answering calls of the other creatures of the circus. In a moment the still night was as full of sound as a house where frozen pipes burst, and water seems to fall everywhere at once.

Keith, who was on the ground and about to crawl through the hedge, remained perfectly still. I knew that he was alarmed. As for me, my heart beat in my throat. I felt sick and afraid for no reason.

" It can't be *us*," said Keith. " Even wild animals couldn't have heard us all this way off. They must be three hundred yards away."

" We can't go on," said I. " That noise will have woken up everybody."

" They'll be lucky if the police don't nab them for letting the animals become a nuisance in the town, waking people up. No, we can't go that way. Our best plan might be the high street, I should imagine," he rejoined.

" Come on, quick," I said, " before anybody finds us here."

We ran back, stumbling over the uneven ground and the rough grass and the weeds. Even although we were safe by the time we had gained the towing-path, still we continued to run. From the church tower ahead, the clock chimed four times loudly and struck the hour. Eleven. We were much relieved that the sinister chimes of midnight did not boom out upon the stillness. We could no longer hear the roaring of the beasts, and the great black bulk of the church, seen south-eastwards in a slant across the canal, was reassuring.

We trotted on and gained the bridge. We climbed up the sloping path which led to the narrow pavement, crossed the bridge and hastened towards the market place. Here a narrow thoroughfare brought us up into the great square where the September fair was held, and where men used to practise their archery and hold the elections.

It took us less than ten minutes from here to get to our home.

We reconnoitred carefully before we re-entered the house. The coast was clear. We climbed up and scrambled in, and were soon in bed. My hands were very dirty. I rubbed them hard on my shorts before I undressed (for I had changed before I went out), and trusted that they would not soil the sheets nor my sweaty cheeks the pillows. We dared not go into the bathroom and turn on the taps.

I lay and listened to the night, but there was no sound. I dreamt about the man with the knife, a dreadful dream that I had to wake myself out of, and, even then, I had to keep myself awake for a time, for fear I should dream it again.

CHAPTER THREE

The Circus

JUNE LOST the argument, for neither Keith nor I was pressed into accompanying her on her duty pilgrimage to her mother's house in Kent. At the last minute she herself decided not to go, and sent a telegram.

We had been roused at six to go and get the hot cross buns. Usually we disliked getting up early, but on three days of the year we were always awake long before we were called. Those days were the going-away day of the summer holiday, Christmas Day, and Good Friday. On this particular Good Friday there were not only the buns but the visit to the circus, so that when June put her head in, and told us to get up and go to the baker's, we lost no time, and by twenty past six were in the shop.

The baker's was at the bottom of our road. We were friendly with Mrs. Banks, who kept it, and she usually had a smile, especially for Keith, but this morning she was different. She served us with the buns as though she had something on her mind, and was giving us twenty-two buns at eight for sixpence instead of the usual twenty-four.

" Two short, please, Mrs. Banks," said I. She jumped nearly out of her skin.

"God forbid, duckie!" she said; and then she seemed to recollect herself. "What was that you said, ducks?"

"I think you've only given us twenty-two," said Keith, who had also counted.

"Bless us, have I?" She took them all out of the big bags and counted them. "So I have now. Shows how *my* mind's working, don't it, just? There you are, ducks. Now mind how you go, and don't you hang about the streets."

"It isn't likely," I said. "Not with *these* to take home, Mrs. Banks." I paid her the one and sixpence, and we went home as quickly as we could, but Keith said, before we got half-way:

"I wonder what's up with her? Do you think the cat has had kittens again?"

"She wasn't *afraid* about that; she was only annoyed," I said, "because Winkie was supposed to be kept at home."

We enjoyed the buns, and then went out before we could be asked to wash up. We did not go near the circus tents and caravans, because we did not want to get known as we were going to crawl under the canvas that afternoon. We went in the opposite direction, through the Butts, and across the market-place, and beside the Magistrates' Courts, until we came to the high street.

We crossed the high street, ducked down Church Alley and came out on to the Leys. Here we met Fred and Arthur Bates.

"Heard about the Ripper?" asked Fred. "There won't be any circus this afternoon."

Up to that time it was the most terrible news I had ever heard, for we were too young to have been told outright about the deaths of our parents. We had found that news out gradually, and by putting two and two together; but this was a bolt from the blue.

"No circus?" said Keith. "You're rotting."

"No, that's right," said Arthur. "There's been an awful murder right in the circus ground, and the police are there. Been there since midnight, someone told me. Everybody knows, because Mr. Simkins was to leave some milk, and he couldn't leave it himself; the police had to take it in, and the clown and the lion tamer and the chief man have all been taken to prison, and the lady rider hasn't stopped screaming yet, because it's her sister what's been killed and all cut up in pieces, you can't hardly tell it's been a woman."

" I seen the blood," said Fred.

" He thinks he has," said Arthur, " and my mum says he isn't to be thwarted."

" But they *must* have the circus," said Keith.   " How do they get their living and pay Mr. Taylor for the field, if they don't have the circus when they come ? "

" *I* dunno," said Arthur.   " Come fishing for newts up the canal ? "

We had our own reasons for wanting to go along the towing-path to the scene of our night adventure, but we did not want company.

" No.   I want to see the body," said Keith.

" Garn !   You can't see the body.   They've took it away in a sack for the doctor to look at."

" Why ?   Mightn't it be dead after all ? "

" Oh, yes, it's dead.   It's all in bits, I tell you.   But the doctor can make out what it was done with, if he's careful and tries his best."

" *Done* with ? "

" *You* know—an axe, or a carving-knife, or a sharp-edged spade or a native weapon, or a—or a—what else is there ? "

" Kukri, kris, Japanese sword, Persian dagger, French rapier, dah, beri-beri——"

" That's a fever," said Arthur.   " Our teacher told us.   Well, anyway, the doctor can tell quite a lot from the remains."

" But where *are* the remains ? " asked Keith.   " At the doctor's house ? "

" Shouldn't think so.   I expect they're at the police station or the cottage hospital."

" Oh, I suppose so, yes.   Well, see you later."

We went on towards the confluence of the canal with the river, and the other two went back to the high street to cross the narrow bridge and get on to the towing-path.   We could have gone with them as far as the high street.   It would have been our quickest way back to Mr. Taylor's field, but we wanted to get away as soon as we could.   Arthur was all right, but Fred was both young and spoilt.   We did not want *him* hanging round. I often thought that Arthur had nearly as bad a time as a girl, having to look after Fred and not thwart him.

We crossed one of the mouths of our little river, as it ran beside the canal which had been cut from it, by means of narrow lock gates which were not used for boats but only to regulate the water. Then we had to cross two bridges. Once across these we ran up a narrow path between the two basins where there was a village of disused hoppers and barges, and came past the little public house called the *Brewery Tap* and into Catherine Wheel Yard. This alley led up to the high street, and very shortly we were on our way up the Half Acre to Mr. Taylor's field.

Sure enough, the show was packing up. The big marquee was already partly taken down, the other stuff was being packed, and a big waggon full of monkeys (which they usually sent on ahead as an advertisement) was being pulled out of the gateway by a team of piebald ponies.

There were several policemen about, keeping the gate and watching the packing-up, and there were people hanging round at the road's edge to see what could be seen. We could hear the lion roaring, and I said I supposed he had smelt the blood. We got near some of the groups of people to try to hear what they were saying, but I do not believe they knew much more than we did about the murder. Possibly, it occurred to me later, not nearly as much.

Keith drew me away, and we walked up the road towards the Manor House, Mr. Hopkinson's big place opposite where the canal and the river made one of their separations and formed a wide, long island in midstream.

" You don't think we ought to tell those policemen about the fellow with the knife ? " he said.

" I hardly think so," I answered. " For one thing, I want to get on his trail before we tell them anything, and find out where he gave us the slip last night, and, for another, we must wait for the detective."

" What detective ? "

" They always put a Scotland Yard man on to a case like this."

" Why can't Inspector Seabrook see to it ? "

" For one thing, I don't believe he's had a detective training; and, for another, it isn't a person in this town who has been murdered."

" But she was murdered *in* this town."

" I know, but I believe it makes a difference. Anyhow, let's get on the trail. We don't want to waste any time."

" Do you know," said Keith, as we broke into a jog-trot and began to ascend the long hill past Mr. Perry's field and Mr. Viccary's farm, towards the station, " I'm not at all sure this isn't better, in a way, than the circus. After all, the circus only lasts one afternoon, and it's an awful sweat to get in unless you pay. This murder might last us all the holidays."

He was usually philosophical, but this time I thought he might be right. Besides, it gave me some solid satisfaction to be on the right side of the law for once.

Our outing covered the same ground as we had traversed overnight, but nothing could have seemed more profoundly different. We had no time to lose, because we knew we had to be home by about eleven to help Jack plant the potatoes, but, even without that necessity for haste, I do not think we would have loitered.

We did not climb the allotment fence in daylight. Beyond the allotments, double gates gave on to a cart-road. The farm to which it led was off our beat, being well on the further side of the little river, and having neither fruit trees nor root-crops. We were trespassing the moment we got over the gates and on to the cart-road, but we had frequently been that way before, usually to bathe in the river, and sometimes had caught and ridden the horses which grazed in the meadow.

This time we stopped for nothing, but as soon as we had climbed the second gate we branched off through the scrubby bushes that grew round about some elm trees, ran down a slope on which hawthorn bushes grew, and found ourselves on a steep, good path which led beside the river.

We were soon across the bridge where the river joined the canal, and where we had seen the man, and then we went very slowly.

"'I don't see where he could have left the towing-path," said Keith, " unless he bogged his way through the pond."

Along by the side of the towing-path at the place where we had lost sight of the man with the knife was a long stretch of duckweed-covered water, very dirty and muddy, the home of all kinds of small water-creatures. It was not so much a pond as a long, wide, shallow ditch, for it covered a distance of more than sixty yards along the canal bank, and was not more than twenty feet wide. A low sparse hedge of hawthorn divided it from the towing-path, but there were gaps in the hedge, and, had it not been for the water, it would have been easy enough for the man to have left the path and struck up over the meadows to Mr. Taylor's field, which was divided from the lower fields nearer the canal by a wooden fence which a child of six could have climbed.

We satisfied ourselves that the man must have crossed the pond.

" You'd have thought we'd have heard him splashing," said Keith; but a worse thought occurred to me.

" Suppose he didn't cross the water, but heard us coming behind him and lay flat behind the little hawthorn hedge ? Do you think we'd have seen him ? "

Keith thought not, even by moonlight, particularly as we were not expecting to find him.

" I don't like the idea of that," he said. " It means we walked right past him, and, when we were gone, he went up to the circus and did the murder."

" He might just as easily have murdered *us*," I said; but Keith did not think so.

" Nobody ever murders boys," he said. I found. this a reassuring thought. Come to think of it, nobody ever did murder boys. I wondered, contemplating the dirty pond to see whether newts were stirring, whether boys were too valuable or too insignificant to be murdered, and could come to no conclusion, for Keith said, " Come on, Sim. Those beastly potatoes."

So we jog-trotted home. Jack kept us hard at it until half-past one, and then we had a good dinner of cold ham and hot vegetables, and my favourite treacle pudding, and Christina cheered us up still more by giving us our Easter eggs ready for Sunday morning, and then we were free for the rest of the day,

since even June could hardly expect us to wash up when we had
had to plant the potatoes.

We went straight up to Mr. Taylor's field to see whether the
circus had gone, and were just in time to see the main part of the
procession move off. The roundabouts and swing boats, which
the circus people always brought with them, had not even been
unpacked. The big marquee had gone, and so had some of the
caravans, but all the animals except the monkeys were there, and
we had a good view by climbing the railings and standing
balanced with our feet between the spikes at the top. Keith
got his feet stuck because he was wearing his sandals, which are
broader than ordinary shoes, and a man lifted him straight up
in the air to free him.

" And now you be off home," he said when we had thanked
him, " else the killer might cut your tails off."

" Please, sir," said Keith—although the man was only an
ordinary navvy, we thought—" have they found the murderer
yet ? "

" Not likely to. Nothing to go on," said the man.

" No clues, do you mean ? "

" Not unless somebody actually saw him do it. And those
circus people are funny sort of cusses. Not a word to say for
themselves. Likely as not a revenge job, and, if so, none of
them's likely to split, without it's a rival."

We could make nothing much of this, and decided to put it to
Christina when we could get her alone; not that we could, very
often; at least, not half often enough.

" Do the police know which way the fellow went when he'd
done the murder ? " I asked. The man tipped his cap from the
back of his head, scratched his head, looked at me, and said:

" Now what on earth made you ask that ? "

" I was wondering whether they'd found the weapon he
used."

" No, they haven't. But the doctor says it was a knife
like they use for cutting leather. Know the sort of thing I
mean ? "

" Oh, yes," we said; for Jack had one, and used to buy pieces
of leather from Mr. Grinstead, the cobbler, and mend the soles
of our shoes.

" I suppose there would be a reward, if anyone found it ? " said Keith. The man laughed and began to slouch away.

" You'd better find it and see," he said, over his shoulder.

" We shall meet that fellow again," said Keith, as we turned to run after the procession and catch it up before it got to the high street. " He's either the murderer or the detective, and, so far, I don't know which."

" What about hunting for the knife ? "

" Could do, when the police have cleared off from the field."

" Which way do *you* think he went ? "

" Don't know, but I bet you anything the knife is in the canal."

" If it is, we'll never find it."

We ran on, and caught up the procession. We looked at the faces of the men driving the waggons and the big traction engine which pulled along the train of heavy red and yellow vans which held the parts of the roundabouts and swing-boats, and at the faces of the women who sat beside them, and at the young boys and men dangling their legs over the dashboards and shafts, but you could tell nothing from their guarded gipsy eyes. One spat at us when we came too close. They looked sour and unfriendly, but that gave nothing away, because naturally they were angry and sulky at not being able to hold the circus and the fair. Some people said they had lost more than twenty pounds, and others said nearer two hundred. It all sounded a good deal to us. We made hardly any distinction between the two sums. Whichever it was, it was enough to make anyone sulky to think of having lost it.

We went with the circus as far as the bridge over the Wyden, and came home down Green Dragon Lane and the top of Clayponds. It was near enough to tea-time for us to decide to break our journey at the house and call in for something to eat.

" Hope Christina is at home," said Keith.

I hoped so, too, but we were disappointed. There was no one at home except June and little Tom. June cut us some bread and butter, stuck the jam-pot on the table, and told us we could make ourselves some cocoa if we liked. She was going out.

" You'll have to look after Tom," she said. " I'll be gone about an hour and a half. I'm going round to Mrs. Galloner's to see if she's going on all right after coming out of hospital."

"What on earth possessed us to come home?" said Keith disgustedly, when the front door had closed behind her. "We might have *known* she'd find us something beastly to do."

"Tom isn't beastly, and it's coming on to rain," said I. "Let's play trains with him. He likes that."

So we collected chairs from all over the house, and Tom was pleased. We made a good deal of noise, and Tom fell off once and bumped his head, and bellowed a bit, but we hoped the bump would not be noticeable. It was no good asking him to say nothing, because the last time we did that and he had promised, he had said straightway, as soon as June came home:

"Tom is a good boy. He promised not to say and he won't say."

Well, of course, she wanted to know what it was he had promised not to say, and boxed our ears and called us deceitful when she knew. We did not like her ways much, but Jack had said to me once that it was hard on her to keep house for so many, and I think both Keith and I felt sorry for her in a way. Jack went out without her far too often, we thought, and never took any share in helping to look after Tom. She was good to us, in her fashion, not loving, but, on the whole, fair. I think she was older than Jack. Somebody said she had caught him. I do not believe it. Jack could always do what he liked where women and girls were concerned. Since Christina had come we thought that sometimes he regretted his marriage.

"There's one other thing," said Keith, "although I don't know that it has any meaning."

"What?" said I, giving Tom a piece of chewing gum to keep him quiet. He was not really allowed to have it, so, of course, he loved it. We had trained him very carefully not to swallow it, so I am sure it could not have hurt him. We had taught him to make pennies with it when he had chewed all the flavour out, and he thought this was a necessary part of having chewing gum, and loved to press a coin on to the mess he took out of his mouth, and watch the pattern come. When he was tired of playing with the gum, Keith would take it away, and we would pretend to help him look for it. He would soon forget what we were supposed to be looking for, particularly when he got a little piece of cheese to eat. Cheese was another thing he was not allowed to have, but it never seemed to upset him. We had taught him to call it Cow, which was a word he could easily say, and one which conveyed nothing to June. She was rather a stupid woman, and did not understand Tom, and never would.

" What ? " I repeated, when Keith did not answer.

" Well," said he diffidently, " correct me if I'm wrong, but didn't you think once again of the remark that woman kept making when we were at the entrance to the circus ground last night ? "

" ' Don't you be so silly. Don't you never. It don't do to believe all you hear, 'specially not in a pub,' " I repeated slowly.

" That's it. Don't you think somebody had made a date with her, or something ? Or promised her something, to decoy her ? "

" We can't tell that. It's possible. Still, the other circus people will have told the police all there is to be told," said I.

Later on, we were not so certain that they had.

CHAPTER FOUR

The Death of a Tight-Rope Walker

CHRISTINA CAME in at six and took over Tom, but we found we did not want to go out again just then. June was gone longer than she had said, but not longer than we expected, for, short and sharp as she was with us and even with Jack, she dearly loved gossip with her women friends, although she never really took to Christina.

At half-past six Christina put Tom to bed. We helped her give him his bath. He enjoyed that, and so did we. Then we mopped up the kitchen while Christina took him upstairs, and at seven Jack came in, and he and Christina sat and talked.

They talked first about what sort of a day they had had, but the talk came round to the murder, as we had known it would, and we lay on our stomachs, half under the kitchen table, pretending to read our library books, and listened as hard as we could.

They had forgotten, I think, that we were there.

"Yes, it was a horrible business," said Jack. "Jack the Ripper all over again, so I'm told. Not much doubt it was a revenge job. You know what these circus people are. They've got the chap they think did it, a Portuguese fellow called Castries. It seems he was sweet on the girl, and another fellow was hanging round her, and got in the way, and looked like taking her from under Castries' nose, so he knifed her and carved his trade mark on her face after she was dead. Really a ghastly business. Sorry it had to happen here. She had been a pretty girl, they say, but you'd never have guessed it."

"Does he admit he did it?"

"Well, I was talking to Seabrook, who made the arrest, and it doesn't seem he admits it. In fact, Seabrook says that if you didn't know what liars and hypocrites some of these foreigners are, you'd think the fellow was really upset about the death and determined to find the murderer."

"You would have thought he'd have killed his rival, not the poor girl."

"That's what he said to Seabrook. Of course, as Seabrook admits, there's something in it, but these foreigners do such queer things. And he may have been afraid of the other fellow, of course."

"But wouldn't he have cause to be even more afraid of him, once he had murdered the girl?"

"Well, you or I might think so, of course, but I doubt whether these more hot-blooded people think ahead as far as that. Anyway, I'm glad they've got him. He's a scoundrel."

"I suppose it is certain he did it?"

"We can't tell that, of course, until we know more about it. But when I'd come away from Seabrook I happened to meet Crayton. The local paper is coming out big with it, of course. So I sounded him, thinking he'd have all the best of the news, and *he* said the evidence was presumptive and that so far he did not believe a single witness had come forward. Anyway, the inquest is bound to be adjourned after evidence of identification."

" They'd have to prove possession of the knife. It *was* a knife, wasn't it ? "

" Yes, it was. The kind a snob uses to cut leather. I've got one, as a matter of fact. I'll show it you, and then you'll know what to look for when you're taking your long walks, because the knife has not been traced. According to both Seabrook and Crayton, it can't be shown that Castries had anything but a pocket knife, but you know what these foreigners are ! Probably festooned with knives. I suppose he got rid of it in the canal or somewhere. Easy enough round here. I doubt whether they'll ever come across it, but that proves nothing."

" Aren't they bound to find something against him, apart from the fact that the girl may have been in love with someone else ? "

" I don't believe so. He's got a motive, you see, and, in a foreigner, as I say, a pretty strong one. These fellows will do anything when they're jealous."

" What time . . . ? "

" About half-past eleven, the doctor thinks. At least, so Crayton told me."

" Where does this Portuguese say he was when it happened ? "

" In bed. That's all he can say. It's all the majority could say for themselves at that time of night, I should think."

" Yes. Mightn't it be true ? "

" It might be, if he hadn't a motive for the murder, but, then, you see, he has."

" But that is the only thing they've got against him ? "

" It will probably be enough."

" It doesn't seem much to me. It seems to me that the rival would have almost as good a motive. Could he be certain that Castries wouldn't, in the end, cut him out, just as much as the other way round ? "

" Yes, perhaps, if he'd been another foreigner. But he happens to be English, you see."

" I call that rather prejudiced."

" Of course it's prejudiced. I'm an Englishman, too."

They both laughed, but Christina still said it was not good enough, and then Jack saw us and ordered us up to bed.

" But it's not our bedtime for another hour," said Keith. I

nudged him, and we put away our books and went up to Christina to say good night.

" You can take your books and keep the light on a bit," said Jack. He was just to us, on the whole, and often kind, but there is no denying he was hasty. Besides, I think he wondered what June would say if she knew that he and Christina had been discussing the murder with us there. She had brought us up to believe in fairies and storks and all that muck. Fortunately it had not done us much harm.

We went up to bed, but did not undress. We sprawled on the bed with our books, and, after a bit, Keith said:

" I wonder what she did in the circus ? "

" Let's go and ask Jack," I suggested.

" He'd only tell us to mind our own business, I expect."

" Let's try. I don't mind going. What can I pretend I've gone down for ? "

" Our Easter eggs. They're on the piano really, but you could pretend you thought you'd left yours in the kitchen. He can't say much about that; he knows Christina gave them to us. Be careful how you go in. They may be saying something you're not supposed to hear, and he won't like that."

" Should I knock on the door ? " I asked.

" Good heavens, no ! " said Keith. Although he is a year and ten months younger than I am, there have always been some things he has known better than I have. " Show a bit of gump."

" I'm sorry," I replied humbly. Here, it seemed, was another of those *gaffes* which I was always on the verge of committing. ' Born with two left feet,' Jack called it, and June said, ' Another brick.' Christina once said, " You'll never make a diplomat, Sim, and I think I'm glad of it." But it all came to the same thing, and I did not usually lose much sleep on account of it. It was no more a failing than being born cross-eyed, I thought. We knew a boy whose cross-eye had been turned straight at the hospital, so I did not worry about my lack of tact. I supposed it would right itself in time.

I nipped down, made plenty of clatter on the five steps which led down to the kitchen, and opened the door.

" What do *you* want ? " growled Jack.

" My Easter egg."

" On the piano, Sim," said Christina.

" Thanks," I said, and pretended to make off.   Then I turned back.   " Had a bet with a chap to-day," I said carelessly. " He said the girl who was murdered was the bare-back rider, and . . . she . . ."

" Bed ! " said Jack.

" I couldn't get it," I said, returning to Keith with the one egg which I'd gone in and got from the piano; but when Christina came up to bed she put her head round the door and whispered :

" She was the tight-rope walker, Sim.   Your brother told me so.   And the Portuguese is flush of money, and the dead girl, they think, had been robbed."

It was no wonder we liked her.   She was the nicest girl I had ever known.

" Here, Christina ! " I said.   " Come in a minute and talk to us.   We haven't seen you all day ! "

" That's not my fault," she said, laughing and coming in and shutting the door.   " I can't see in the dark.   Where are you ? "

" Here," I said; and pulled her down on to my bed, and put my arms round her.   She smelt good, and her hands were small and soft, not big and always half-covered with cuts and scratches and callouses, like mine.   She always seemed clean and fresh, and made me think of the cool bunches of bluebells that we used to gather in the woods beyond Dead Man's Island and bring home on the backs of our bicycles for her to put into jars.   I tried to pull her down to lie beside me, but she would not let me do that.   She had never known us as little boys, and it made a difference, I think.

Keith came over, then, and sat on the end of my bed, and cuddled her.   She put an arm round each of us, to keep us warm, she said, and we both put our arms round her because we loved her.   Keith said it, and she kissed him and laughed. Then she kissed me, too, and pushed my hair the wrong way, and said:

" Well, and what have you been doing with yourselves ? "

Before I could stop him, Keith was telling her everything.

" You're not making it up, Keith, are you ? " she said at the end.

" Not a word, cross my heart," said Keith.   " It all happened. We saw the man, and we saw the knife, and he disappeared along the towing-path, and that would have been about half an hour before the time of the murder.   We heard the animals roaring at him, too."

" How far away, when you saw the knife ? " she asked.   We worked it out.

" Twenty or thirty yards.   He was leaning on the coping of Dead Man's Bridge."

" Do you think you'd have seen a thing no bigger than a leather-knife at that distance ? "

" The moon shone on the blade and it glittered.   It couldn't have been anything but a knife."

" Well, I know you've got eyes like hawks, but . . ."

" Anyway, we lost him all right, along the canal," I said. " And we believe he may have crossed the ponds and got into the circus that way.   What was the woman doing out in the field at that time of night ?   Do you know ? "

Keith's eyes met mine.   We were both thinking of the drunken woman's remarks.   It seemed as though they had had no bearing on the matter, however, for Christina replied:

" Yes.   The girl she slept with said that she went out because she felt sick."

" And was she sick ? "

" I don't know."

" We could find that out.   They don't clean up sick in a field."

" Oh, darling, don't be horrid."

" It isn't," said Keith.   " Detectives investigate everything."

" You see, Christina," said I, " our point is this: if the murder was done by the chap they say, he wouldn't need to go snooping along by the canal bank, and get to Mr. Taylor's field in that roundabout way.   All he had to do, being on the spot, was to lie in wait for the woman and knife her as soon as she appeared."

" Yes," said Christina.   " I see that.   But you can't prove, you see, that the man with the knife was the murderer."

" We're pretty sure the girl had made a date to meet somebody, anyway," said I. "The tale about feeling sick was probably just a yarn." And I emphasized what the drunken girl had been shouting.

"It might have meant anything," said Christina.

"I know," I said. "But you do agree it looks fishy on the face of it, don't you?"

"It was certainly very near the time of the murder that you saw that man with the knife."

"And he was behaving suspiciously, I should say," said Keith.

"Well, why not tell the police? I'll come with you to the inspector, if you like. I know him pretty well."

We knew she did. He was only thirty-two, and a bachelor, and was the sort of man who might have been an officer in the Army.

It was agreed that the three of us would go to the police in the morning, and it was just as well that we were prepared for this, for the news next morning was terrible. There had been another murder in our town, and this time it was one of our own people; and this time it could not have been done by the Portuguese circus fellow, for he was in prison. Moreover, it was a murder of exactly the same pattern as the first. The whole town had the news, and June came in from her Saturday shopping with it. She seemed scared, and said she wished Jack were at home. I wished Christina were at home, too, but for a very different reason. The person who had been murdered was another girl. We knew her by sight. She was the barmaid at the *Pigeons*, down near the market. She was twenty-three, and rather a jolly sort of girl. Jack liked her. He liked almost everybody, and he often used to have his glass of beer there on a Saturday when he left work. It was on his way home, and he liked the fine old inn. It had been a coaching inn, and the girl was killed just outside the back door which led on to the cobbled yard.

There was a big open archway leading from the market into the yard, and it led to lock-up garages, where people could put their cars on market days if they did not want to park them in the yard. In the days of the coaches the garages had been stables, and there were still a couple of built-out windows on the first floor of the inn from which, it was said, the passengers on the top of the coach could receive refreshments without coming down, for some of the coaches only halted for a quarter of an hour or so, and then went on to Oxford.

At the back of the inn there was a very curious, round tower, rather like the keep of a castle; but there was a large sash window in it, and by the side of it, in a flat piece of brick wall, a door. Out of this door the barmaid had come to go home, for she was newly married, and did not sleep on the premises. Before she could get to the archway which led to the market square, she had been killed.

We gathered very little from June, but, as soon as we had the news, we went by way of the Butts to the market square, only to find the most enormous crowd of people, almost like fair-day, gathered about the entrance to the yard. The police were there, too, keeping sightseers back, and the inn itself was packed with men who wanted to hear what the landlord had to say. There were more than forty public houses in our town, but the *Pigeons* had most of the trade that day, although by about nine o'clock at night the people, Jack said, would be finishing up their drinks and going elsewhere.

It was the landlord who had been called by the potman to see the woman's body. He was thankful it had been he and not his missus, he said. She was having hysterics in the second floor front bedroom, as it was. The window was open at the top, and you could hear her making a noise like the whooping cough. She had been like that for hours, said the landlord proudly. She was always one to take things to heart.

We hung around to hear all that people were saying. Almost the whole town was there. We saw nearly everyone we knew, and everyone had something to say about the murder.

The best tale came from our friend Mrs. Cockerton at the little antique shop. She lived some distance away from the *Pigeons*, and that was why, she said, she patronized it. She thought it was more respectable to go a distance for her glass of port or sherry, rather than to visit one of the public houses near at hand. I could not then, and I cannot now, follow the line of her reasoning, but she said that, in better days, she had always kept port and sherry in the house, and had never dreamed that, later in life, she would be reduced to calling at the *Pigeons*, or anywhere else, for her dock glass at eightpence.

"And, even at that, it's an imposition, Mr. Innes, for it used to be threepence when I was a younger woman. Not that I ever bought it, of course, but it was always advertised outside. Ah, those were the days! There were none of these noisy, smelly buses in those times, but gallant coaches through from London to Oxford, with the post-horn blowing and the whip cracking, and the horses at a spanking gallop, noble beasts, and the best for everyone at the inns."

"But you didn't live here then, Mrs. Cockerton," I remarked.

"Not here, Mr. Innes. I lived out on the Shooters Hill road; but the coaches came by, through this old town, just the same."

"Did you ever see a highwayman, Mrs. Cockerton?" asked Keith. It was that which brought us to the murders.

"No, no, Mr. Keith. I was after the time of the highwaymen. But I did know of a murderer who used to lurk on the Heath."

"We've got one lurking here, it seems," I said. She looked at me sharply.

"Lurking? What makes you say that?"

"I thought it was your word, really. But surely it must be right. He *must* lurk, and then come out on these poor girls."

"It may not be the same man, Mr. Simon Innes."

"Oh, come, Mrs. Cockerton," said Keith, in the grown-up way that usually made her laugh. "They say the two murders were just exactly alike."

"Well, I think I *saw* something last night," said Mrs. Cockerton. "But, mind, not a word to a soul. I don't want police round here. It's not respectable."

"We're going to the police ourselves this afternoon, when Christina comes in from work," I said importantly.

"You *are?*" Mrs. Cockerton opened her eyes very wide. They were faded blue and yet looked dark, like cornflowers closing after the end of their flowering. "Story for story, Mr. Innes."

"Yours first," said Keith; and he sat on an old wooden chest

at the back of the shop to hear it. She had two more swords
that day. They had come in on Holy Thursday, after we had
gone home. One was really a bayonet, a heavy, gleaming thing,
with a Paris mark on the top of the blade near the hilt, and a
badly-rubbed sheath with a square ring to hitch on a belt. The
other was a light curved sabre. I could not place it. It was
less than twenty-three inches, sweetly balanced, a weapon for a
boy or a man, with a cutting edge sharp as a razor and a swing
and a grip good for horseman or foot, or, possibly, an imaginative
hunter of murderers.

" Be careful with that, Mr. Innes. I don't like it," Mrs.
Cockerton remarked, as, from a standing position, I drew it out
of the scabbard and swung it, whistling, through the air. " I
should call it a scimitar, young gentlemen. No Christian had
the forging of that steel. It is unholy, and of the Mohammedans,
Mr. Innes."

" I'd give my soul for it," I said.

She did surprise me then.

" Take it, and welcome, Mr. Innes. There is, I fear, something unlucky about it, although your young innocent heart will
come to no harm. I shall be glad to get it out of the shop, for
all that I gave six shillings for it in Camberwell."

" You'd bought it, then, before we came in on Thursday ? "

" Oh, yes, and a great deal besides." She saw Keith fingering
a horse-pistol, one of a pair. " Those do not match, Mr. Keith.
Never tell me. A bad bargain I made over those. You'd
better have one, and match your brother with his sword."

I was cutting the air with the scimitar. " Look at the curve
on the blade, and look at the leather wrist-strap ! This has been
used from horseback, or I'm a Dutchman ! " I cried.

" You might be worse, Mr. Simon. A courageous race,
obstinate, great-hearted and canny. None of that could be said
of the wretch I saw last night."

" Whom did you see, and where was he lurking ? " asked
Keith. " And are you really giving Sim that sabre ? "

" And you the horse-pistol ? Yes, Mr. Keith, I am. And as
for the story, such as it is, you shall hear it."

" You went to the *Pigeons*," said Keith, prompting her, " for
your glass of port or sherry."

" Port, Mr. Keith. The sherry they had opened was a rather inferior Amontillado. I prefer an Oloroso, and, in any case, I like a better wine. A profit of fifty per cent., Mr. Keith, on every bottle they sell. I cannot think why my good friend Inspector Seabrook allows such things to go on."

" So you had port," said Keith. " A dock glass ? "

" Yes, a dock glass, Mr. Keith. Not a lady's measure, but what would you ? A very choice ruby wine of the upper Douro; not a vintage wine; that one does not expect; but drinkable. Oh, yes, drinkable." She seemed to be tasting the port in retrospect, and we did not interrupt her musings. " So, then," she continued, briskly, " the clock chimed loudly. Ten o'clock. Time for me to be off. The moon was rising. It was all beautifully light. I stepped out into the market square and the moon shone full on the clock above the balcony. Ten minutes to ten. The *Pigeons'* clock, of course, was a little in advance. That is usual, and did not surprise me, but it was time I was on my way home."

" But what did you *see ?* " asked Keith. We seated ourselves on an old chest at the back of the shop, and gazed at her in the liveliest anticipation.

CHAPTER FIVE

The Death of a Barmaid

" I'M COMING to that," said Mrs. Cockerton. " You know my habits. I like a walk. It is dull in the shop all day with nobody to talk to and all these old things that have seen other days and other ways and would tell of them if they could, and on moonlight evenings I take my way along Manor Road, at times, for a breath of air; for it is all nonsense, gentlemen, to dread the night air as our grandparents used to do. The night air is as fresh and sweet, and often a great deal more holy, than any air met with by day.

" I left the *Pigeons*, as I say, at ten minutes to ten by the clock on the Magistrates' Courts, and made my way to the Manor Road by crossing the market-place and coming up by Doctor Thom's house at that old iron bar-gate which leads from the market to the Butts.

" As I came on to the wide square of the Butts the moon was beautiful. I could see it shining in the Bregant down by the Boatmen's Institute, and the spirit moved me to turn aside from my planned walk and take a turn by the water.

" Now, as you know, gentlemen, one cannot get along by the Bregant itself just there, but must cross the miller's bridge by the Boatmen's Institute and then, further on, the lock gates controlling the canal. All this I did, for the sake of the moon on the water, but when I reached the towing-path there was a knot of men gathered, and I scarcely liked to proceed, for there is considered something remarkable, I do not know why, about a woman who walks by night, and for her own pleasure, alone, without husband or lover.

" So I made to return by the way I had come, but then asked myself why I should follow the dictates of a popular prejudice rather than my own wishes, and so went on, to be called after by one of the rough fellows, but not unkindly, to the effect that I should look out for the Ripper along there.

" The idea this conjured up was so unpalatable, gentlemen, that nothing but obstinacy, engendered by the fact that I was born in better circumstances than those in which you find me, caused me to continue along the towing-path.

" You know the walk as well as I do. I was about to pass under the railway arch which carries the Great Western line across the canal, when I was aware of a person in the shadows and the horrid sound (in the circumstances) of a knife being sharpened on a stone.

" I make no excuses. I turned in my tracks and ran back towards the high street, imagining all the time I could hear footsteps behind me. The knot of men had dispersed, otherwise I would have flung myself on their protection. I did not dream of crossing the lock-gates and the footbridge on my return, but hurried up the slope of the road bridge and came out where the old chapel used to be, and so to the bustle of the high street, glad (for the first time, I think) to see street lamps as well as the moon, and to hear the noisy buses and grating trams instead of the little sounds of the flowing water."

"But you didn't see the murder?" demanded Keith, disappointed. "And you don't *know* that you saw and heard the murderer under the bridge?" He went on to tell her our story.

"It proves it," she said at the end. "He lurks along by the canal. The police should know, but I do not intend to be involved. Say nothing to them of what I have told you to-day unless they ask you about me. If they say I was seen along by the water last night, you have my answer, gentlemen, and I look to you to make it quite convincing."

"And when you passed the *Pigeons* on your way home last night, Mrs. Cockerton, what time was it then? Did you notice?" I enquired.

"Yes, I did notice," she said. "It was twenty-past ten. I had gone no distance, you see. The bar was still open. Plenty of people were about. Bessie, the girl who was murdered, would still have been serving, no doubt."

Well, that was her story, and that would have been the end of it but for Keith. He was turning over some odds and ends of junk in an old chest well in the darkest corner of the shop when he picked up a gleaming knife with the point stuck into a cork.

"Did you know you'd got this?" he asked.

"Good gracious alive! It's been lost for years," said Mrs. Cockerton, coming and taking it away. "That's my late husband's pruning knife, Mr. Keith. I wonder how on earth it got into that chest? I don't believe I've seen it since he died."

She took the knife and drew the cork off the point.

"It would make a jolly fine advertisement," said Keith, "but perhaps you'd hardly care to use it."

"Use it for what, Mr. Keith?" She put back the cork and rubbed her thumb over rust at the base of the haft.

"Why, to put on a bit of black velvet, or something sinister, right in the front of the window, and . . . you needn't even label it, you know."

"I don't understand in the least, sir."

" Well, it's awfully like the leather-knife, don't you think, that the Ripper is supposed to be using ? "

She went quite pale, and put her hand against a marble-topped washstand.

" To think of the ideas that go through boys' beautiful heads ! " she said, almost whispering the words. Then, seeing us look frightened, I suppose, she rallied herself, and even laughed.

" You'd best be off home to your dinner. To Saturday's early dinner. Sausage and mash, I wonder ? "

" No, it's stew, I think," said Keith, " and a lump of pease pudding. Do you like pease pudding, Mrs. Cockerton ? "

" Dearly," she answered. " It is, to make bold with a quotation, ' wholesome and filling, and cheap.' It is protein, my lords and gentlemen. Protein. Body-building. You were best to have a bit of paper to wrap up that sword and the pistol. You were better not to carry them naked and gleaming through the streets."

" Funny," said Keith, as we went home. " Did you notice she called the barmaid Bessie ? Her name was Ruby, wasn't it ? "

" I believe that's what Jack used to call her, but you can't go much on that."

" I wonder whether that really was the murderer by the railway bridge over the canal ? "

Our Saturday dinner was always at twelve, for Jack left the market at a quarter to, and came home on his bicycle by way of North Road and up Walnut Tree, and along Braemar. His market was not the one by the *Pigeons* in the old part of the town, but the fruit market, London way, just past the new bridge over the Wyden.

Christina left work at twelve, and it took her an hour to get home, so she had her lunch at an A.B.C. on Saturdays, and we rarely saw her much before two. Jack and June went out at a quarter to two, so the two of us washed, and put on our best suits, ready to go to the police station with Christina when she came home. She gave us a last look over when she arrived, got herself ready, and at three o'clock we set out. We went through Braemar Road and down Drum Lane to the police station, and

Christina took us in at the double gates by which the inspector's car went in and out, and knocked at the side door of the house.

The inspector had a very good flat above the station, and his old mother looked after him. The rooms were extremely large, the largest I had ever seen in any of the houses or flats in which people actually live, and the drawing-room was papered with life-sized parrots on great sprays of wild roses and poppies. Christina said this wallpaper gave her the horrors; the inspector said it gave him a change from his work, which was apt to be dull; his old mother said that the parrots were cheerful. Keith and I thought it the handsomest and most interesting wallpaper we had ever seen. As Keith said, there was nothing niggling about it. The inspector said he hoped not. There had certainly been nothing niggling about the price. It was a most expensive paper, but his old mother had fancied it, her sight being rather dim, and so that was that.

Christina knocked at the door, and old Mrs. Seabrook opened it. She asked us in, and said that Evan was out, but was expected back as there was a 'phone call coming through from Wallingford.

We had not been in the drawing-room long enough to count more than a fifth of the parrots when Inspector Seabrook came home, and had to take us down to his office so that he could take his call as soon as it came. He took us in by the back way, so that we did not need to go through the outer office or the Charge Room, and then he gave Christina an armchair and us small hard chairs, and asked what he could do.

"You can listen to a story that might mean something or nothing," said Christina. "It isn't my story. It's theirs."

"Fire away," said Mr. Seabrook, "and no lies, in which are included embroidery, exaggeration, loss of memory, the glossing over of sin, mental observations, and deviations from the normal, the withholding of salient facts for the sake of politeness, and all literary and historic allusions unless they have particular and peculiar bearing upon the matter in hand. Got it?"

"Yes, sir," I said; and thought: "You silly swine!" He was too much inclined to show off. As soon as I mentioned the time he began to make notes, and he did not interrupt once or

ask any questions, until I had finished my tale. This I thought
more intelligent than his wont.

" Now you," he said, nodding at Keith.

" Nothing to add, sir, thank you," Keith replied, " except
that we are accidentally in possession of coborra . . . corroborative
evidence, the source of which we are not at present at liberty to
disclose."

The inspector grinned.

" I'll accept that, *at present*," he said. So Keith, mentioning
no names, told him of Mrs. Cockerton, and of how she had
heard the knife being sharpened underneath the canal railway
bridge.

Inspector Seabrook listened with the close attention he had
given to our own story, made a note of the time, and then took
my name and address, although he knew them quite well.

" And now you know so much," he said, " I'm going to trust
you with more. But, mind . . ."

At this point his 'phone call came through and Sergeant Hobbs
took us back to the drawing-room, where old Mrs. Seabrook
gave us a piece of cake and got Christina to pick up a stitch in
her knitting because she herself could not see it very well.

" And I do hope, dear," she said, " that you won't go
walking alone while these nasty things are going on. It really
doesn't do."

Curiously enough, Inspector Seabrook said almost the same
thing when he came up. We had tea with the Seabrooks,
balancing very thin china cups and saucers on our knees, and
trying to eat cake without making crumbs on the carpet, and
when we were wondering when the inspector would keep his
promise and tell us a bit more about the murders, he said suddenly, when his mother went out of the room:

" You know, Christina, I wish I were your father or brother
or husband, to give you some advice."

" I'll try to take it, Evan," she said. He looked very pleased
at that.

" It's only this: don't walk about the town at night without
somebody with you. And let the somebody be a man,
if you please. We're up against something pretty bad, I'm
afraid."

" What do you mean ? "

" A monster. Probably a lunatic of the most dangerous kind . . . a mass murderer. I don't want to frighten you, of course . . ."

" But you *are* frightening me," she said. " Do you mean this isn't the end ? "

" We're afraid not. Scótland Yard are sending us a man, and I must say I shan't be sorry to have him turn up. You boys keep this under your hats, and, listen: don't go trying any private detective work, or any nonsense of that sort. You go indoors before dark, and stay indoors. Understand me ? "

We said we did, but we did not make any promises. What we wanted was not to waste time talking about our own safety, which did not interest us much, particularly now that Mrs. Cockerton had given us the horse-pistol and the scimitar, but to hear how the barmaid had met her death. We were comparatively fortunate.

" It appears, from what we have been able to deduce," said Mr. Seabrook, " that these two women, the circus girl and the barmaid, were not marked down in any way as victims. The murderer merely killed them because opportunity offered. The circus girl had no business to be out in the field at that time of night. The girls had all gone to bed early, to be ready for the late nights and hard work of the holiday week-end. She had sneaked out, it seems, to meet a man, although that was not stated at the beginning; we had to drag it out of the other people with whom she shared a caravan. Well, she met a man all right, although not the right one. The right one was this foreign chap that we pinched on suspicion and now shall have to let go."

" You don't think," said Christina, " that the second murder was premeditated, and was deliberately a replica of the first ? "

" No; and for a very good reason. The only people who knew the full details of the first murder were myself, Sergeant Hobbs, Constable Dewberry, Doctor Mains and this fellow we got our hooks on. There were some artistic embellishments and so forth. I can't go into details, and, in any case, I ought not. But you can take it from me that only the same hand could have reproduced quite so faithfully all the fancy work. No. We have one murderer, not two. It makes our task at once easier and more difficult. Easier because one man ought to be easier to find than two, particularly if this isn't the end of his run; more difficult because there won't be much to go on so long as he chooses his victims pretty carefully.

" You said the victims *weren't* chosen," muttered Keith.

" In the case of the barmaid, she was the last person but one to leave the premises. It was half an hour or more after closing time, and, except for the barman, Travers, who left even later, and was the person to find the body, all the others slept in the inn. This woman was just sheer, plumb unlucky. The fellow was lurking . . . possibly in the hope of stealing, for the contents of a cash-box seem to be missing . . . and she seems to have walked slap into him as she came down the steps at the back of the house."

" Surely she called out, or tried to attract attention? " Christina enquired.

" It seems as though she didn't have time. Nobody in the house can remember hearing a thing. The landlord, Knowles, and his wife, were cleaning up a bit in the saloon and the private bar, Travers, the barman, had swabbed down the counter in the public bar after Ruby, the girl who was killed, had put the cash-box away, and nobody else was about the place at all, except the housemaids, who had gone up to bed. Their room over-looks the high street, and would be quite out of earshot of the yard, particularly if trams were going by, and all three bars are on the front or side of the house. There's nothing at the back except the kitchen and scullery, the tap-room, the little room leading to the cellar, and that round-turreted guest-room which was unoccupied, and in which they keep the takings from the public bar until they can be banked."

" And hasn't the knife been found? "

" No. That's one thing that makes us suspect that the fellow is a homicidal maniac, and may easily do the same thing again, and more than once, if he isn't discovered and arrested. Of course, he may have chucked away the knife, but we've more than a notion that he hasn't. These criminal lunatics get a fixed idea, and are, of course, regardless of their own safety.

He must be a lunatic, because he has gained nothing by these murders except the dubious satisfaction of slaking his thirst for blood. Robbery may have been a secondary motive, perhaps, for, in each case, money is missing—how much we do not yet know. The circus girl is supposed to have saved a few pounds which have disappeared since her death, but anyone may have had those, not necessarily the murderer. And now, of course, the next job will be to deal with a whole crop of accusations and rumours," Mr. Seabrook went on. " We shall learn, no doubt, of men with fiery eyes, and people who mutter and growl at the passers-by, and all sorts of junk . . ." he stared at us for a moment . . . " will be dragged from the canal and brought here for us to identify."

He sighed.

" Poor Evan," said Christina. " Well, we mustn't take up more of your time. Come along, boys, and let us get home before dark."

It was then not five o'clock, and, as we had questions to ask the inspector, we were not inclined to allow Christina to hurry us home.

" If you please, Mr. Seabrook," said I, " what makes you think that the robberies were either only a secondary motive, or else the work of a thief who was not the murderer ? "

" I can't go into all that with you, Simon," he replied. " Whoever killed those girls killed them because he did not like girls. You won't understand, so don't bother your heads about it."

" But the robberies," I persisted. " Even if one of the circus people could have known of the tight-rope walker's savings, and had stolen them from her before the police were shown her body, that wouldn't be quite the same as in the case of the barmaid, would it ? "

" Why not ? " asked Mr. Seabrook snappily.

" Well, you wouldn't suspect Travers, the potman ? " I urged. " You said he found the body. Would he have robbed poor Ruby ? And did someone break into the *Pigeons* and steal the contents of the cash-box ? Somebody told me——"

" Yes," said Keith. " The cash-box. Would anybody have dared—— ? "

Mr. Seabrook looked somewhat harassed.

" Poor Ruby herself may have done a bit of robbing before she was killed, but that is not public property at present, so don't pass it on," said he. " Run along now, boys. I'm busy. Mind, Christina, and don't go running your head into a noose."

" Does he think *you* did the murders? " demanded Keith, grinning, as soon as we got outside.

Christina did not answer, but hurried us up, as though it were already dark and there might be murderers lurking in every doorway we passed.

June scolded us when we got home. She was angry, I think, when she knew where Christina had taken us.

" You'll get there soon enough on your own account, I have no doubt," she said nastily, when Christina had gone to her room; and we had to give her our word that we would not go out again that evening.

" A nice thing," said Keith, disgusted, " if all the rest of the holidays we're going to be gated after tea."

" Cheer up," said I. " You know our methods. Apply them."

We rarely contested an order from any of our elders. Prohibitions wore off if not challenged. We went upstairs to Christina, who had bought some toffee and nougat on the way home. None of us mentioned the murders for a time. I was wondering what the Scotland Yard detective would be like, and Keith said afterwards that he was wondering how hard you could hit a man on the head with the butt end of a horse-pistol without actually killing him. Christina, I think, was wondering why the inspector had told us so much about the murder of Ruby, the barmaid, for, just as June called us down to a very late tea, she said:

" I wonder whom he suspects? He's got something up his sleeve, Sim. You two *will* be careful, and not do anything silly and dangerous? "

" They are not necessarily the same thing, Christina," I replied. " It's you I'm worried about. No more dances and theatres, unless you're met at the house and escorted back to it."

She went out comparatively often, sometimes with girls from the office whom she met at the theatre, or in some tea-shop up in Town, and sometimes with her young men, of whom, to our amusement, she had several. Jack was thinking about her, too, for he said to June, directly after tea:

" You two girls had better stay indoors from now on, after dusk, unless I'm with you."

" You know how often *I* go out after dusk, either with or without you," said June resentfully. Christina said nothing. Jack gave her a glance, and then helped me with my model of a frigate. He was often out in the evening without June. He used to go with young Danny Taylor and the boys, and spend rather more than he should. Ours was a quiet town, and Jack and his friends were neither wild nor troublesome; but Danny and some of the others were discontented; Danny because he was living in expectation of inheriting his father's money and property, and dared not offend the old man by asking for a larger allowance, or even by choosing a wife. They all drank a good deal, too, although we never saw Jack the worse; but it all accounted for a nagging tongue in June, and the fact that we had to take a lodger. In our street people prided themselves on keeping the house to themselves. It was a grievance with June that we could not do the same.

CHAPTER SIX

The Temporary Disappearance of a Husband

AFTER TEA Jack sent me out to get an evening paper. June objected to my being asked to go, and said that the streets might be dangerous. It is true that the sun was setting, for we had had tea rather late, but I agreed with Jack, who turned angrily on June and said:

" Don't make a fool of the boy ! He'll be all right. He's my brother, and I won't have him made soft and cowardly by women."

" No, you'd rather have him murdered by men," said June sharply, in her shrill, unpleasant voice. " All right, then, send him ! I wash my hands of it."

We were all glad she did, and Keith offered to go with me as far as the newsagent's. It was at the top of our road, just into Field Lane. The sun was almost gone, and the moon was not due to rise for some time, for it was still sufficiently early in the year for the evenings to draw in soon after seven o'clock. Full moon had been on the previous Thursday, the night of the first murder.

We got the evening paper, and took it in, and then Keith said, as we sat at the kitchen table with our library books whilst June did some of the mending, Christina darned a tiny hole in the top of one of the stockings she was wearing at a dance that evening, and Jack stoked the fire for the bath-water before he settled down to the evening paper:

" What did you think of the law and the prophets ? "

June, who could not always follow our conversation, and was annoyed when she could not, said sharply:

" Don't be blasphemous ! "

I said, replying to Keith, and taking no notice of June, " Not much. What did you ? "

" Ditto. San fairy ann, so far as I'm concerned."

" No slang in this house ! " said June.

" French," said Keith without looking at her. " Ask Jack. If you ask me," he added, continuing our conversation, " if some can brave the elements, so can others."

" I'm not too happy about that. Goes out better ? "

" I think not. Apron strings too tight."

" John Knox was right."

" I've always thought so."

" Speak up ! " said June. " There's nothing so aggravating as a muttering noise in the room."

" Leave the kids alone," said Jack. " They've got to have *some* private life, even if *I'm* not allowed any."

" Then they can go upstairs and have it in their bedroom, and you can go off to the *Pigeons*, or wherever you want to be."

We guessed that our brother and his wife had fallen out over Christina's going to the dance. Jack, no doubt, wanted to take

her, and then go out with the boys, and then meet Christina
when the dance was over, to bring her home. It was natural
enough, except that we guessed there would be someone else to
bring her home. She was going to the dance at eight, and it
would close down at twelve.

The dances in our town were held at the Baths. In winter
our swimming-bath was closed, and a floor was put down over
the top of where the water had been. Then the hall could be
let for concerts and dances. The bath would be open again for
swimming by the end of the Easter holiday, and this was the last
dance of the season. But for that, I do not think Christina
would have troubled to go; but she had promised some of her
friends that she would be there, and as some were coming from
a distance, she did not want to disappoint them, particularly
as one of them was bringing an extra man to be Christina's
partner.

It was most likely that she would come home, although it was
such a short distance, in a car. That sort of thing always
irritated June, although she pretended that it was because Jack
had to leave the front door unbolted; but, then, so he did if
Christina went to a theatre. We noticed that when she came
back on foot from having gone out with girl friends, June never
appeared to mind the door being left undone, although she got
home considerably later from the theatre than she did from the
dances, for the station was at least a mile from our house, whereas
the Baths Hall was only at the top of the road.

" I suppose," said Jack, confirming my ideas, " you really are
set on this confounded dance, Christina ? "

Christina bit off the end of her silk sewing thread, looked up
at him and smiled. She did not answer.

" You boys go with her as far as the hall, and see her inside
before you leave her," he said to us.

" No ! " said June loudly. " Nothing of the sort ! They're
to go to bed."

" All right, then. I shall go," said Jack. " I'm not going to
let a girl of twenty walk even a couple of yards after dusk with
that gentleman loose in the town."

" Oh, don't be so silly and melodramatic ! " said June.
" You'll make Christina look a fool ! Still, please yourself !

The thought that the man might just as easily break in here and murder your wife and child wouldn't weigh with you, I suppose ? "

" All right ! All right ! " said Jack. " The boys shall go. As you say, it's only up the street. It can't hurt Christina, so, presumably, it can't hurt them. That's logical."

We got our caps, and waited at the front door for Christina. She had gone upstairs to put on her long dress, and I wanted a kiss, and to smell the scent she put on when she went to a dance.

" Shan't be long," I said to June. She sniffed, and said she did not care how long we were. She washed her hands of it.

" Oh, for goodness' sake think of something else to say ! " said Jack, exasperated. The last I saw of her was of pursed lips and eyes which she was blinking to keep from crying. I did not care for June, and neither did Keith, although she was nicer to him than she was to me, but I sometimes thought Jack was unkind.

Christina was soon ready. She came down in a pale green frock we had not seen before, and had a small fur cape on her shoulders, and she carried a little handbag that seemed to sparkle with diamonds.

" You look expensive," said Keith.

" Do I ? " She laughed, and bent down and kissed his cheek. He gave her a hug and she pulled his hair. He smoothed it down, ready for his cap, and then she put her arms round me, and I hugged her harder than I meant to, so that she lost her balance and came into my arms. I kissed her hard on the mouth, in the way I had seen a man do before she smacked his face. That had been after a dance. She did not attempt to smack mine. She said, pushing me off and laughing :

" Oh ! Oh, darling, you'll be all over lipstick ! " She took out her handkerchief and tilted my face to the light. But I dragged out my khaki-coloured rag and scrubbed my mouth with it. I was blushing, but I was far more pleased than put out of countenance by the incident.

We accompanied her to the Baths Hall. The street was almost empty, but that was not unusual at that time of evening, especially at that time on a Saturday. We went right up to the entrance with her, and saw her safely inside. Then we looked at one another, and began to trot towards the high street.

We had not far to go to our old friend's shop.

"Just to see if she took the hint," said Keith. She had no blind to her shop window, and it was not yet absolutely dark. The sky was clear, and, although the moon was not up, there seemed the promise of light in the sky. By straining our eyes we could see the knife in the window.

"Wonder how soon she put it there?" said Keith. "I *said* it was a good advertisement. Bother to-morrow being Sunday! I want it to be Monday, and things to happen. Who wants to go to Sunday School twice in the day? And morning church? It's an imposition. Soon I shall strike for my rights, or become a Roman Catholic."

"How would that help?" I asked.

"They need only go to church once a year. Think of it! Only once a year!"

"Are you sure?"

"Ron Edwards told me. His father's a Catholic. *He* only goes once a year, although, come to think of it, Ron himself goes every Sunday. It's like the old law about right of way, I think."

"Oh, I see," said I. "Still, it seems a bit mean, once a year. What does he do about the collection and missionary money, and the Sunday school treat and all that?"

"Well, I don't know. As I say, it's the *father* goes once a year, not Ron. But even Ron only goes once on Sunday, I believe, and gets out of Scripture at school. He says he isn't allowed to pray with heretics and use the ordinary Bible. I kicked his shins, but he still said it, so I think it must be true."

"I always thought Catholics were *more* in the thick of religion than we are, not less."

"Perhaps it's thicker, the bit they *are* in. And, after all, they do believe in hell, which we don't have to. That must make a difference."

We trotted home.

"Well, you've been long enough," said June. "Bed, as soon as you've bathed. And *not* two in the bath at once. It's very dirty."

" Willie Bathurst has to bath in his sister's dirty water," said Keith.   " He doesn't mind the scum, but he objects to its being cold by the time he gets in. The water, I mean, not the scum."

" Don't be disgusting," said June.

We were in bed by half-past nine, having had our cocoa brought up to us by Jack.   Christina did it whenever she was at home, and sometimes June brought it up, because she had a horror of our catching cold after a bath, and she did not want to have us in bed with pneumonia. We drank the cocoa. I said:

" I wonder what Christina's doing now ? Don't they do anything at a dance except have dancing ? "

" Shut up," said Jack, " and give me that cup. Are you going to be all night ? "   He did not stop for a chat, and at ten we heard him come up the stairs to bed. He had come in rather late that evening, and seemed to have something on his mind.

" Suppose nobody *does* bring Christina home ? " said Keith. I had had the same thought myself.

" It's only down the road," I felt bound to point out.

" Ruby Thingummy was only outside the back door," said Keith.

" There'll be plenty of people."

" But they nearly all go the other way, towards the high street. Hardly anybody comes past this house. You can hear the row when they come out, and then you don't hear any more."

" That's true.   Can you keep awake until twelve ? "

" I don't know.   Perhaps we ought to get up,"

" Let's take it in turns to be on watch."

" All right, then. Toss for innings."

I lost, and took first knock. For some time I sat by the window. The moon began to show, a great orange ball, among the trees, and it quickly changed its colour to the pale and smaller light that we knew best.

Time passed very, very slowly. There were no sounds at last except the little noises of the night and Keith's even breathing from his bed, except that once I heard a whistle which sounded outside our front door. I looked at my luminous watch, and suddenly remembered that we had not brought Keith's Easter egg upstairs. I had brought mine up on the previous evening, but his was still on the piano in the drawing-room.

I crept out to go and get it, and, on the landing, fell over the baby, Tom. He must have got out of his cot and started to go downstairs.

He began to cry, because he was afraid. I don't think I hurt him. I was only in my socks. I took him to his parents' door and knocked. June's voice, very sleepy, said, " Come in." Then she said suddenly, " Where's Jack ? He hasn't come to bed yet. What's the time ? And you're dressed ! What's going on in this place ? "

" I don't know," I said, confused, remembering the whistle I had heard.

" He's gone after that girl ! " she said. " I thought there was something in it when he said he wasn't ready to come to bed. Here, you go after him, do you hear, and bring him back ! You say that, for all he knows, Tom might have broken his neck ! My word, when I get him home ! "

It seemed that she had forgotten about the murders. Still, it was an excellent opportunity to call at the Baths Hall and bring Christina home, and saved breaking out of the house and perhaps being caught getting back.

I got out of the room as quickly as ever I could, and went back to Keith. I roused him.

" Got to get to the Baths in a hurry. Come when you feel like it, Keith."

" Right," he said, very sleepily, and I did not wait to hear more. It was not that I intended only to take the message. I wanted time enough to give Jack a chance to make up some excuse. Wild tales of elopements, and of stealing girls from their homes came into my mind. At the age of thirteen I myself felt fully capable of such deeds; I wondered whether Jack were the same. I had never thought of my elder brother as a Lothario, Romeo or Don Juan; neither were these my heroes. I doubt, indeed, whether, at that age, I even knew their names; but I had read of damsels in distress, and sometimes thought of Christina in that guise.

I went out by the front door, closing it carefully behind me. Jack and Christina would each have a latch-key. I ran swiftly to the entrance to the Baths Hall, and the sounds of dance music filled the air and deprived, no doubt, the more sensitive residents of sleep.

At that time of night the doorkeeper had gone off duty. There was no one between me and my objective but the cloak-room attendant. She came out to the turnstile as she heard it click, and guessed from my face, I suppose, that I was no ordinary gate-crasher.

" What's up, duck ? " she kindly enquired. We knew one another quite well, for in summer she issued the tickets of admission to the swimming-bath.

" Is my brother inside ? " I demanded.

" Not to my knowledge he isn't. Go to the door and have a peep. Nothing gone wrong at home, I hope ? "

" No, except . . ." I groped wildly in my mind for some reason which should satisfy the questioner without disclosing the truth. " The baby's taken bad," I blurted out, " and he's wanted to go for the doctor."

" Dear, dear ! The croup or something ? "

" I don't know, but I do want him quickly."

" Help yourself, duck." She released the turnstile and let me pass through. As it happened, a waltz was on, and in a moment Christina, looking lovelier than ever, came dancing to that end of the hall. I would have liked to stay and watch the scene. I had never been present at a dance and had often wondered exactly what went on at such a function. However, I stepped just on to the floor and said:

" Christina ! "

She heard at once, excused herself to her partner, and smiled at me, as though she did not in the least object to having her fun interrupted by a dishevelled boy in a sweater and flannel trousers.

" Good heavens, Sim ! " she said. " What on earth are *you* doing here ? "

" It's Jack ! " I said. " June has discovered he's come out. Hadn't he better get home ? "

" I should think so, darling. But where is he ? "

" He's here. Or . . . isn't he here ? "

" He certainly isn't. Look round for yourself. Can you see him ? "

The dance ended. The couples walked back to the chairs, and some went out to the bar. There was no sign of Jack, although some of his friends were there.

" Here, Jerry," said Christina to her partner. " You know Jack Innes by sight. Go into the bar, and see if he's there, by any chance.

" The baby's ill," I said. " He's wanted at home."

" O.K.," said Jerry, and sauntered off. People looked at me, and I began to feel rather uncomfortable. Christina drew me over to two chairs at the end of the hall.

" He won't be long," she said, " but, Sim, I'm sure he isn't here. Tell me what's the matter, and what's happened."

I told her about little Tom, and June and my mission, but did not mention the whistling at the door.

" She thinks he's with you," I said crudely.

" Oh, dear ! " said Christina. " How awkward ! Look, I'll come back with you, Sim, if Jack isn't here—and I'm perfectly certain he isn't."

Nor was he. Jerry returned at that moment, and reported no sign of Jack anywhere.

" I even went and called out round the Gentlemen's," he said *sotto voce* to me. " You've drawn a blank, old fellow, I'm afraid."

" I'll have to leave, Jerry," said Christina. " I can't let Sim go home alone. June will be in a stew. We'll have to see what can be done."

" O.K.," said Jerry, " I'll come with you. I don't like what I hear of this township after dark."

" Don't trouble. It's only up the road."

" No trouble at all. This dance is nothing to me if you're going to leave."

" I must just let the Singletons know, then."

She went off to find her friends, went into the cloakroom for her cape, and soon we were outside the Baths.

June almost went off her head when we returned without Jack, but apologized to Christina.

" He was very funny about your going alone and coming home alone," she said. " And you know what he is when he gets an idea in his head. But what am I to do ? I can't think what can have happened. I feel so lost and bewildered. Think for me, quick, and tell me where he can be."

" Come now, Mrs. Innes," said Jerry Charteris. He was a fine young fellow, one of our professional footballers, and a handsome one, too, and very much attracted by Christina. " Take time to think. Go over in your mind. There'll be something to give you a clue."

But although June tried hard to collect herself and to think, it was obvious that she was far too much upset to be of much help.

" I can't think . . . I quite thought . . ." she said; and she looked at Christina. Christina returned the look steadily, and then smiled and gently took her hand.

" Don't worry, June dear," she said. " He can't be far off. He'll be home and you'll think yourself a silly to have worried.

" You get back to bed," said June to me.

" If there's anything you can think of that I could do," said Jerry at once. I did not wait to hear the answer, but went upstairs for Keith.

" There's only one thing for *us* to do," I said. " We'd better go out and find him. June's right. There's something very funny here."

Keith dressed hastily. We took the horse-pistol and the sabre in case we met the murderer, and tied them round our necks with the cords out of our pyjamas, and made sure the weapons were tied firmly. Then we raised the bedroom window at the bottom, and dropped to the scullery roof. From there an easy waterpipe led to the ground, for we recollected in time that the cover had been left off the water-butt.

In five minutes' time we were out of our road, and were walking in the flood of moonlight round the outside of the library grounds towards the Butts and the high street.

" Where do you bet he is, Sim ? " Keith enquired.

" Don't know. Can't think. Don't hurry too much, or else, if we meet a policeman, he might think us up to no good."

We walked briskly but not with undue, suspicious haste, down Somerset Road and along the little road which connected it with the great broad square at the western end of the Butts.

The moonlight showed up the sandy surface of the road and swam in the Georgian windows of Mr. MacKechnie's house and

in Doctor Morrison's, too. At the lower end of the Butts the
River Bregant flowed by like a stream of oil, and the Boatmen's
Institute stood up large and black, like a house of evil.

" I wouldn't cross the miller's bridge to-night, not for a
fortune. Not for all the pistols and guns in the world," said
Keith, as we crossed the great square and passed near to the
Voting Elm, and reached the little bar which kept cars from
coming up from the market-place into the Butts.

He voiced my own thought on the matter. We were approaching the *Pigeons*. It was after closing time, but a number of
people were still about in the high street, mostly men, although
we saw one or two elderly women. There were no girls or
young women. They were all safely indoors.

" Well, he can't be at the *Pigeons*," said I. " It's closed.
He's out somewhere with Danny Taylor and his friends. They
came and whistled for him. He's gone to Taylor's to play cards
and have a drink, I reckon, and then he'll call at the Baths to
take Christina home. We'd better get along."

CHAPTER SEVEN

The Death at the Farm

THE MANOR ROAD was almost a country lane. Once past
the town end of it, and the entrance to Mr. Taylor's field, there
were nothing but fields and trees, Mr. Viccary's farm, Mr.
Perry's orchard, the railway, and the cart-track leading to the
Bregant, until one came to Mr. Taylor's farm. On either side
of the road were elm trees and a hawthorn hedge, a deep narrow
ditch on the one side and a broad and grassy one on the other.

The moon put black shadows in the hedges, and a mist rose
out of the river and over the fields. We walked in the middle
of the road, Keith holding his pistol by the barrel and I with my
sabre at the ready. We did not talk. We kept watch on the
treacherous roadside for the murderer. It was not a pleasant
walk.

We mounted the long and gradual slope, and, when we reached Mr. Viccary's farm, wondered how much farther we should have to go. We were counting on meeting Jack on his homeward way.

" Better go as far as the station, perhaps," said I, " and hang about for him there. He can't be long now." So we passed the farm buildings lying quiet and dark-roofed in the moonlight, the old, white-fronted house forming the middle block between the cowsheds and the stable, and climbed the last rise to the station. Here we stopped, for, coming towards us up the opposite rise was a man.

" If it isn't Jack, and he goes for us, slice at his arms," said Keith, " while I get him on the skull with my pistol butt."

We had both concluded that on that lonely country road the only other man we were likely to meet was the murderer. Neither of us was anxious to encounter *him*, but fortunately Jack it was, and very much surprised he was to see us, and, it was very evident, not too pleased.

" Confound you! You *have* mucked things up! " he said ill-temperedly. " What the devil am I going to do now ? "

" Say you heard the call of the wild," said Keith, not meaning to be cheeky; and got a cuff that sent him half across the road.

" Here, leave him alone! " said I. " It isn't our fault you're in a mess." He did not reply to that, and the three of us walked back in silence; all the way to the house not one of us spoke a word.

Keith and I went up to bed. What happened then between Jack and June I do not know. Christina went upstairs when Jack came in. There was one thing, however, which I had noticed before we left them. Jack's coat-sleeves were wet almost half-way up to the elbow, as though he had been washing in the river with his jacket on. I asked Keith whether he had seen this. He said that he had, and that he wondered what Jack had been doing.

Jack's own story (which we heard at the Sunday breakfast table) was that he had slipped out, intending to see Christina safely home, at five to eleven in mistake for five to twelve. Discovering his mistake when he got to the Baths Hall, he decided not to return home, but to go for a stroll, and call for her on his return.

Having been interested in our story of the man with the knife, he had crossed Mr. Perry's field, slipped in some mud and got his hands black and also the knees of his trousers, and had cleaned himself up as best he could in the river. It was all reasonable enough up to a point; but, as Keith said when we took up Christina's breakfast and sat on her bed to watch her eat it, how was it that, even allowing for the fact that he had fallen and made himself muddy and had washed off the mud in the river, it had taken him at least an hour and a half to get from our house to the river and back as far as the station ? We knew also that he must have told a lie about the Baths Hall. We could be certain that he had not called there that evening at eleven o'clock or at any other time.

" What it comes to," said Keith, when, hounded thereto by our elders, we were on our way to church (having been fortunate enough, for once, to be too late to go to Sunday school because we had been allowed to investigate our Easter eggs), " is that Christina was only an excuse."

" But, look here," I said, " that won't wash. He'd have thought of a better one than her."

" How do you mean ? " asked Keith.

" Well, he gets into a fearful row with June whenever he's a gentleman to Christina."

" Granted. That proves my point." He always had a better head than mine, although in some ways I had the more vivid and purposeful imagination. " You see, he wanted a *foolproof* excuse, and wanted it badly. He knew June would fall for anything involving Christina, and yet *we* knew he went nowhere near the dance."

" Of course," I said doubtfully, " he may not have meant that he actually *went* to the hall."

" He meant us to think he had, Sim. He must have been up to something pretty bad. And who came and whistled for him ? And why ? If it had been Danny Taylor he could have said so. June loathes Danny and that gang, but she'd rather that than Christina. And he looked pretty groggy, too, when he came in."

At this point we met Fred and Arthur Bates coming out of Sunday school, and a crowd of other acquaintances, some going in to the service, others going home or for a walk. We suspended our conversation in order to pass the time of day.

" Coming to church ? " I asked.

" Garn ! " said Fred. " What you take us for ? "

" Christian gentlemen," said Keith, whose witticisms were greatly appreciated in our circle, especially since I had taken to clumping the heads of those who thought it funny to try to clump his.

" But the murder ! " said Arthur. " Me and Fred's missing church this morning. Our mum said we was to. We're going to Mr. Viccary's before all the blood dries away."

I thought all Keith's blood was going to dry away. He suddenly clutched my sleeve and said :

" Take me to a drain. I'm going to cat." And cat he did, some on his Sunday suit.

" Good Lord ! " I said. " What's the matter ? Wasn't your egg all right ? "

" Oh, yes," he said weakly smiling. " Sim, we must get to Viccary's farm as well. You can swear I was sick. For one thing, it's true, and, for another, it's a cast-iron reason for not going into church. Even June wouldn't think I ought to be sick in church."

" I can't see the point," said I. " But as you say."

" Of course you can see the point, ass ! You think it over. But don't breathe a word to a soul, except to me. We're in this, up to our necks. Are you prepared to commit the crime of perjury in defence of an elder brother ? "

Then I could see it, of course.

" But Jack didn't do it ! " I said.

" Probably not. But we know he came this way, and *we know he washed in the river*. Come on, quick."

We met Bob Cammond on the way. He came out of Park Road as we passed along the top of it. He was a Baptist.

" Hullo, you Immersed Believer ! " said Keith, with a grin. Bob answered with dignity :

" Not until I attain the age of . . ."

" Puberty ? " said a boy called Kenneth Matthews.

" Don't be a lousy swine," said Arthur Bates. " Everybody knows your school-teacher told you the word, and, my belief, it's a dirty word, at that."

" He means consent," said Teddy Anderson.

" That's girls," said Bert Cordery. Arthur Bates changed the subject without appearing to do so.

" The innocent blood of a murdered maiden can never dry up when once spilt," he solemnly averred.

" What murdered maiden ? " asked Ross Cavanagh. This was what Keith and I had been waiting for. We scarcely breathed whilst Arthur replied:

" Mr. Viccary's dairymaid. She was saying good night to Bill Chitton at about eleven o'clock, so Mr. Carew told my sister, when the Ripper came along and done her in.'

" With Bill Chitton there ? " demanded Kenneth.

" Course not, you fool. Bill had gone by then. Well, so long. See you later."

Keith and I walked up the road with hearts of lead. We found ourselves joined again by Bob Cammond.

" Funny about your brother Jack and the dance," he said, as we passed the entrance to Mr. Taylor's field and found ourselves opposite the first of the elm trees that screened Mr. Hopkinson's wall. " Jerry told my brother Ken. Ken said he was sorry for Jack's wife."

Keith and I glanced at one another.

" Just here, Bob, a minute," I said. He came behind the elm trees, and we got him between us and the wall. We socked him. He bled. He was plucky enough. He was fourteen, big and stout. But we knew what had to be done.

" And now, you rat," said Keith, " you can take that back, and swear on your oath you heard nothing."

" What should I know ? " snuffled Bob. He did not snuffle for fear, but because his nose bled all down his Sunday suit.

" If our brother goes after Mrs. Cavann it isn't any business of yours," said I, upon inspiration. I had heard June say that Mrs. Cavann was not a bit better than she should be.

" I never said nothing about him and Mrs. Cavann," protested Bob. We had each got hold of an arm and were hurting him badly.

" And you'd better not," said Keith. " We can't have it known. Our family credit is involved."

Bob said he saw it. We let him go, and, when he had mopped up a bit on our handkerchiefs as well as his own, the three of us went on to Mr. Viccary's farm. It was past Mr. Perry's orchard and well past the wrought-iron gates of Mr. Hopkinson's house.

A policeman was standing at the gate. We knew him. He was Tony Martin's brother. But he took no notice of us, nor we of him. There were plenty of sightseers, but nothing in particular to see. A low stone wall with a wooden gate divided the midden from the road, and a clock on the old house showed the time. The house, the cowsheds and the stables were familiar, smelly and quiet. The windows of the house were closed, and some of the blinds were drawn down.

" That was her bedroom," whispered Bob, pointing to a little room over the porch, " and that's where she breathed her last."

He indicated a spot about midway between the wicket-gate and the house, and over towards the cowshed.

We stood and stared reverently at the place where, as we then supposed, the murder had been committed. Then I tried to fit in what we knew of Jack's movements on the previous night, and Keith said later that he had been doing the same. Nothing made much sense. So far as we were aware, Jack had not known the dead girl. There seemed no reason why he should have decided to murder her.

Nobody asked where we had been. Nobody seemed interested in whether we had been to church or not. Keith was reduced to pointing out the stain on his suit, and saying that we had gone for a walk to give him air after he had been too ill to go to church.

" We went as far as Mr. Viccary's farm," he said in a warning tone to Jack. Jack did not say a word, but June said:

" Yes, you would ! Anything to get in people's way, and make yourselves a nuisance, I suppose ! "

So we knew that she knew about the murder. Keith said to me, up in our room:

" We ought to tell her. We all ought to know where we stand."

" There'll be a row," said I.

" I know. But we ought to get the whole thing quite clear. If he didn't do it, he didn't, but if he did he'll need her on his side."

So he told June. She listened with a hand on her breast, and said, in a whisper, when we had done:

" He was at the dance with Christina. We must all remember he was at the dance with Christina."

" Other people know that he wasn't," said I. We explained it all to her.

" I see," she said thoughtfully. " Yes, I see." It was at that moment that we knew, I think, why Jack had married her. " I'll have to think it out. It looks bad. Mind, I don't believe it, but there were his sleeves, soaked through. And, of course, he's got a snob's knife."

" We ought to find that knife," said I. She looked at us almost hopefully.

" You two can look, while he and I have a sleep this afternoon. He keeps it with his tools, down in the cellar. He's discontented and wild, but he isn't bad. I *know* he isn't bad."

So we knew she thought he could have done it, had there been motive enough.

" Do you think she was going to have a baby ? " said Keith to me.

" We could ask Mr. Seabrook," said I, " if you think he'd tell us."

We always enjoyed the cellar. From the hall five steps descended to the kitchen, and just outside the kitchen door was the cellar door, under the staircase.

We gave Jack and June half an hour, making sure that Jack had seen us settled down with Keith's frigate for which we were making the masts and spars, and for which Christina had promised to cut out and sew the sails.

She had gone out with Jerry, we did not know where, but it was safe to assume that she would not be in to tea. Tea, on Sundays, was at five, and we rarely finished in time to go to church. It was not a high tea, such as we often had on Saturdays, especially if Jack had been to football, but there was usually lettuce or watercress, radishes or mustard and cress, two kinds of cake, jam tarts from the pastry left over from the tart at dinner, jam, honey, bloater paste, possibly fruit and cream. We liked to take our time over it, and June liked to have the table and her cooking praised and appreciated, and, with Christina out of the way, she was always better tempered. We usually enjoyed our Sunday tea.

At the end of the half hour, and with a lively sense of the fact that tea would be ready in two and a half hours' time, we commenced our search of the cellar. It went under the front two rooms of the house, and therefore was very large. Eight wooden steps led down to it, which, with the five steps down from the kitchen, made the cellar high and easy to use. Except for the light which came in through a grating to the back room, it was pitch dark unless the cover was off the coal shoot. This was in the front cellar, for the coal shoot was beside the front door.

We had a candle, but did not light it until we were down below. Jack's tools were in the back cellar. We opened the chest, and then the leather bag, but there was no sign of his snob's knife. I began to be afraid. Keith, looking white-faced in the candlelight, went over everything again. It was of no use. The knife had disappeared.

" When did he sole any shoes ? " I asked at last.

" He did a pair for himself a fortnight ago," said Keith, " and I know he had the knife then, for he scored round the edge of his shoe placed on the piece of leather he bought off Mr. Grinstead. I watched him do it."

" And did you see the knife after that ? "

" I don't remember. Do you ? "

" His initials were on the handle."

" His initials ? "

" Yes. I asked if I could cut them on with my penknife when I had it for my birthday. Don't you remember ? "

" His knife could be traced to him, then ! "

" Well, it could, anyway, couldn't it ? You needn't blame me."

" Fingerprints, you mean ? Yes, if anyone wanted to be nasty, but, even then, the police don't——"

" The police aren't nasty. It's their job."

" I didn't mean the police. Some snooping person, who'd got a down on him, perhaps."

" But who'd have a down on Jack ? "

" Oh, plenty of people, I expect. Everybody has enemies. June's down on him, for one. But she wouldn't down him over this."

" I'll tell you what," said Keith. " We can't leave matters where they are. We've got to find his knife, you know."

" If it's where we think it is, the police will have found it by now."

" Sim ? "

" Yes ? "

" Why do we think it was Jack ? "

" We don't. Of course we don't really. It's just because . . . well, it *was* rather funny, that walk, and mistaking the time, and his sleeves all wet where he'd washed his hands in the river. It's so queer, when you add it all up. Plus the whistle. Who whistled for him ? Was it the woman herself ? "

We added it up in silence. Then I snuffed out the candle and we went up the steps to the kitchen.

" Well ? " said June, the minute she got us alone.

" It isn't there, June," said Keith, speaking gently. She looked at us both, and did not know what to say, but she went white all round her mouth and under her nose. It was dreadful.

" It will have to be found, and quickly. What can we do ? " she said. " I won't believe, I *won't*, that he is as wicked as that ! But he *didn't* go to the dance. I've found *that* out all right ! "

" You would ! " said Keith unkindly; and she did not answer a word.

" She hates him, but she'll back him up," said I, when we were alone.

" I wish we *knew* something," said Keith.

Christina came home at eight o'clock, after Jack had gone out and as the people were still drifting along from church. It was the custom in our town for the younger grown-ups to go for a walk after church up the Manor Road, and across the fields, and along by the river and canal. But on this particular Sunday I do not think anyone went.

We were all glad to see Christina; first, to know that she was safely home; secondly, because the house was very uncomfortable with Jack and June in the mood they were in towards one

another. June, as we knew, was no longer angry with Jack; she
was afraid for him. Jack was sulky, because he thought she was
still annoyed, but underneath the sullenness, which he made
unnecessarily obvious and annoying, we could tell he was very
uneasy.

Immediately tea was over . . . and I cannot more vividly
describe the feeling of tension in our house than by saying that,
although it was easily the best tea, even for a Sunday, that June
had given us since Christmas, I did not enjoy a single mouthful.
. . . Jack said to me, trying to speak carelessly:

" Oh, Simon Legree, go down the cellar, old man, and bring
me up my snob's knife, do you mind ?   You'll find it in the tool-
chest, with my bit of leather apron and the bradawl. I think
I'll clump your school shoes before you go back."

" What! On a Sunday ? " said Keith. We scarcely knew
what to do, as we knew the knife was not there.

" What's it got to do with you ? " shouted Jack. I got up
from table and slowly went down the cellar.

" Here! Wake up, boy! You've forgotten the candle ! "
cried Jack. " Or have you turned into a tom-cat to see in the
dark ? "

" It's you that's the tom-cat," I muttered as I came back into
the kitchen and lighted the candle. I caught Keith's eye, but
neither of us made any sign.

" Sorry, Jack," I said, coming up at the end of ten minutes,
during which, for my own satisfaction, in case we had overlooked
the knife before, I had made a most careful search.

" Hell ! " said Jack; and he took the candle from me, and
went down the cellar himself. June began to cry. Keith said,
in an urgent voice:

" No, don't! We'll manage. Don't you worry."

She pulled him against her, and went on crying into his hair.
I was glad it was not I she was fond of. Keith bore it well, and
got away when he could. Jack came up swearing, and then
said he must have lent the knife, and June had better remember
who had had it so that he could ask for it back on the morrow.
Knowing what we all knew, it sounded unconvincing. Then I
suppose he noticed what we looked like, for he suddenly said:

" By heck, no ! I took it with me when I went out to meet

Christina. Fool that I am! I must have dropped it somewhere! I must find it! It might be awkward."

He went whistling out of the house, and we did not see him again the whole of the evening. It was after he had been gone for about ten minutes that Christina came back from her outing.

Not much to our surprise, the two of them sent us out of the drawing-room and told us to play in the kitchen and to make up the fire, and not to come back until we were invited. We knew that June was going to confide in Christina, for girls and women, it seems, even when they hate the sight of one another, will usually tell one another their troubles, and, more curious still, will receive true sympathy and pity.

We did not mind being turned out whilst they talked. The kitchen was a good long way from the drawing-room, and down five steps besides. We put the table into the scullery, piled the chairs on it, took up the hearthrug made of pieces, and got out the gloves for a spar.

When we rested, Keith said:

" It means thieving, but I don't see anything for it but to thieve."

" It's a mercy we know where it is," said I, with complete understanding. " One will have to be the decoy duck, and the other sneak it away."

" And come back innocently later ? "

" I hardly think so. Don't want to make that connection. Better have gone out for the day. Plausible enough, on Easter Monday."

" But will she open ? "

" She opened on August Bank Holiday."

" Didn't she say it was a pruning knife, though."

" It looks exactly like Jack's. Get it home, and get his initials and fingerprints on it, and who's to know the difference ? "

CHAPTER EIGHT

The Knife

THERE WAS no moon that night. It would not, in any case, have risen very early, but heavy dark cloud covered the whole of the sky, and by morning a good deal of rain had already fallen, and it looked like a wet Easter Monday.

We went to bed on the Sunday night at nine. At half-past eight Jack had returned. He was in a vile temper, beneath which we deduced that there was fear, answered us with a snarling negative that sounded more like an oath when we asked whether he had found the knife, and asked to have supper early, as he wanted to get to bed.

We waited until ten before we sneaked in to see Christina. She had a part to play, and we wanted to find out whether she was willing to play it. She was not in bed when we went in. She had her dressing-gown on, and was seated in front of the mirror brushing her hair.

" Well ? " she said. " Time you were asleep."

Keith took the brush from her hand, and I drew up a chair and sat astride it, my arms along the back.

" This is a law court," I said. I think she knew at once that we were serious.

" Could I finish my hair ? " she asked. " I don't know why it is, but hair never seems the same if one doesn't tidy it up in one operation."

Keith gave her the brush. She did not keep us long.

" Get into bed," he said. " And you can lie down if you promise you won't go to sleep in the middle of what we're saying."

She promised, and took off her dressing-gown. I hung it up behind the door. She got into bed and lay down, and we tucked her up, and then we sat on the bed and told her about the lost knife.

" Um ! " she said when we had finished. " I don't like the

sound of it much. Of course, *we* know Jack couldn't have had anything to do with it, but, all the same, it's not going to look too good if the police get hold of that knife. I wonder where on earth he could have dropped it ? "

" It's worse than we've told you," said Keith.

" The police have found the knife ? "

" We don't know about that, but we do know Jack washed in the river, and wetted his jacket sleeves almost up to the elbow. And we know he didn't go out to bring you home from the dance."

She sat up in bed.

" Who knows that, besides you two ? "

" Why, no one, except, of course, June. She's sure to have noticed his wet coat."

" He's safe enough with her. You don't know whether he had already met anyone, though, before he met you two at the station ? "

" No, we don't *know*," said Keith. " But somebody came and whistled for him. Sim heard the whistle."

" And what are you going to do now ? "

" Get hold of another knife, if we can, and cut his initials on the handle."

" But . . . anyone buying such a knife . . . it would cause comment. The police would find out."

" We're not going to buy it," said Keith, " so don't ask any more questions. Your share of the business is quite different. It's something that only you can do."

" And that is ? "

" Swear, if you're asked, that he called for you at the Baths Hall, and stayed there until you came home."

" But Jerry, and others, know he didn't ! I *can't* promise. It isn't that I wouldn't. You both know that. But it might not be the best thing. And this knife business. I don't know quite what you're up to, and maybe I'd better not enquire, but take my advice and drop it. You can't play tricks on the police. Evan—Mr. Seabrook—isn't silly, and he *can* be rather hard."

" Do you want to see Jack in prison ? " demanded Keith.

" Let's get this straight," said Christina. " You two surely don't think *Jack* committed those murders, do you ? "

I looked at Keith, and Keith at me.

" I don't see why he shouldn't have," I said slowly.

" Well, you would see if you knew anything about him at all, you little cuckoo! " she retorted. " Or about the murders either. You can both take it from me that Jack is as innocent as you are, and that I would swear to anywhere. Take my advice, and leave things just as they are. You can't do Jack any good, and you might do tremendous harm."

" All very well for her to talk," said Keith gloomily, when we were back in our room, " but what the police go on is evidence, and evidence is just what they've got, once they find that knife with his initials cut on the handle."

" Will they recognize his initials ? "

" There can't be all that number of people with initials *J. I.* It's not a very common combination, and this isn't a very big town."

" You think of everything," I said, feeling gloomy, sleepy and ill-tempered. " What are we going to do, then ? "

" What we've planned, of course. It's the only thing. But first I think we ought to do something else."

" About Jack ? "

" About Jack. Do you think he's innocent ? "

" Well, I can't see what he'd want to murder people for."

" Except June, at times."

" Yes, but that's only figuratively speaking."

" I know. We swear to believe, then, that he hasn't committed any murders."

" But what *was* he doing up the Manor Road last night ? And why should he take that knife ? It isn't as though it was a penknife."

" That's one thing we ought to find out. And I don't think it's much good to ask him."

" He's worried about the knife."

" Well, anybody would be. You can't go by anything like that. He's got sense, like everybody else. *Somebody* did the murders, and if his knife gets found . . ."

" The police may have found it already."

" I know. There's no time to lose."

" You don't think Christina may be right ? "

" No, I don't. Girls never face realities. Their heads were not made for facts. All girls are more or less ostriches."

" Yes, you're right about that. All right, then. What time in the morning ? "

" No hurry. She won't open until nine, or maybe half-past. She isn't an early riser."

" You don't think there's anything peculiar about her having such a knife in the shop ? "

" Among all that junk ? It's hard to say. She explained it. She ought to have the benefit of the doubt."

" Like Jack ? "

" Well, I can't see a woman—especially an old woman—killing three girls who would all be stronger than she is."

" Not if she took them by surprise."

" Something in that, of course. But I don't see Mrs. Cockerton . . . no, I *don't*."

" All right, then. Neither do I. Said prayers ? "

" Shan't say them to-night. After all, we are going to steal."

" Don't thieves ever pray ? "

" I don't see how they can. They would probably be struck by lightning."

" But we're stealing in a good cause."

" I don't believe you can."

" Well, it's not to benefit ourselves."

" It might be argued that it was. If Jack were hanged, or even imprisoned, you know, we'd be rather left in the cart. We'd have to support June and Tom, and June might have to work until we could get ourselves jobs."

It seemed inevitable that we must regard ourselves as outside the pale of good Christians and honest men. I was averse to going to bed without saying my prayers, but Keith's stern logic was unanswerable. I wondered what would happen, supposing I died in the night. I put this point before Keith.

" It's most unlikely," he said.

" The murderer might break in and kill us all."

" Well, we can take it in turns to do sentry duty, if you like."

But the risk of being murdered scarcely weighed with me against loss of sleep.

" Let's take a chance," I said.

We were up at seven, and we took cups of tea to Jack and June, and then went in with another cup for Christina.

" It's nice," she said.   " Thank you.   What are you going to do with your Bank Holiday ? "

" What are you ? " asked Keith.

" Oh, I don't know.   Jerry wants the river and Bill wants a cinema up in town and Rex wants a matinée and dinner out in the evening.   I don't know which to say."

" I should have Rex," said Keith, " and make hay while the sun shines.   There won't always be all this competition."

She laughed.

" I notice you two don't offer to go out with me," she said. She drank her tea, and Keith put the cup and saucer on top of the chest of drawers.

" Lie down again," I said.   " You'll get cold."   I loved to see her in bed.   She woke up looking clean and fresh, not frowsty and sweaty like us.   My brown hand on her smooth, soft arm was hot against her cool and lovely skin, and looked dirty, although I had washed before getting the early-morning tea.   I took it away, and she half sat up and stretched her arms and pulled me down beside her, my head against her shoulder and her arm round my neck.   I felt dizzy for a minute, and put my arm over her and pressed my mouth against her breast.   I did not know how to kiss her, and would not have dared, just then, even if I had known how.   Keith jumped on the bed and kicked his shoes off.   They fell on the floor with a bouncing, thudding sound.   He put his head in Christina's waist, and she laughed, and rumpled his hair.

" There won't be Jerry and Bill and Rex when you're married to *me*," said I.

" What do you pretend, Christina, when we get on the bed with you like this ? " asked Keith, as he wriggled because she was tickling his neck.

" That I'm your mother," she answered seriously.   I knew she meant it.   She hated it because we had not a mother.   She wanted to be mother and sister and everything else in the world except what I wanted her to be.   I knew I was in love with her, although it was a secret—the only one—that I ever kept from Keith. In his own way I think he felt the same, but he was younger. She did not mean as much to him. My day-dreams were full of her presence. A thousand times I rescued her from drowning, from burning houses, from tigers and bandits, and these dreams always ended the same way. She fell asleep in my arms to my gentle assurance:

" You're safe now, Christina, quite safe. Don't cry any more now. You're quite safe."

We had seen her cry only once, but I did not forget it. I felt I would rather die than see her afraid or in pain.

Keith sat up and jumped down. He put on his shoes.

" I've just remembered I saved you a bit of my Easter egg," he said. " I'll go and get it."

I felt ashamed at once. I had saved her none of mine.

" I say," I said. " I never thought . . ." I turned half over, and put my arm over her body. She kissed my cheek, and then freed herself, pushing me away.

" You'd better go with him," she said.

" Why ? "

" Well," she said laughing and sitting up, so that I had to sit up, too, or roll off the side of the bed, " you're almost a man, and I ought not to be in bed with a man, do you think ? It's me I'm thinking of; not you."

She laughed again. I blushed. There was a mixture of yearning and pride in my mind. Jack had told me one or two things. They had not meant much at the time. They hardly bore any relation to the dirt one heard at school, or to the strange, delicious, half-guilty, half-agonizing feelings which Christina's presence and the scent of her hair, the warmth of her body, her round, smooth arms, and the nape of her neck could induce.

I got up and went to the mirror; studied my boyish eyes, round chin and undisciplined hair.

" Sim," said Christina. I turned. " You and Keith aren't going to try to do anything about another knife for Jack ? "

" We are," I said. " It will be all right. Don't worry. You keep out of it."

" Don't do it, Sim.   It will only complicate matters.   Promise me, Sim."

" I can't," I said.   " He's my brother, and we've all got to do what we can."

" At least tell me what it is you're going to do."

" You know too much already.   We thought you'd stand in with us, you see."

" I'll say what you want me to say about the dance, if you'll give up the idea of stealing this knife.   I'm sure you'll only get into trouble, and make matters worse than they are."

" That's our look-out," I said.   " We ought never to have told you about it.   It wasn't fair."

Keith came back with the piece of chocolate egg.   She and he ate it between them.   Keith offered me some, but I refused. We acted in such matters in obedience to tribal laws to us considerably more binding and very much more important than any of the ten commandments.   I had had my egg.   I could not accept a piece of his.

When they had finished, we went back to our room and dressed for breakfast.   Breakfast was at eight.   Jack said:

" We're going to the Zoo."   He did not sound cheerful about it.

" Don't want to," said Keith.   " We're going fishing."

" That you are not, then," said June.   " You ungrateful little beasts ! "

" Oh, let them do as they like," said Jack.   " My idea was they'd like it.   If they don't like it, why, let them please themselves.   I shall be at work to-morrow."

I suddenly saw that he wanted a good excuse to get out of the town.

" Why don't we go to mother's ? " said June, as though she had had an inspiration.   They were still arguing when we got up from the breakfast-table and slipped out.   We took our rods and a landing-net for the look of the thing, and because, if our nerve did not fail us, we thought we might do some fishing after we had stolen the knife.   We hoped very much that Jack and June would go to her mother's.   It would suit us very well indeed to have them out of the way, and Christina out with one of her numerous friends.

We left the house at five to nine, and went straight to the ferry with our rods. Ferry Lane went down by the side of the fire-station and was just about half a mile long. At the end of it there were sheds and a dump of coal, for it marked a wharf for barges drawn by tugs. The ferry ran from March until October. After that, if you wanted to cross the Wyden you had to go round by the bridge which, properly speaking, was not within the town boundary.

We sat on the wooden pier which ran out from the wharf, and fished for half an hour with our backs to Julius Cæsar's monument. Then Keith put his rod up, hitched our satchel over his shoulder, and walked up the lane towards the high street.

I gave him five hundred seconds, counting " A-one-two, a-three-four," to get the time right, and then I walked after him, matching his pace.

There was no sign of him when I came out by the fire-station, so I strolled along the high street towards Mrs. Cockerton's antique shop.

The shop, as I had hoped and expected, was empty. The knife was in the centre of the window. I had to wait whilst several people went by. I waited several shops further along towards the Half Acre. When the coast seemed clear, I nipped in, put the knife in the sheath we had made for it out of a leather glove with a cork at the bottom, put it in the lining of my jacket sleeve where we had cut the stitches at the shoulder, and then went into the back of the shop and called out:

" Keith, are you there ? You're wanted at home to go out ! "

He came down out of the first-floor room, and Mrs. Cockerton came with him.

" Her lodger's had an accident," he said. " Fell into the canal, and was almost drowned. The rag and bone man, you know."

" Whereabouts ? " I asked, my heart leaping.

" By Dead Man's Island. He thinks it might have been the murderer pushed him in. He's going to tell the police. A big man with a beard, and eyes like living coals."

" Now, don't exaggerate, my dear Mr. Keith," said Mrs. Cockerton. " The poor fellow said nothing about living coals.

He said the man was big and dark, and had an overcoat buttoned to the chin. A very seedy overcoat, he said. It looked as though it might have been slept in on the damp ground."

" And a beard ? " I asked.

" Certainly a beard," said Keith. " He'd need the beard as a disguise."

" I don't think he mentioned a beard," said Mrs. Cockerton. " I don't remember a beard."

" What would you do, Mrs. Cockerton," I asked, " if you were leaning on a five-barred gate, and a man suddenly rose up out of the ditch and his beard suddenly tickled your chin ? "

" Good gracious alive ! " said Mrs. Cockerton, startled. " What a perfectly horrible idea ! All little boys are ghouls ! "

" I suppose, Mrs. Cockerton," said Keith—" you'd better cut back home, Sim, and tell them I'm coming—you wouldn't sell that murderer's knife you've got ? "

" I have told you that it is a pruning knife, Mr. Keith, but I would not sell it, no ! Not while there's all this hue and cry."

" No, I suppose it wouldn't do. People might think whoever bought it must be the murderer. Did you hear someone else had been murdered ? Mr. Viccary's dairymaid, I think."

" Yes, I did hear . . ." she said. Her voice then tailed off. She had just become aware that her knife was no longer in the window. I wished I had taken my departure when Keith opened the way for me to go. But I had not gone, and I could not go just then. It would have looked bad, I thought.

" It was rather beastly, wasn't it ? " said Keith. " The way she put her hand over her mouth, and said through her fingers, ' *Now* what shall I do ? *Now* what shall I do ? ' I tried to ask what was the matter, and why she minded the loss of the knife so much, but the words rather stuck in my throat, and, anyway, she didn't want *me* to say anything."

" It was beastly," I agreed, " but what could we do ? "

" Nothing. There was really nothing we could do. Then she said, ' These souvenir hunters ! I remember I went to a play. Now, what was it called ? They sold the people pens. Now what *would* that play have been called? It was very good. Quite an atmosphere, I remember.' What play would it be? Do you know?"

I did not know, but it worried me that we could not pay for the knife. She must never know who had had it. I thought of the noose round Jack's neck.

"We've got to see it from Jack's point of view," said I, firmly. I had been influenced by Mrs. Cockerton's loss, but I was, on the other hand, tremendously pleased with my feat of *legerdemain* in lifting the knife from the window. "What did you talk to her about while I was getting the knife and putting it down my sleeve?"

"Oh, the murders," said he, surprised. "What else *is* there to talk about?"

"And has she any ideas?"

"Only this tale about the murderer pushing her lodger into the canal."

"I don't believe that, do you?"

"No, I don't. *I* think the man drinks."

"And fell in, you mean? Much more likely."

"You don't think *Jack* pushed him in?"

I visualized the lodger, a scrawny individual in a collar a size too large; a hairy, dirty, rag and bone man who ate in the little cookshop along the high street, and slept in Mrs. Cockerton's little back shed, paying a few shillings a week for rent. He called himself a second-hand clothes dealer, and sometimes we used to meet him pushing an old barrow which, as often as not, had rabbit skins hanging from the handles.

"He looks a murderer," said Keith, voicing my own thought. "And if anybody did push him into the canal, I expect they did it to make sure he got a wash. It's very queer how the canal keeps cropping up in all these murders."

When we reached home—and we did not go there straightway —we found, to our great relief, that the others were out.

"We can fish again this afternoon," said Keith. "It will be a good time to work out our plans."

"We must put the initials on the knife before we do anything else, you know," said I.

"And wipe all the fingerprints off it. It wouldn't do for the inspector to find Mrs. Cockerton's fingerprints on that knife, as well as yours and mine."

I got to work on the knife, and made a good job of Jack's initials. They were easy enough to do, and did not take long. Then we wiped the knife hard all over, and took it in turns to handle both haft and blade, because we deduced it did not matter how many of our prints were on it, provided that Mrs. Cockerton's were not, and then we put it down in the cellar among the tools.

" And if even Jack himself can tell that knife from the other I'll be sugared and shot," said Keith triumphantly. As he said it, there came a knock at the door.

My conscience was by this time so tender that I jumped. Keith said:

" Police. Go canny. Don't give anything away. Or shall I go to the door ? "

" I stole that knife out of her window."

" Yes, but I am an accessory before and after the fact."

" I'll go," I said, as the knocking was resumed rather louder. We had returned from the cellar to the kitchen. I went up our five stairs to the hall with my heart beating thickly and the feeling that my knees would give way.

Inspector Seabrook was there, in plain clothes. We looked at one another. Then he asked:

" Is Christina at home ? "

This simple question took me aback. It was, I suppose, the very last thing which I had expected him to say.

" Er—no. No, she isn't," I answered. " Will you come in ? "

It would never do, I reflected, to appear to be afraid of him. We did not want to put ideas into his head. Unfortunately it was at once clear that the ideas were already there.

" I'd be glad to get one or two things cleared up," he said, taking off his hat and following me into the drawing-room. " I don't know whether you can help me. Is Jack at home ? "

" No, they're out. Everybody's out, except us."

" Get Keith in, will you, then ? "

I went to the kitchen. When I came back with Keith, Mr.

Seabrook was standing by the window looking at June's new curtains. She had made them and put them up for Easter. An uneasy and foolish suspicion that on them he had discovered some clue to Jack's guilt or to mine crossed my mind like a blow across the eyes.

" Sit down, you two," he said. We sat, like two culprits, on the settee. He took an armchair, leaned back, and crossed his legs. It was something in our favour, I thought, that he did not produce a notebook. " Now, as you know," he said slowly, looking up at the ceiling, " we've had a spot of trouble round here. First, there was the business on the circus field; next, the performance at the *Pigeons*; third, this spot of bother at Viccary's farm."

" Why don't you say murder ? " asked Keith. The inspector stopped looking at the ceiling and looked at my brother instead.

" I don't say murder because it isn't a nice word," he replied. " But, if you prefer it, I can use it."

" I do prefer it," said Keith.

" Like to call a spade a spade ? "

" Well, that's preferable to calling it the grave-digger's tooth-pick," said Keith. Mr. Seabrook studied him carefully. Then he said:

" I accept the correction. Well, now, cast your minds back to Sunday . . . no, Saturday night. You first, Simon. Give me an account of what you were doing at eleven o'clock on Saturday night. And mind it's the truth. I shall check it."

" You'd have a job," said I, " because, as far as I know, I was in bed."

" Subscribe to that ? " asked Inspector Seabrook, looking at Keith again.

" Of course I don't," said Keith. " All I can do is to tell you that I can't disprove it."

" Sleep in a different room ? "

" No. But I do sleep."

Mr. Seabrook studied him again, and got up.

" I'll call again when the others are at home," he said. " You're both a sight too cheeky for my liking. You can't play tricks with the police, you know."

" We don't mean to be cheeky," said Keith, " but if you suspect one of us of committing the murders, oughtn't you to have warned us that anything we say will be taken down and may be used in evidence ? "

" Not until I arrest you," said Mr. Seabrook, grinning. " What I might have done is to have warned you that there was no need for you to answer my questions unless you wished, and that you were entitled to ask for your solicitor to be present."

" Thanks," said I. " We will remember." He aimed a friendly smack at my head, and got up to go.

" You might tell Christina I called," he said carelessly. " Who is she out with ? Do you know ? "

" It was a choice among Jerry, Bill and Rex," said Keith, " but we don't know which one it was."

" You don't know where they were going ? "

" Jerry the river; Bill a cinema; Rex a matinée and evening dinner," said I. Inspector Seabrook nodded, gloomily I thought, We were very glad to see the back of him. He was not really a good-humoured man.

" We found your knife, Jack," I said.

" Found my knife ? " He looked startled, but it did not make the impression that I should have expected. " But I don't see—that is—Good Lord ! "

He went out of the kitchen and we could hear him rushing upstairs. In a minute he came down again, looking worried.

" What do you mean . . . found it ? " he asked. Keith said :

" We put it down the cellar, with your tools, where you always keep it."

" But . . . where did you pick it up, then ? "

" Oh, up the street. You must have dropped it."

" Yes, I did drop it," he said. He went down the cellar. June looked at us. She was darning socks, and had kept her head down, and her eyes on her work. Now her eyes and mouth and the tilt of her head were one agonized question. Keith nodded.

" We've doctored it," he said. " No one will know the

difference, but we had to get his finger-prints on it before the inspector comes again."

" Oh, my God ! " said June, in a whisper. " To think of little boys like you ! "

" We're not little boys," said Keith; and I remembered what Christina had told me, and said nothing. Jack came back almost at once, but the knife was not in his hand.

" Look here, what *is* this ? " he demanded. " That isn't my knife. You'd better put it back where you found it, or take it to the police station. What do you mean by saying that it is my knife ? You know perfectly well that my knife had a darker handle than that, and the blade was longer."

June looked at him and put down her work.

" You'd better get this straight," she said. " Your knife has gone from the cellar. I suppose you took it with you on Saturday night. I suppose you dropped it. I suppose the police have it by now. I suppose they will ask you to explain how you came to be carrying it along the Manor Road. That's what you've got to think of, my lad."

Jack passed a finger round the inside of his collar.

" It's all easily answered," he said. " My knife went from the cellar because I took it from the cellar. I took it on Saturday night when I went out for a long stroll before meeting Christina. I took it because of this beauty lurking about. I'm not a nervous man, but I don't pretend to be able to cope with an armed maniac single-handed and without any kind of a weapon. I did not know I had dropped it, but, if the police have found it, I have the reason I've just given you to explain it. I can't see any difficulty."

" No ? " said Keith. " Then you listen to this: so far, there does not seem to be any clue to the identity of the murderer. Your knife is the kind of knife the police doctor thinks was used. Your knife is found. You walked right past Viccary's farm on the night of the murder. You went down to the canal, along which the murderer is already known to have his haunts, and wetted your coat-sleeves almost to the elbows, washing yourself where you say you fell over and got muddy. You didn't go out for Christina. You went out on a secret whistling signal, and went jolly quietly, at that, so that nobody heard you go."

" *What !* " said Jack.   He saw it all right.   " Say that again, Keith.   Slowly."

Keith said it again.   A lawyer could not have done better. He had all the horrid logic at his fingers' ends and he let Jack have the lot.   You could watch it sinking in as you watched Jack's face.

" But Seabrook's a friend of mine.   He'd never suspect me," he said.   June threaded her darning needle.   It seemed to take all her attention.   The colour came into Jack's face.   He scowled as he watched her trying to thread the needle.

" Give me that ! " he said.   " I don't know why women are so helpless ! "   But when he took the needle and wool, he dropped the needle because his hands were shaking.   Keith bent down and picked it up.

" Better let her do it herself," he suggested, handing the needle back to June.   Jack gave her the length of wool without a word, and we all watched her thread the needle.

" You don't think I did it ? " said Jack slowly.   " You couldn't think that, so that's all right.   If Seabrook comes here I shall tell him the truth and be . . ."

" Hanged," said Keith.   " Don't be such a fool, Jack.   Why shouldn't it be you, as much as anyone else ?   Did you handle that new knife much in the cellar ? "

" Yes.   I turned it over, and cut a bit of leather to test the edge."

" By candlelight ? "

" No.   I took it into the front cellar.   The coal shoot was open.   There was plenty of light from that."

" Then your prints are on the knife.   That's something."

" Now you can all stop arguing," said Jack.   " I'm perfectly unconcerned with any crimes.   You can go and put that knife where you found it.   I shall just tell Seabrook what happened. I've made up my mind.   It's of no use to cheat the police.   It would only come back on me in the end."

We gave up trying to persuade him, and he had just told Keith to go down the cellar and get the knife and bring it up to him, when once again there came a knock at the door.

" Christina, I suppose.   Forgotten her key," said Jack. " Here, don't you kids go.   It's getting dark.   *I'd* better go."

He went. We heard Seabrook's voice. In a minute the gas went on in the drawing-room. Jack called:

"Come in here a minute!"

Seabrook and a constable were there . . . Billie Knowles' brother Herbert . . . both looking too big for our front room. They greeted June, and Herbert Knowles looked sheepish. He and Jack had been boys at school together not so many years before.

"Take a seat, Mrs. Innes," said Mr. Seabrook. "You boys, stand by. I shall have to ask you some questions in a minute. Now, then, Jack, I want you to look at this knife. No, if you don't mind, don't touch it. It has your initials, as you see. Can you explain how it came to be by the canal bank, on the other side of the station bridge, half trodden into the mud?"

"Why should I explain it?" asked Jack. "You've nothing on me."

Beads of sweat stood out on his forehead and under his nose. He had given in already. That was plain. There was something he had to fear. His talk had been nothing but bravado. I looked at Keith, and he at me. We were in despair. Jack was in the mood to blurt out anything.

CHAPTER NINE

The Dark of the Moon

"WHEN DID you last go along that way?" enquired Seabrook. Jack moistened his lips.

"Last Saturday night," he said.

"Any special reason?"

"No. I went for a stroll."

"Taking your snob's knife with you?"

"No," said Jack, glancing at Keith. "No, I took no knife. Why should I?"

"That's what you've got to tell us," said Inspector Seabrook.

The line of his jaw grew hard and his eyes suspicious. " That's just what we want to know, Jack Innes. Why should you ? "

Jack went to pieces.

" You fool ! " he said. " I took no knife, I tell you ! I've got my knife down in the cellar."

" Mind if I come with you and look ? "

They both went out with him. June was twisting her handkerchief in her hands. Keith said, under his breath:

" He's mucking it up. He's windy. He'll land himself properly like this. He doesn't know what witnesses they've got. He ought to stall, not try to bludgeon them like this."

The three came back in less than a minute and a half. Seabrook looked worried. He carried the stolen knife.

" So you swear this is yours ? " he said. I knew, by the way he said it, that something was wrong. " You'll have to come with me, Jack, I'm afraid."

" Then I go with him ! " said June. " The idea of arresting my husband ! You ought to know better, Evan Seabrook ! You, that call yourself his friend ! "

Mr. Seabrook looked very uncomfortable, and mumbled about his duty, and Jack and June went off with him.

Christina came home at just after nine, while the other two were still out. She was escorted to the door of our house by Rex. His real name was Robert, but he was usually called Rex by his friends. We did not like him much, and I do not think Christina liked him very much, either. His father was the bank manager, a grey-haired, quiet sort of man who grew roses and some very good delphiniums with which he took prizes at the flower show. Rex did not want to be in a bank, so he was in a shop in Town which sold cars. He always wore very expensive suits which were not made by Mr. Westbrook, our tailor in the high street, but by a tailor in the West End. Mr. Westbrook said they were cut by the Jews. I do not know how he knew, and I did not know Rex well enough to ask him whether it was true, or in what respects a suit cut by the Jews was different from any other, but there was no doubt that clothes worn by Rex were not like the other young men's clothes.

Jack said Rex was a poop, but I think that was partly jealousy. Rex earned a good deal of money and spent most of it. He said he should never marry, and would not think of saving. He spoke of saving as though it were an ungentlemanly action. I asked Christina once what she really thought of him, and she said he was all right to go out with.

We had been talking to Christina for an hour when Jack and June came back from the police station.

" I'm not arrested," Jack said, " but I've been told pretty straight to watch my step; I gave Seabrook a piece of my mind, but there's something on his, and I wish I knew what it was."

It was at this point that June sent us upstairs. She gave us a piece of cake, too. We sat on my bed and ate it. Keith said:

" I wonder what the snag is ? "

" I can make a guess," I said, " but it wouldn't be right."

" Shoot," said Keith, putting the last crumbs in his mouth.

" That knife we boned from Mrs. Cockerton's shop . . ."

" Well ? "

" *That's the knife the murders were done with*."

" How could it be ? "

" I told you it was only a guess. Well, not even a guess. Nothing as definite as that, because if I really thought that was true, I should go to Mr. Seabrook to-morrow and give myself up."

" Good Lord, we'd be sent to Borstal or prison or something, wouldn't we ? "

" Probably. Better than Jack being hanged."

" Well, we needn't worry. He isn't even arrested, and he won't be."

This was not much comfort, and I could not sleep for thinking about the two knives and wondering whether we had done the best thing after all. It seemed as though we had. It seemed to me that if Jack's knife only had turned up, the police would have had no option but to hold him. With the two knives the police were confused. The thing I did not like about it at all was the fact that it was when Inspector Seabrook had seen the second knife that he had taken Jack to the police station.

I lay awake and went over everything again, but it still seemed to me that I had hit upon the right idea.

The real murderer had also lost his knife, and Mrs. Cockerton's lodger, the rag and bone man, had picked it up, not realizing what he had found. In this case, my skeleton theory, propounded to Keith, was correct. I lay awake for a long time, working out whether to point it out to Mrs. Cockerton or not. It meant making a clean breast of our theft, that was the trouble. I had decided not to say anything about it when I heard Christina come upstairs. I heard her bedroom door close, and crawled out of bed. Jack and June, I knew, had been upstairs more than an hour. I had heard them talking for a time, and then, I suppose, they went to sleep.

I listened at the top of the stairs and could hear nothing; so I crept down, barefooted, entered the kitchen and made a pot of tea.

" Christina," I said at the door. She was doing her face.

" Good heavens, Sim ! " she said. " What on earth are you doing in here at this time of night ? "

" Made tea for two. Got something to tell you," I replied. I told her all, and emphasized my theory about the murderer's knife.

" Too much of a coincidence, Sim. Things don't happen like that," she said, when I had finished.

" Then why did Mr. Seabrook look so peculiar when he saw the knife we had pinched ? "

" You must have imagined that his look altered. Besides, if the police haven't seen the murderer's knife, how could Evan know that there was anything important about the one you stole ? You're romancing, Sim. You must be. Drink your tea and go back to bed, darling. I'll go and see Evan in the morning before I go to work."

" You'd better not. You'll mess everything up," I said. " I'd like you not to interfere. I wanted your advice. I don't want help. We've got to see which way the cat jumps. There's something on Jack's mind, Christina. He's got something to hide. He isn't in a position to tell Mr. Seabrook how he came to lose his own knife, and he clung to the one we gave him as though it were a lifeline. Don't interfere."

" All right," she answered. " We'll wait and see what happens. But I'm glad I know all about it. It was nice of you to tell me."

" And you won't make a move without telling us ? "

" I shan't ask your permission, you know," she said, wiping stuff off her face.

" No, but you'll just put us wise ? "

" Yes, of course I will, Sim. You can trust me."

I kissed her. She was impulsive, though, and I wondered whether I ought to have told her anything.

Keith's holiday lasted until the following Monday morning. There seemed to be no more news, and, except that the streets and alleys were absolutely empty by eight o'clock except for stray cats and one or two people who pretended not to care about the murders, the life of our town went on as usual. Children were forbidden to play down by the canal, but, on the whole, they took no notice, and the boys had a game called ' Murderers ' which frightened the girls and led to some quarrels between parents and ended in some of the boys getting into trouble with their fathers.

Keith and I, sometimes by ourselves and sometimes with some of the others, ranged the riverside and the canal and played down on the Leys, fished and bathed, and carried on much as usual. June, glad to get rid of us, I think, used to give us some sandwiches and money for ginger beer, and turn us out after breakfast, and not expect to see us again before tea-time.

For the first three days we went nowhere near Mrs. Cockerton. Robbing her, even of so small a thing as the knife, was on our consciences, but on the Friday we had a windfall, for we sold three golf balls we had found, and got a shilling, and Keith suggested that we should go and spend it at her shop, as a slight recompense for the knife.   We would have given her the shilling, but could think of no reason we could put forward which would cause her to accept it.

" So we had better choose something she could not otherwise sell," said Keith, as we went along New Spring Gardens, and out into the high street to her shop.

We looked in the window for a long time, making up our minds to go in.   We were so long about it that she saw us there and came out to the door to greet us.

" A strange thing has happened since you were here last," said she. I felt quite sick with suspense, and Keith said afterwards that he felt so weak at the knees that he thought he could not continue standing on his feet. She beckoned us into the shop. " You know that knife, that you persuaded me to put in the window ? " she said.

" I know," said Keith, pulling himself together. " It wasn't there the next day."

" The day you last called, Mr. Keith."

" Yes. The day I last called."

" You wouldn't know about this," she said, turning to me. " But my lodger has a very strange idea. Do you know what he said ? "

We shook our heads, although I jumped at once to what it was.

" He thinks it was the very knife used by the murderer, and that the murderer must have stolen it from my shop, and then, with the coolest assurance, returned it after the murders. What do you think of that, I wonder ? "

" I think it might be possible," said Keith.

" It was the biggest surprise in life when you found it among my old rubbish. Such a surprise that I'm wondering now whether I ought to tell that nice young inspector that it once belonged to my dear husband."

" As long as he doesn't suspect you of doing the murders," said Keith, rather quickly.

" Good gracious ! " said Mrs. Cockerton. " Oh, yes ! Dear me ! I never thought of that. One wouldn't suppose that anyone would suspect me, but . . ."

" It would sound pretty bad, your having it on your premises," said Keith, " if it *were* the knife used by the murderer."

" Then I certainly shan't say a word," said Mrs. Cockerton firmly, " and I am much obliged for your quick wits, I am sure, my dear Mr. Keith."

With an exchange of compliments, we took our leave.

" It would never do," said Keith, " for her to go blowing the gaff at this stage of the proceedings, do you think ? "

" Of course not," said I. But neither of us felt at all happy about deceiving our friend. Keith, however, had had another idea.

" I could bear," said he, " to get a line on her lodger."

" The rag and bone man ?   He'd probably chase us away."

" Yes, but he wouldn't suspect us of *knowing* anything.   You know, Sim, it's odd about her having that knife.   It must have come from somewhere, and you and I have been through her stuff so often and so thoroughly that I don't see how we came to overlook it.   Somebody wished it on her, and that somebody must have been the murderer."

" Then why should she have told us in the first place that it was her late husband's pruning knife ?   I think we ought to put Mr. Seabrook on to it."

" In that case, what about Jack ?   And, although I don't want to over-emphasize it, what about ourselves ?   I think a spot of *private* investigation is called for here.   And it *may* have been her husband's knife, you know."

We returned to the shop, but Mrs. Cockerton had a customer, and we were obliged to wait.   The customer was an unusual-looking old lady with sharp black eyes, a yellow face, hands like claws and a general expression of knowing all about you and making allowances.   She was turning over some oddments on a tray.

We were always interested in strangers.   We watched whilst the old lady picked up the paper-weights, brass door-knockers, broken fans, second-hand cigarette cases and candle-snuffers, which, among other objects, were heaped on the tray, and then returned to a small object striped and pointed, having a face on it with a very large eye.

" What are you asking for this ? " she enquired.   Her voice surprised us by its lovely quality.

" Three and sixpence," said Mrs. Cockerton, glancing at us to ask us not to point out that she usually asked one and six for everything on that tray.

" Nonsense," said the old lady.   She took a magnifying-glass from her pocket.   " To begin with, you've no business to keep a thing like this in the window, and, to go on with, you should at least put a price on it which is, in some measure, commensurate with its value."

" You could have it for two shillings if you really wanted it," said Mrs. Cockerton.   The old lady put it into her hand and cackled.

" Do you know what you've got there ? " she asked. " That is a terracotta figurine from Mycenæ. I saw one very much like it in the National Museum of Athens. How do you come to possess such an object, I wonder ? "

" My husband had it given him," said Mrs. Cockerton. " Do you mean it is valuable ? "

" It is, at any rate, worth more than three and sixpence," said the old lady. " I'll send my friend, the Assistant Commissioner, to look at it. He is, besides being a policeman, an expert on early Ægean art. Would you care to have him come and see it ? "

" A policeman ! " said Mrs. Cockerton. " Oh, dear me, no ! Not on top of the knife and these dreadful murders. You take it, if you want it. I've had it for years and years. I'll give it you. It is lucky to give presents to strangers."

" Interesting," said the old lady. " Serve these boys, and then you and I must have a talk."

" We've got a shilling, Mrs. Cockerton," said I. " What can you do us for a shilling ? "

" Oh, dear, you know what there is as well as I do," she replied rather shortly. She seemed to be upset about something.

" Can we scout round, then ? " I asked. Taking her permission for granted, we went the round of the shop, and then to the room upstairs.

" It must be something we don't really want, and something she isn't likely to be able to sell to anyone else," said Keith. " We don't want to profit from the shilling."

In the end we selected a dirty but fairly big bit of lace which we found draped over an antimacassar on a broken armchair.

" Can we have this for a shilling, Mrs. Cockerton ? " I asked, when we went downstairs.

" Now what in the world do you want that for ? " she asked. " What's come over you to-day ? "

The old lady took the lace from my hand and grinned.

" A bargain at a shilling," she said. " Sell it to them, Mrs. Cockerton, and I shall make an immediate repurchase."

" It's good lace," said Mrs. Cockerton. " My husband bought it for his mother."

Keith turned on the old lady.

" What would you give for it ? " he asked.

" Thirty pounds. It is Point d'Alençon," she replied. She took a notecase out of her skirt pocket, and counted out the money before our astonished eyes.

" I won't take it," said Mrs. Cockerton.

" You know," said Keith, when we left the shop after Mrs. Cockerton had given way, " I feel better now about the knife. Mrs. Cockerton wouldn't have sold that lace but for us, do you suppose ? "

" I am sure she wouldn't," said I. " And we still have our shilling. Let's spend it on toffee and chewing gum for us, and a piece of milk chocolate for Christina, and a sherbet dab for Tom."

" He chokes on sherbet."

" He likes it, though."

" I wouldn't risk it. We've enough on our hands as it is. Buy chocolate buttons."

" All right."

" But we still haven't got any further," Keith remarked, when we had gone into Albany Road to buy the sweets. I did not reply. We strolled up the high street until we had passed the Half Acre opening and were opposite Catherine Wheel Yard. " Let's cross the bridges and the lock, and go round by the Leys ? " I suggested.

Catherine Wheel Yard was a narrow alley leading to an iron foundry and the canal. Usually we made the round in the opposite direction, but on this occasion we dropped down its cobbled slope and stood for a while on the first of the two bridges, for here the little River Bregant made one of its mouths to the Wyden, and the canal had been cut alongside. There was a lasher going under the bridge, and in the slipway beyond was a hopper with a broad-beamed dinghy on board.

" Wonder who that belongs to ? " Keith enquired. We debated whether to get aboard the hopper, but did not do so, as a man in fisherman's boots came out of one of the buildings on the wharf.

We walked on over the bridge, along a narrow path and over the second bridge. Here the water eddied in a rusty channel, and the barges were aground upon the mud. We never loitered just here, as we had never been able to find out whether the public were allowed to use the bridges. It was an odd little corner of our town, and the people who lived around that spot were by no means always friendly, and always looked suspiciously at strangers.

About fifteen yards from the second bridge were the lock gates. I glanced round, and was about to cross, when Keith pulled my shirt. Immediately I went to ground in an elder bush and looked to see what he had seen. It was Mrs. Cockerton's lodger, the rag and bone man. He tossed something into the water by the lock gates, and then peered into the depths.

" We ought to get that, whatever it was," said Keith, when the rag and bone man had gone across the lock and was trudging along the towing-path towards the Leys. " Did you spot what it was ? "

" Only a bit of rag. Looked like pink silk," said I. " Let's have a look." We stepped on to the thick wooden barrier, leaned over the rail and looked down. We could see what the man had thrown in. The water, coming up against the gates, was holding it firm.

" How to get hold of it ? " said Keith. " Too public a place to go in."

" Dangerous, too," said I.

" We could manage, if it wasn't so public."

" I doubt it. Dashed silly to get drowned."

" A long stick ? "

" A fishing-rod might do it, but, by the time we got home and back, no doubt it would be gone."

" One stay on watch and the other go ? "

" All right. You call." We left the narrow lock gates, and tossed our dud coin. We kept it for such occasions, and sometimes to lend to June for the gas meter when she was out of a shilling.

" Heads ! "

" Heads it is. I'll go, then." I went quickly. There was no time to hang about. I was fairly certain that by the time I got back the bit of stuff would have vanished, sucked under the gates, but there was just the chance that it would not. I loped across the bridges and trotted up the alley, watched my chance to cross the high street, continued my run up the Half Acre, rounded the library at last, passed the Baths, and went into our house the back way.

June was in. She said:

" What do you want ? Messing all over the house in your dirty shoes ! "

" Fishing-rod," said I, and took the stairs three at a time. Our rod had once been a good one. It was one which a yachtsman had given us. He had used it for sea-fishing. He had caught mackerel with it off Norfolk and Suffolk. It was nine feet six inches long. I think it was really a trout rod. I took it from the corner where we kept it, and ran out at the front door in case June should ask me to go on an errand. She did call after me, but I pretended not to hear, and was half-way up the road before she got to the front gate.

" Good work," said Keith, when I joined him and we had put the rod together. We had Ix gut and a Number 10 short shank hook. " Hope nobody thinks we're fishing," he added, getting out of the way while I made the cast.

The wind was blowing south-west, almost dead against the set of the stream. The water was sluggish and deep. I cast from the bank, and let the line drift down. I had to make three casts, and Keith, I know, was itching to have the rod. There was rather a lot of drag, but, fortunately, no weed, and I managed to hook the silk firmly, much more firmly than I had expected to be able to do. The difficulty then was to get it away from the lock. I played it carefully at first, then worked it clear of the gates, and reeled in.

Keith got down flat on his stomach and helped to draw it to the side. We unhooked it and laid it on the bank. It was easy to see why my hook had taken so strongly. The silk was part of a lady's corset, and was strongly provided with eyelet holes, into one of which my hook had been caught.

" Mr. Seabrook ought to have this," said Keith, as I put up the rod. " Let's take it along to show him. It must be important for that chap to have tried to get rid of it."

But Mr. Seabrook was not at the police station. We left the

pink silk with the sergeant, who seemed amused about it, I suppose because it was part of a lady's corset, and went home to dinner.

June had put Tom up to the table in his high chair, and Tom was glad to see us. It was washing day, as Monday had been the Bank Holiday, and Tom hated washing days just as much as we did. We had stew, from the Sunday joint, and potatoes, and a piece of cake for pudding, and a spoonful of jam on it because it had gone rather dry. Then June asked us to take Tom out for a couple of hours because he was fractious and naughty. We were not often asked to mind him, and he never objected to any kind of amusement which we considered good for him and entertaining to ourselves, so we agreed to take him with us, and June washed him and put on his gaiters, and off we went, with the push-chair for when he got tired.

" Let's go to the Baths," said Keith. " Mrs. Swainton will mind him."

Mrs. Swainton was the wife of the Bath superintendent, a very young, good-looking woman with two little children of her own.

" No money to go swimming," said I. But (not knowing, of course, where we were going with her son) June came down handsomely with sixpence, and we could get in for twopence as long as we went before two, and we would not have to pay for Tom, so, regardless of our stomachs, much distended with stew, we sneaked up and put on our trunks, tied our towels round under our shirts, wore our jackets and went out quickly before we could be asked where we were going.

Tom had a grand afternoon. Mrs. Swainton undressed him and put him on a little pair of breeches which she said would not hurt getting wet, and let him play in the slipper baths while we swam. We went to have a look at him afterwards. She had let him have warm water in one of the baths, and her little girl was looking after him and helping him to sail paper boats. He slipped over twice while we played with him, and we fished him up yelling with laughter.

Mrs. Swainton dried him and dressed him. He would not come out when *we* told him, but she picked him up quickly before he knew anything about it, and stopped his bellowing by giving him a spoonful of condensed milk. We

did not take him back until half-past four. His hair was dry
by then.

Nothing important happened all that week. Keith had to go
back to school on the Monday, but my school did not open for
another week and a half. He had sat for his Free Place during
March, but had not heard whether he had passed. I had won
my Free Place the year before, which made me rather old for
my form. Keith, if he passed, would be rather young for his,
but there was no chance of our being together, as I did not want
to do badly in the summer examination and get left down.

I was at a loose end on the Monday, after he had gone back,
and I planned that on the Wednesday I would go along to the
park to try for a game of football with the boys. Mr. Fothergill
always carried on with football until the end of May because he
did not like cricket. At the end of the football season he began
coaching for the sports, so the school never got much cricket.
Jack, however, was keen, and had coached us a bit, and I was
hoping for my House colours as we were short of bowlers in
Nelson, and I had, for my age, pace, and could keep a good
length. I got out my bat on Monday morning and oiled it and
looked it over, and took Tom down to the shops to get him out
of June's way for the washing. She had been almost gentle
since the business of Jack's knife, and I felt sorry for her.

In the afternoon I went to meet Christina at the station, and
we walked back instead of her taking the bus as usual. I told
her about the corsets, but she did not think it important.

" I suppose, as it was only part of a garment, he could not sell
it," she said. I said I thought all the rags a rag and bone man
collected were sold to make paper. We had heard nothing
more from the inspector, however, so I thought that perhaps she
was right and the garment had no importance.

Tuesday dragged. I made a few models, but it was not much
fun without Keith. On Wednesday I went to the park and
got a game, and hacked Alec Piper on the shins, which led to a
fight afterwards. June was annoyed because I had blood on
my shirt. Keith said, " The Ripper in person," and got his
head smacked by Jack. On Thursday I went out for a ride and
got a puncture, and on Friday I did a few errands, and June

gave me fourpence to go to the pictures. In all, it was a very tame week, and I did not look forward to the days which must still elapse before I returned to school.

Fortunately there was my holiday task. I read the set book and wrote an essay on local geography, and felt rather pleased with myself for being industrious. Then I pushed a few weeds and leaves between blotting-paper, put some heavy books on the top, wrote out the name-tabs for them, and even put my initials inside my new gym. shoes and my white P.T. shorts.

Then I sparred with our old gloves, and split a panel of the bedroom door. After that I gave up indoor amusements and pestered June for the money to go swimming. She suggested I waited for Keith, and gave me the money for both of us; not a word about the bedroom door, either. I was sympathetic. She must be horribly worried, I thought. Yet we had heard nothing more about the murders, nor had we any hint that Jack was still under suspicion.

I went for a prowl round the police station after that, and saw (as I found out afterwards) the Scotland Yard detective. He was in plain clothes and was with the yellow-skinned old lady who had bought Mrs. Cockerton's lace.

CHAPTER TEN

The Old Woman

AT WHAT point the people in our town began to dread the nights of the full moon I do not know, but the whispers, the rumours and the panic gradually grew.

I had homework every night which had to be done, but Keith was free as soon as his school closed, and he brought home reports, at first from the boys, and later from people in shops and round the houses. He was interested, and used to wait at the bus stops and in the cinema queue, to hear what people would say, but how and where the rumours began, whether someone was making mischief, or whether people had deduced from the beginning that the Ripper would continue his' work when the moon was bright again, neither he nor I could discover.

Once we had both returned to school our opportunities for sleuthing were few until Saturday came round. Police enquiries, we knew, were still going on, because Mrs. Cockerton told us that her lodger had been questioned by the inspector.

She did not mention corsets, and neither did we, but we concluded that the sergeant must have shown what we had found to Mr. Seabrook, and that he considered our discovery of some importance.

People then began asking why no arrest had been made, and all sorts of stories were put about that things were being hushed up because someone of importance was implicated. All sorts of names were mentioned, including that of our Member of Parliament, but he was known (by those who *did* know) to have been in Scotland over Easter, and the editor of our local paper, calling himself *Gadfly* in a special column of gossip which he wrote, had to give a thinly-veiled warning to people not to talk scandal.

Jack was not bothered any more.

" I expect the inspector is keeping Jack up his sleeve in case he can't find another scapegoat," said Keith. We felt uncomfortable.

" He should arrest the rag and bone man," said I. " The obvious criminal. People who drop things in the canal on purpose can always bear watching. Remember that woman with the baby ! "

" The obvious criminal is never the real criminal," said Christina, to whom I made this remark.

" That's in books," retorted Keith. " In real life the obvious criminal is almost always the real one. The woman with the baby certainly was." This reference was to the only previous bit of excitement in our town.

But nothing much happened until, with the next full moon, on a lovely, calm night of early summer, the murderer chose his fourth victim, and killed a pretty girl called Bessie Gillett in Saint George's Court, a very narrow alley almost opposite the police station.

It was at this point that I got to know the Scotland Yard detective whom I had seen in company with the old lady we had met in Mrs. Cockerton's shop. She introduced me to him, as a matter of fact, and, later, he came round to see Jack. It happened that on the Wednesday of the week following my return to school, when Keith had been back for more than a fortnight, we had been set some mathematics for homework which, since I had not attended to the lesson, I could not fathom. I sat at it for three-quarters of an hour, as it was for Mr. Short, whom I hardly liked to offend. He had already threatened me with detention, and of all things I loathed it was being kept at school on a summer evening.

Finding myself as much at sea at the end of the time as I had been at the beginning, I enlisted Jack's sympathy, and put my work before him. He spent about twenty minutes on it, then said he could not help me.

Christina was not in. She would have seen through the stuff in ten seconds. I decided to put it aside until she came home, and then get her to give me the solution.

I was honest over my homework as a rule. If I had been helped, I wrote this, neatly, at the foot of the exercise. The masters usually played the game by us, not always to their advantage, for if your father or older brother had done the whole thing for you, you still wrote *Helped* and it saw you through until the mid-term tests bowled you out. Few masters ever queried it, or asked to what extent the work had been done for you.

On this occasion, however, I did not even intend to say that I had been helped, since I realized that the homework had been set on the lesson we had received that day, and I would be expected either to have followed Mr. Short's exposition, or to have asked him to repeat such parts of it as I had not been able to grasp. Mr. Short was an able master, but not good-tempered or gullible. He was apt to round on one with a swift question on the work in which one claimed to have been helped, and, if the correct reply were not forthcoming, would ejaculate, ' These amateurs ! '—meaning our parents and friends—and keep one behind from a games period or a music lesson (the great rag of the week, for which we had a visiting teacher who was despised by the rest of the staff) in order to bring one's knowledge to the point he thought it should have reached.

I put aside my mathematics, therefore, for Christina, and took out my French. Here there was little difficulty, and I was sailing into a piece of translation with the aid of a good dictionary belonging to Jack when the telegraph boy came to the door.

Christina, the telegram stated, had met old friends of her family, and was staying the night at their house in Kensal Rise.

I have never seen anyone more upset than Jack. I was somewhat upset myself, since I saw no chance of getting my mathematics done, and was resigned to facing the just wrath of Mr. Short on the morrow.

Suddenly inspiration took me. Mr. Seabrook had once told me that he was studying trigonometry, and liked it. To a man capable of such mental flights, my elementary problem must seem child-play.

Leaving Jack cursing and fretting over Christina's absence, and threatening to go straight over to Kensal Rise and bring her home—fortunately June was putting Tom to bed, and did not hear his remarks, which were made to Keith and me—I slipped out of the house with my books and, trotting along Braemar Road and along Drum Lane, was soon at the police station, and was fortunate enough to find Mr. Seabrook at home.

He was having a late tea, and with him was the earnest-looking man who looked very much like a lawyer whom I had met in company with the old lady in Mrs. Cockerton's shop. She was with him again.

I was for backing out, but Mrs. Seabrook had pushed me in, cut me a slice of cake, put me on the end of the settee next to the black-eyed old lady, and poured me out a cup of tea, before I could utter a word.

" Well," said the black-eyed old lady, " and what is troubling us this time ? "

" Maths," said I, trembling with fright.

" Ah," she responded. " Maths. Eat your cake. What of these murders ? "

Whatever a grown-up person might have thought, it all made

sense to me. I grinned at her gratefully, ate my cake, had another piece, drank my tea, and rested content. My homework was going to be explained to me, and I was also to be called into consultation about the murders.

Of course, the murder of Bessie Gillett had not taken place at that time. It was reserved for that same evening. I am glad to say that none of us, except the old lady, had the slightest idea that it was about to take place. When I had finished my tea and she had enquired my name and such particulars of my family as old ladies deem essential to their understanding of a child or an adolescent—in which last class she appeared to place both Seabrook and the man from Scotland Yard—the old lady we had met at Mrs. Cockerton's introduced me in these words:

" Detective-Inspector Cosgrove, allow me to present Mr. Simon Innes. Mr. Innes, this is Detective-Inspector Cosgrove of the C.I.D."

Of the two of us, I think the Detective-Inspector was the more alarmed.

" Ma'am ! " he said, in protest.

" Oh, nonsense ! " said the old lady. " He is one of the actors in the piece, and a very intelligent fellow. He has something to tell us, I feel sure. He may be able to prevent the next murder."

" Sure he's got something to tell us," said Mr. Seabrook. " This boy has been in on the matter from the very beginning. I would like you to hear his story."

I had not expected this, and was not prepared. However, all three of them looked at me and were silent, and I felt constrained to begin.

I told them a very great deal. Why, I do not know, except that the atmosphere was sympathetic and kind. I talked of our determination to see the circus on Good Friday, of our desire to enlarge the hole in the big marquee, of our Holy Thursday jaunt, and all the rest.

Nobody interrupted. The black-eyed old lady made notes. When I had done she questioned me. During her questions the Scotland Yard man took notes. Mr. Seabrook did not question me or take notes.

It was soon clear that the old lady knew what she was talking about. She took me through my statement in the most business-like way, and, apart from the fact that I was dreadfully afraid of saying anything which might be prejudicial to Jack, I enjoyed myself, and warmed up to what she wanted. She picked out the salient points with a skill and a grasp of the facts which astonished me. It was surprising, too, how many of these salient points there seemed to be, and how little importance Keith and I had attached to them.

" Just one or two points, dear child," she said.

" Yes, ma'am ? "

" My name is Bradley."

" Yes, Mrs. Bradley."

" First: you say that you have had the free run of this antique shop ? "

" Yes, we have."

" You turned over all the stock, at various times, no doubt ? "

I felt uncomfortable, and kept a wary eye on Mr. Seabrook. We were getting dangerously near the matter of the stolen knife. I did not care for the opening to the conversation.

" Yes," I admitted. " We generally had a good look through her stuff."

" You think you could swear to what she had in the shop on the Thursday of the first murder ? "

" Oh, yes, I think so, Mrs. Bradley."

" Good." To my great relief she gave up that side-line and branched off into another. " You proposed to go to the circus."

" Yes, ma'am. Yes, we did."

" What was the price of admission ? "

" Threepence, for boys." As we had not, in the end, worked our way under the canvas, I felt fairly safe in answering this question.

" Had you threepence ? "

" No—well, not at that time. We—we had to wait until Saturday."

" By which time the circus would have come and gone ? "

" Yes, I'm afraid so. Still, that couldn't be helped."

" You naughty boy ! " she said, wagging her forefinger at me. I felt, however, that in her I had an ally. She turned to the men and asked for a map of the district. Mr. Seabrook pulled out a plan of our town and the country which immediately surrounded it, and pointed out the various places connected with my story and with the murders. " Now," she continued, " tell me again exactly what you did on that Thursday night."

Then she took the inspector's map, and we got down on to the carpet (watched, I imagined, by the parrots which crowded the walls), and she made me put my finger on every spot I had named and say how long it had taken us to get there. When it came to Dead Man's Bridge I had to describe very carefully where we had gone to ground, and how far off the man had been.

Then she took me back in my story to the Thursday evening. " This man who spoke of the big cats being murderers," she said. " Had you ever seen him before ? "

" No, but perhaps I don't know everybody in the place, although I think I know most, except, of course, for the people who live on the Leys."

" Have you ever seen the man since ? "

I said that I had not. As a matter of fact, until I had told her the tale that evening, I had forgotten that we had ever seen the man.

" I want you to look out for him," she said. " Now, the tiger of the circus. *Was* it a lad in the skin ? "

" Oh, no, I shouldn't think so. That was only a tale among the boys."

" I wonder why they picked upon the tiger ? I must ask Mr. Seabrook whether there is any likelihood of that little rumour being true. Now, the man with the knife. You saw nothing more of him that night ? "

" No. Nothing at all."

" But you've not much doubt about what he did ? "

" I do know he couldn't have been in front of us, walking along by the canal. We'd have been bound to see him."

" Quite. Now, these mathematics of yours." And in five minutes she had not only done the rider but had explained the theorem so that I never afterwards forgot it. I thanked her with all my heart.

"Reciprocal kindnesses," she responded with her harsh cackle, "are the oil of life, child. You help me with my murders, and I help you with your homework."

"*Your* murders?" I asked. "I thought they were Mr. Seabrook's and Mr. —— Detective Inspector Cosgrove's murders, ma'am."

"Mine as well. I'm a consulting psychiatrist to the Home Office, and when things become a little abnormal they often send me along. Mr. Cosgrove, in fact, is here merely to keep a fatherly eye on the proceedings." She looked at me with her sharp black eyes. "It is fun, and we must have it together, but, first, we must be frank with one another. Can you be frank, do you think, child?"

"Yes, I suppose so," I muttered; and I cast a glance at the detective, and at Mr. Seabrook.

"Oh, not in front of *them*," she said, with another cackle. She prodded me in the ribs with a finger as bony as that of the witch who prodded Hansel. "In any case it is time you went back to your home, and I to my hotel. We have not seen the last of this business, and to-night we have the full moon. Where should you suppose the next attempt will be made?"

"I'm sure I don't know," said I. "Do you think there will be another attempt? Lots of people think so, but I just thought they were scared."

"There is almost sure to be another attempt," she said. "And I don't see how to prevent it. Where can I meet you to-morrow?"

"I have to be at school until four, and it takes me three-quarters of an hour to get home. I have to come by train, and walk from the station. And then . . . I've my homework to do. But I'd be able to do that later on in the evening if we could meet directly after tea."

"Excellent! I will meet you in the reading-room of the public library as soon as you have finished your tea. I shall get you to show me the neighbourhood. By half-past seven you will be free. I will arrange with your headmaster to have your homework excused, unless you think it particularly important that you do it."

" It's only an English essay to-morrow night, and a page of history swot," I responded joyously. " I can easily miss all that. It won't make the slightest difference."

" Consider it arranged, then."

I was jubilant. It never occurred to me that she would be unable to do as she said. Neither was I wrong in my assumptions. My homework was formally excused until further notice, my form master, Mr. Rogers, remarking, in his jocose way, that I was fortune's favourite, and that I must be sure and speak up for him at the Old Bailey if he happened to be laid by the heels.

I ran all the way home, put my newly-acquired knowledge into my geometry exercise book, and went off to bed without a murmur of protest. June and Jack were arguing about Christina's going off like that for the night, and Jack was saying that it would be all right, he supposed, so long as Christina did not take it into her head to come home, after all, after dark, but that he did not like it.

June pointed out, snappily, that it would be a full moon. Jack looked at her, whistled a bar or two under his breath, and then said:

" That's what I mean."

Keith and I, when we got to our room, discussed whether Christina were likely to do anything so foolish as to return from the station late at night, but we decided that she would not. If she had had any idea at all of returning, she would not have sent the telegram, we thought. It had cost one and threepence, and nobody, as Keith pointed out, would spend one and three-pence for nothing.

Much comforted, I said my prayers, got into bed, and then told him about my evening.

" Am I in it as well ? " he asked, as soon as I had finished.

" Sure," I said. " I don't detect without you."

" Will the old lady mind ? "

" Call her Mrs. Bradley. No, I don't think she'll mind. She seems rather odd, but a thoroughly good sort. Old ladies usually are. See you in the morning."

It was our usual good night.

I had the news about Bessie Gillett as I went up in the train. I was rather late that morning, and missed walking to the station with the two or three boys who came my way. I almost missed the train, and would have done, except that the guard waited. He groused, but he was a very decent man, and never made us late for school.

"Thought you weren't coming," he said, as he pushed me in, shut the door, blew his whistle and waved his flag, all in one operation.

"That's what we all thought," said Sparks. "Heard the news ? Another murder. The worst of the lot. And almost opposite the police station."

CHAPTER ELEVEN

The Death of a Nursemaid

"Tell us ! " said I. "Where was it, and who was murdered, and what time ? Was it another Ripper murder ? Are the police on the job yet ? "

"Look here," said Sparks, "whose murder is it ? Yours or mine ? "

He was a slow-moving, slow-spoken, fattish, white-faced boy, brilliant at Latin, which he took with the post-Matric form. His father was a clergyman. Sparks was a year older than myself. I was abashed.

"Go on, Sparks," I said humbly.

"The murder," said Sparks, "took place in a low alley called Saint George's Court, almost opposite the police station. The victim is a girl of nineteen of blameless type . . . at least, it is believed so. . . ."

"Come off it, Sparksey," said one of his friends. Sparks eyed the interrupter with dignity, and, turning again to me, continued:

"Of blameless type, being one of our own parishioners. Her name is Bessie Gillett. She makes a slight but honest living by acting as children's nurse at the Manor, residence of Mr. E. N. K. Hopkinson, sometime of the Foreign Office, her charges being the two small grand-daughters of Mr. Hopkinson, his daughter's children.   The post was not of residential type, but the deceased used to attend daily at the Manor House for the purpose of taking the two little girls for a walk, or of amusing them in their nursery should the weather chance to be inclement."

" Come *off* it, Sparksey ! " said the interrupter, " and get on with the stuff. We want to hear about the blood."   Sparks appealed to the compartment.

" Gentlemen, do you, or do you not desire to apprehend the circumstances which led to this bestial crime ? "

" *Rather !* " said the rest of us in chorus; and two of Sparks' admirers put the heckler under the seat, and thoughtfully shoved his handkerchief in his mouth to lessen his powers of obstruction.

" It so happened," continued Sparks, " that my excellent sire, who, as those among you who profess the faith should be aware, is vicar of the parish of Saint George in the East, chanced to be passing by the mouth of the alley on his way home from attending the sick-bed of one Annie Varley, bedridden since Michaelmas twelvemonth, when he heard the sound of running feet. He halted, he can scarcely say why, and a young man named Harry Eldon came out of the mouth of the alley and collided with him, not seeing my father in his haste and terror.   When he recognized him . . .

" ' Quick, vicar ! A doctor ! There's a dreadful accident ! ' he gasped.   Fortunately the two of them were within a stone's throw of the surgery of Doctor Seattle, and they, with the doctor, were soon upon the scene.   The poor girl's death from knife wounds could be assumed immediately.   And now, gentlemen, our destination, I perceive.   More upon the return journey, if it please you."

We badgered him for details all the way up to school from the station, but I do not think he knew any more. His father, naturally, had not described the girl's injuries, but they must have been rather terrible, as he did admit to us, in ordinary conversational terms, that his father had refused any breakfast except two cups of coffee, and looked as pale as a ghost.   It also appeared that Harry Eldon, a young bricklayer's labourer who lived in Albany Street, was being held by the police for questioning.

I did not see Sparks on my journey home from school. I was anxious to get back and have my tea and meet Mrs. Bradley at the library, so I ran my hardest to the station and caught the early train, which, as a rule, only the Form II boys were out early enough to catch.

I had finished my tea by a quarter-past five, and had been in the reading-room eight minutes when Mrs. Bradley came in.

"Excellent," she said. "I thought I should have been first. Let us walk up the Manor Road, and as we go you shall answer my questions and direct my attention to such aspects of the crimes as seem to you germane to our enquiry."

So we walked from the library grounds on to the Manor Road and strolled towards the station.

"Now, let us see," she said. "We have not yet, I think, discussed the very interesting statement which you made respecting a man who lifted your younger brother off the fence when he had caught his foot. You remember?"

"Yes," I answered. "We thought he must be a detective in disguise, or perhaps the murderer." And, at her request, I detailed again the conversation we had had with the man.

"You say you came to the conclusion that the man was either a detective in disguise or the murderer. Yet, when you first met him, you thought he seemed to be an ordinary workman," she observed.

"Yes. But it was when he seemed to know about the knife that we realized he was something other than that."

"I don't see your reasoning, child."

"Perhaps we did rather jump to conclusions," I admitted. "But, you see, we had a special interest in the knife when we heard the kind of knife it was."

"You believed what the man said, then?"

"Yes, we did. And, later on, you see . . ." I paused, regarded the pitfall gaping at my feet, and was silent.

"Ah, yes," she said. "Your elder brother owned a similar knife. Now two such knives have turned up, both bearing your brother's initials. Very odd, is it not? Almost more than coincidence, that."

I felt extremely uncomfortable. I suppose I looked it, too, for she added kindly:

"There is often a great deal to gain by being frank. I do not press you, of course. You know your own business best, but . . . could we not do without one more mystery in this very complicated affair?"

I made up my mind.

"Yes, ma'am, we could," said I. And I recounted to her the whole history of the two knives, so far as it was known to me.

"I did ask you, did I not, whether you could swear to all the articles which comprise Mrs. Cockerton's stock?" she asked, at the end.

"Why, yes, you did, Mrs. Bradley."

"And this knife was not among those articles on the previous Thursday afternoon?"

"No, I am sure it was not."

"We will assume then, as Inspector Seabrook has done, that the knife found (and removed) by you, was the weapon with which these fearful crimes were committed. There was blood where the blade is rivetted on to the hilt. It proves to be human blood, but not of the same blood-group as that of the girl at the farm. The knife picked up along the road we are now following showed no trace of blood whatsoever."

"So Jack didn't commit the murders!" I exclaimed. "I mean . . . it can be proved he didn't commit them."

"It *could* have been proved, before you tampered with the evidence, my poor boy."

I was overcome with dismay. My next words almost choked me.

"You mean that Jack may be hanged because of our stealing that knife?"

"No, no. We will see that he isn't! But it is as well not to try to defeat the ends of justice. The object was laudable, the means deplorable, the outcome rather a nuisance. Never mind." She cackled heartily, startling the ducks on Mr. Hopkinson's lake which we happened to be passing at the time. "You mustn't worry," she added. "All will be well. It is just as well that the truth of the matter has come out. Detective-Inspector Cosgrove will interview your brother later on."

"You guessed the truth, ma'am, didn't you?" said I, feeling suddenly certain of this. "You saved Jack from being arrested! Perhaps from being tried for his life!" I felt overwhelmed with gratitude towards her, and continued, almost hysterically, "I'll sign a statement for the police! I'll do anything! I suppose I can be sent to prison," I added. I had time to wonder whether Christina would trouble to visit me there.

"I don't think a statement will be necessary," Mrs. Bradley observed. "You may have to submit to a few harsh words from the inspector. I do not think prison will be necessary, as you are a First Offender."

I thanked her humbly for this consoling statement.

"And now," said the old lady, having paused to allow me to recover, "the field where the first murder was committed I have already been shown. The back of the *Pigeons* inn I have also seen. This, I presume, is the farmhouse, and the body was found . . ."

"Just there," I said, pointing to the place. We rested our arms on the low brick wall of the midden and contemplated the yard.

"Cow-byres and stables," said my companion. "What kind of farming do they do? All dairy-farming? If so, why so many horses?"

"Mr. Viccary lets out horses to shopkeepers with vans, if they don't want to buy their own, or have nowhere to keep them," said I.

"Excellent," she replied. "There would be no lack of people with a right to enter the farmyard, then, I take it? A stranger would not be challenged?"

"I don't know much about it, ma'am, I'm afraid."

"Let us see," she said; and before I realized what she was going to do, she had pushed the gate open and was walking up the flagged path which divided into two portions the trampled mud of the yard. I darted after her.

"Shall I come, too, ma'am?" I asked.

"Why not?" enquired Mrs. Bradley. "Two sets of ears and two ripe intelligences are always better than one. What you obtain, I may miss, and *vice versa*."

The farmhouse was a very long, low building separated from the farmyard by a small garden in which was a white-painted wicket-gate. From this a very short path of bright red bricks led to a broad front door. Above the door was a clock, and above the clock, in a little alcove, was a large china picture like a dinner plate in white and blue.

Mrs. Bradley knocked at the door, and Mrs. Viccary's daughter Anna opened it. I knew Anna by sight, although I had never spoken to her. The Viccarys came to our church, and Anna sang in the choir.

There had been a rumour, some months before, that there was an understanding between Anna Viccary and Danny Taylor, but nothing had come of it. There was talk that the Viccarys did not like Danny, and that the Taylors did not think the daughter of Mr. Hopkinson's groom was good enough for their son.

It was easy enough to imagine Anna giving in to her parents, but not easy at all to think of Danny giving in to his.

The next thing we knew was that Danny was meeting the dairymaid, Marion Bridges, who was several years older than he, and, in most people's opinion, nothing much to look at. Danny was a handsome lad, and his wild ways and daring actions had made him a great many friends and sympathizers, as well as a good many enemies. Jack was, perhaps, his greatest friend. June hated and feared him, because he had an Irish tongue and swayed Jack any way he pleased. June always thought he would get Jack into trouble before the finish, an opinion which she voiced whenever she was angry with Jack, and which annoyed and irritated Jack a little more every time he heard it.

Anna did not seem surprised to see us. She smiled politely and asked what she could do for us.

"You can tell me whether your maidservant left any will," said Mrs. Bradley.

Anna looked surprised and alarmed. She was a big, fair-haired girl with simple manners and a face which gave away her thoughts.

"Would you come in, please," she said. I was for hanging back. At the age of thirteen my dislike of entering the houses of people I did not know very well amounted almost to morbid dread. But Mrs. Bradley took me by the arm and pulled me in with her.

Anna took us into a pleasant room overlooking the yard and on the same side of the house as the cowsheds.

"Ah," said Mrs. Bradley, walking to the window, "an excellent view of the spot."

I saw Anna's hand go to her mouth as women's hands do when they are going to scream. She made no sound, however, beyond a slight choking, and went hastily out of the room. I could hear her calling her father. In a moment Mr. Viccary came in.

He was not much like his daughter. She took after her mother. Mr. Viccary was a short, thin man, slightly bow-legged, as I believe grooms usually are. His farm belonged to Mr. Hopkinson, who let him have it at a very low rent because of his years of service. He was nearly sixty years old, for he had not married until he was forty, and Anna was now a girl of about eighteen. I suppose it was because he had been a groom that, he was able and willing to keep so many horses for hire.

He came in smacking his hands down the seams of his breeches, for he was wiry and energetic. If he had nothing to do, he invented movements and gestures to use up his surplus energy.

"Well, good morning, ma'am," he said, looking bright and brisk, "and what can we do for you to-day?"

"You can read my credentials," said Mrs. Bradley. "I am here to represent the Home Office. I want to know all you can tell me about your late dairymaid, Marion Bridges, who was murdered on Saturday, April 4th." She handed to Mr. Viccary a letter. I do not know what was in it, but it seemed to convince Mr. Viccary that she was someone to be trusted.

"Scotland Yard, eh?" said he. "I heard there was going to be a detective sent down to help young Seabrook, but I didn't foresee it would be a lady."

"Neither is it," Mrs. Bradley replied. "A detective-inspector from Scotland Yard is keeping an eye on the case. But, as the victims are all, unfortunately, young women, it was thought advisable . . ."

"Oh, yes, I can see that, of course," said Mr. Viccary. "Well, now, ma'am, what did you wish me to tell you? . . . Not that I know much about it, and, of course, I've been put through it already by young Seabrook. She'd been warned, time enough, to be in betimes, us having a good many tramps and such-like through here, it being so near to London, and she was brought to my place, you know, after the poor girl was dead."

"I don't want to know any more about the murder itself," said Mrs. Bradley. "I have two questions that I would be glad if you could answer. First, what kind of young man was your servant's lover? Second, do you know whether she made a will, or had expressed any wish with regard to the disposal of her property?"

"Strange kind of questions, both," said Mr. Viccary. "I would say, ma'am, as you'd been tipped the wink by somebody, like."

"We have our sources of information, of course," said Mrs. Bradley, "but in this case it is merely what the police, I believe, call a check-up. May we first have the details about this young man?"

"Why, everybody knows Danny Taylor," said Mr. Viccary. "Mind you, I'm not saying anything against the lad. Far from it. But when a boy from a rich home . . . his dad could buy me out twenty times and not notice it . . . comes after a girl the like of poor Marion Bridges, well, I'm not giving away news when I say it isn't all it should be. And, the poor girl's condition being what it was . . ."

He gave a sharp glance at me, and raised his eyebrows. Mrs. Bradley nodded.

"I understand," she said. "How long had he been courting Marion Bridges?"

"A matter of seven or eight months. First we noticed was at the last Harvest Festival. Shared the harvest hymn leaflet, they did, and not in his father's pew but in the gallery."

"Significant," said Mrs. Bradley; although how she knew it was, unless she went entirely by the tone of Mr. Viccary's voice, I do not know. It was true enough, however, that, in our church, young couples who were serious about one another usually began to give their elders and contemporaries something to talk about by sharing a hymn-book in the gallery of the church on Sunday evenings. It was the recognized beginning to an engagement. Our church was almost as strictly enclosed for marriages as a village. Wesleyans tended to marry other Wesleyans, and the simplest way for a couple to indicate that a marriage was pending was the custom of sitting together in one of the gallery pews. Everybody had been surprised to see Dan Taylor there with Marion Bridges because all the people in the know had thought it would be Anna Viccary, if once she could make up her mind either to run off with Danny or stand up to her mother and father.

" But what kind of lad is he ? " asked Mrs. Bradley. " You see, Mr. Viccary, I must be frank. In these cases of murder, as no doubt you will have read, a great deal of suspicion is bound to be attached to the last person known to have seen the deceased alive. In this case that person appears to have been young Mr. Taylor."

" What ! " said Mr. Viccary. " Young Danny Taylor ! That's a laugh, that is ! Mind you, I've not much use for that young fellow. Came dancing round my daughter here until I choked him off. But, with all his faults, he's not the chap to do a murder. Never think of him again, ma'am, not in *that* connection. Well, that *is* a laugh, that is ! " And he gave it its due by laughing himself, most heartily. " But, there," he added, coming to himself, for he was a solemn man as a rule, " I've no business to be laughing. I beg your pardon, ma'am, and that of the poor dead creature. You'll be glad to know, I'm sure, she had the best funeral money could pay for, in accordance with her own wish expressed to my girl Anna when they were doing the bedrooms out between 'em. She left money to pay for it, too."

" Ah," said Mrs. Bradley. " Now we come to it, I think. To whom was this money left ? "

" Why, to my wife," said Mr. Viccary in surprise. I was surprised myself. I could not think of anyone else who would be at all likely to have had it, if the girl had put it by for her funeral. " She gave mother twelve pound ten, not more than . . . ah, I recollect now ! Last New Year's Day it was. Mother laughed at her, of course, for the very last thing you'd think of was that tough young woman laying down and dying. But something, you see, foretelled it to the girl. *Must* have done, or why should she have made any such provision ? And her bit of money she had left . . . a matter of eight pound odd . . . for she wanted for nothing here, you may be sure, and never spent half her wages . . . not a quarter of 'em, indeed once she took up with Danny Taylor, for there was never an outing, of course, but what he paid for . . . she put into my missus's keeping, too and all. ' It'll do for my trousseau,' she says, with a bit of a laugh.

" ' I'm in hopes he'll do the right thing, then, and in time,' my missus told her."

" She was convinced, then," said Mrs. Bradley, " that she was going to marry Danny Taylor ? "

" *She ?* We was all convinced of it, ma'am. He only had to pluck up courage to break it to his family, and the deed was as good as done."

" Oh ! The Taylors wouldn't have cared about the marriage ? "

" When I tell you, ma'am, as my girl Anna wasn't good enough for the Taylors, you may guess what they'd say to a dairymaid. Trouble was, I reckon, not so much the money as that the elder son had married a titled lady—or near enough titled, you might say."

" Indeed ? "

" Oh, yes, to be sure. The Honourable Miss Caroline Something . . . I can't remember the name . . . daughter of an earl, so somebody told me. Of course, the Taylors are warm, ma'am, very warm, as I said, but that was looked upon as a pretty good snip all round. He's not been near his home since, but what of that ? The Taylors can spend their summer holidays in a real castle down in the south of England whenever they like."

" I see," said Mrs. Bradley. " Still, it sounds as though Marion was a thrifty sort of girl, now, doesn't it, to have saved more than twenty pounds."

" Bit of a Mrs. Scrooge, I always used to fancy," said Mr.

Viccary. " Got plenty out of Danny, too—watches and jewellery and that."

" And how old was this sensible girl ? "

" Well," said Mr. Viccary, " there, I rather fancy, ma'am, you've hit the nail on the head. It was only my opinion . . . and, of course, I've nothing to go on. Quite the reverse, in fact, because the girl herself used to own to twenty-four. But it's my belief, from what I know about horses, not to say mares and fillies, that another ten years would have been a sight nearer the mark. Still, I mustn't speak ill of the dead, and if the poor girl *could* take a bit off her age and be believed, it's none of our business, maybe."

" All the same, it *is* our business," said Mrs. Bradley to me, when we were back on the Manor Road. " Did the young man really prefer the substantial charms of the thrifty Marion to those of the girl who let us into that house ? "

" I couldn't say, ma'am," said I. " I only know that Christina . . ."

" Ah, yes, Christina," said she. " I've heard a good deal about Christina. What are our young inspector's chances, do you suppose ? Is the girl really as heartless as he makes out ? "

" I don't know, I'm sure, ma'am," said I, indescribably agitated by this description of my sweetheart. " I wouldn't call her heartless at all. Very much the reverse, I would have said. But I only know her at home."

She cackled, and dropped the subject, greatly, I may say, to my relief. It was my hidden desire . . . hidden until that moment of self-revelation . . . that as neither of us would ever be old enough to have Christina for his wife, June would die at some conveniently early date, and so leave Jack for Christina. We should, by those means, at any rate keep her in the family.

I did not voice these thoughts. We had shut the farmyard gate carefully behind us and walked on up the road towards the station. We went past the station itself, and walked on until we came to the cart-road which led down to the little river, and from which one could reach the confluence, at Dead Man's Bridge, of that river with the canal.

" If you please, Mrs. Bradley," said I, " this is the last turning by which we can reach the river until we get into Brelton-by-the-Splash."

" How far is that ? " she enquired.

" About two and a half miles, ma'am."

" Too far.   Let us turn down here."

" We shall be trespassing, ma'am, directly we climb that gate."

" I have a police permit.   I do not know that it entitles us to trespass, but, if we are accosted, we will see."

She climbed the gate as easily as I myself could do.   Her skirt seemed no hindrance, and she did not need my assistance.   Even Christina could have done no better.   I was surprised, but tried not to show it.

The cart-road was wide enough for us to walk abreast.

" What exactly is your line, Mrs. Bradley," I enquired, as we passed a great oak tree at which the cart-road branched away to the right, and a faint track led steeply downwards towards the river.

" My line of investigation, do you mean, child ?   Well, now that I have heard a little of what has occurred, I am . . . I speak, of course, in the strictest confidence . . . I am inclined to begin by investigating, not the murders themselves, with their necessary but, between ourselves, boring sequels of inquests, medical reports, routine police enquiries, and the like, but various puzzling points which the police, so far, have overlooked.

" You see, it is not, in the broad sense, extraordinary that a murder should have taken place on a fair-ground or in a circus encampment.   It is regrettable but not interesting; it is particularly not interesting from the point of view of pure psychology and even purer detection.   Even that a woman should be murdered outside a public house is not a matter for the amateur of crime.   You follow me ? "

" Oh, yes, ma'am," I said eagerly.   " Certainly I do.   You spoke just now of this being in confidence between us.   Mayn't I tell Keith what you say ? "

" Oh, yes.   All good detectives have a Watson."

" Where Keith is concerned," said I . . . for although I was pleased with the flattery, I was far too honest at that age to accept a compliment which was certainly not my due . . . " I am more likely to be the Watson than he is."

" Indeed ? " she said. " Well, pick his brains, then. We shall need every ounce of concentration we possess in order to prevent any more of these horrid excursions into murder."

" Do you think there will be another to-night, ma'am ? "

She pointed to the sky, which was clouding over for rain.

" Not if this blots out the moon, child."

" You think the murderer is a lunatic, then ? "

" In a sense, all murderers are lunatics. Killing is not a sane reaction to the circumstances of life."

We dropped down into the little hawthorn dell which was the shortest cut to the river bank, and I pointed out, in the distance, Dead Man's Bridge. She did not seem particularly interested, so, as we walked on I ventured to continue a previous conversation by asking her why she had decided that the most interesting case had been that of Marion Bridges.

" I thought that the case of Marion Bridges presented features of rare value," she replied, " partly because, to begin with, as soon as we came to this third murder, we were dealing with the kind of people who could be approached from the angle of motive. You see, in every case of murder . . . or, indeed, of any crime . . . there are three possible angles of approach: motive, means, and opportunity. Of the three, it seems to me that motive is by far the most suggestive. Once you know *why*, you are inclined to be able to say *who*. You follow ? "

" Oh, yes, Mrs. Bradley, I do. But you don't think Danny Taylor murdered Marion because she was going to have a baby ? "

" Little pitchers have long ears ! " she retorted. " I shall have to learn more of young Mr. Taylor before I can answer that question. On the face of it, it appears likely."

" Only circumstantially, Mrs. Bradley," I submitted. She poked me in the ribs as we walked.

" You are much too clever for a Watson," she retorted.

" Well, you ought to take evidence of character into consideration," said I, defending my point. " Everybody knows that Danny Taylor is wild, but you won't find anybody in this town to give him a really bad character except, perhaps, my sister-in-law, June Innes."

" Well, well, we shall see," she replied.   " Your brother is his friend.   Do you think *he* knows anything about it ? "

" He knows lots about Danny," I answered, " and, of course . . ."

" And, of course, he did make a most mysterious journey, in response to a most mysterious whistling, on the night this murder was committed."

I was silent.   I could not find anything to say in Jack's defence.   I tried to change the subject.

" You know this last murder, Mrs. Bradley ?   The one in Saint George's Court ? "

" I do."

" Well, don't you think it rather peculiar that the vicar was out so late ? "

She cackled, and told me to lead her back to the Manor Road by way of Mr. Taylor's field.   I pointed out the difficulties of crossing the ditch to get there, but she made light of them, and we arrived, muddy and exhilarated, at the police station, where I took my leave of her.

CHAPTER TWELVE

The Gleaning

I WAS ABLE to put my question to Sparks on the following morning as we went up together in the train.

" Your old man, Sparks," said I.   " Pretty late for him to have been out."

" Upon what occasion, my dear Innes ? " enquired Sparks.

" When that girl was killed."

" Your remark, coupled with the slightly lewd and definitely improper suggestion which it implies, is not in good taste, my dear fellow.   My sire, as I thought I had pointed out, was about his business—that of visiting the sick."

" Yes, but, Sparks—at midnight ? "

" Certainly not at midnight. At twenty minutes to eleven. He timed his arrival in order to remonstrate with the patient's husband for having been out at the public house instead of cheering and comforting his afflicted spouse."

" Oh, I see."

" Clearly, I trust."

" Oh, yes. He had to wait until near enough closing time."

" You fatigue me," said Sparks.

" I see," said Mrs. Bradley, when I detailed this explanation to her. " By the way, I am interested in the result of your fishing expedition. You remember ? "

" I ought to bring Keith," said I. Keith had expressed his disappointment at being left out of our consultations of the previous evening, and it seemed rather mean to be having fun without him.

" By all means, child. Both meet me at the police station at the end of half an hour, then."

I had run into her at the top of our road. I got Keith, and we raced along to the police station, arriving long before the appointed time.

" Let's have a look at Saint George's Court while we're waiting," he suggested. But a policeman was on duty at the entrance. He told us to get along out of it, so we got. " Silly," said Keith, as we crossed the road and strolled down Ferry Lane. " As though there can be anything to find out now."

" I don't know," I said. " Come to think of it, Saint George's Court is a cul-de-sac. What was a girl doing down there at that time of night, I wonder ? "

" Had an appointment to meet her young man, and the murderer turned up instead," suggested Keith.

" Or the murderer *was* her young man," I suggested, feeling excited. " Now if we could find out whether her young man had any connection with Danny Taylor, or even Marion Bridges, we might be getting somewhere."

" Who's Marion Bridges ? " asked Keith. " Oh, I know. The woman who was murdered at the farm. You know, Sim, there's something very fishy about that murder."

"Yes, I told you last night that Mrs. Bradley thinks so too."

"But, Sim, did she ask whether the horses kicked up any fuss?"

"Did she what?"

"Ask whether the horses stamped and whinnied and screamed, and kicked up any sort of row."

"No. Why should she?"

"Don't you see, ass?"

"No."

"Don't you remember the dog in Sherlock Holmes?"

"Certainly I remember the dog in Sherlock Holmes."

"Horses are just as bad as dogs, and far more nervy."

"Nervy?"

"That's the word. Let's put the point to Mrs. Bradley, and see what she says. Besides . . ." he lowered his voice.

"What, Keith?"

"Horses go nearly mad at the smell of blood."

"Do you think Mrs. Bradley doesn't know that?"

"You know her better than I do."

"She doesn't *seem* an old lady who wouldn't know things, but I'd better mention it. Or would you like to?"

"As long as one of us does. It's a point, you know."

"I expect she's allowed for it. Come on. We'd better go back. I should think it's time."

We had not reached the river, but Keith turned as I said the words, and we went to the police station, checking the time by Mr. Cohen's clock as we reached the high street. Mr. Cohen kept the pawnbroker's shop on the corner of Albany Place. His daughter went to Keith's school. Jack had once pawned his watch there. I knew, but June did not. It was one week when he was very short and had promised to go to a dinner. He was chosen to be secretary at the dinner, and his honorarium easily bought back the watch. He told June it had gone to be cleaned. Mr. Cohen let him have fifty shillings and an evening suit. Jack was grateful, and gave Mr. Cohen a red-hot tip on the greyhounds. Then Mr. Cohen was grateful, so it all went very well, without June's interference.

It was within ten minutes of time when we read Mr. Cohen's

clock, so we thought that that was good enough, and went straight on to the police station.

We were shown into the kitchen this time, another magnificent room which the inspector and his mother used as a living-room. It had a kitchen range which seemed to take up almost one whole side of the room, and a huge dresser filled with cups, plates and glasses.

Mrs. Seabrook gave us some jam tarts and a cup of cocoa, and told us that Mrs. Bradley would be along at any minute. While we were waiting, Mrs. Seabrook gave us her view of the murders, which was that they had been performed by gipsies. We thought this most unlikely, but it seemed polite, as we were eating her jam tarts and drinking her cocoa, to agree with her.

" What was the girl Gillett doing in Saint George's Court at nearly eleven o'clock at night, Mrs. Seabrook ? " Keith enquired.

The old lady looked at him over the top of her glasses. One reads of people doing that, but it is surprising how disconcerting it can be. Keith took it well. He did not stare her out, because that would have been rude, but neither did he drop his eyes.

" You're a naughty little boy," she said at last.

" I see," said Keith, as though he had been answered.

" You *don't* see ! " said she, almost in the tone June used whenever she quarrelled with Jack. " You *don't* see ! How can you say such a thing ? "

" Because I *do* see," said Keith. I do not know what else the old lady would have said, because Mrs. Bradley rang the bell at that moment and she went to let her in.

" So that's it ! " said Keith. " I should never have thought it. Would you ? "

" Thought what ? " said I. I was lost.

" That Bessie Gillett was there to meet the inspector," said Keith.

I was not in the least prepared for this, and so contested it, but Keith would not be deflected from his idea. Mrs. Bradley came in alone. We heard Mrs. Seabrook go along to the drawing-room.

" Well," said Mrs. Bradley, as we made way to give her the

easy chair by the fireside—for Mrs. Seabrook was one of those people who believe in fires until the weather turned warm; she was not like June, who would never light a fire once the spring-cleaning was done and the sweep had been—" and what have you been saying to our hostess, my dear Holmes ? "

She looked at me, but Keith told her.

" Ah," she said, regarding him playfully, " but your deductions are not quite correct. Bessie was certainly there to meet a man, but that man was not Mr. Seabrook."

" Mrs. Seabrook thinks so," said Keith.

" *C'est un enfant terrible*," said Mrs. Bradley. " But to business." She took out her notebook and a pencil. " First, we must, I think, disregard any local rumours that these are a series of Ripper murders."

" What exactly *are* Ripper murders ? " asked Keith.

" They are the crimes of a maniac, and therefore are not, in the legal sense, crimes at all," Mrs. Bradley answered. " They are evil deeds committed by one not in his right mind who has, first, loved women not wisely but much too well, and then (to offset a passion not of this world but of the devil), disliked them sufficiently to believe they are better dead."

" Were Burke and Hare rippers ? " asked Keith.

" Certainly not. Their one aim and object was money, and they strangled or smothered their victims."

" Does this man murder for money ? "

" I think so. I am working on that aspect now."

" But Marion Bridges left only enough money for her funeral and eight pounds over," said I, " and the money wasn't stolen."

" True. The barmaid was leaving with her wages and the contents of the till, though," said Mrs. Bradley. " But that, like all other information I shall give you, is, of course, confidential."

" Of course ! " said we, in chorus.

" Then, if you can find out who knew that . . ." suggested Keith. Mrs. Bradley shook her head.

" There is nothing whatsoever to prove that anybody knew it," she said. " So far as we have ascertained at present, it may have been a last-minute impulse on the part of the unfortunate girl to rob the till before she took her departure."

"Thinking the theft would not be discovered until Tuesday morning," said Keith.

"The pubs all open on Sunday and Easter Monday," I pointed out.

"But the Banks don't," said Keith. "It was most unlikely there'd be any check on the money until Tuesday morning."

Mrs. Bradley nodded.

"We had got that far," she said, "but no farther. There seems no way of discovering whether anybody knew she had the money. She has carried that secret to the grave."

We considered this point solemnly.

"But, even so," said Keith, "she was murdered for *some* reason, wasn't she?"

"Quite so."

"I suppose it *is* all the work of one man?" I put in. "At present I don't see much connection between any of the deaths. What had a circus lady to do with the barmaid, or the barmaid with the farm-girl, or the farm-girl with the children's nurse?"

"You have put your finger on the most puzzling point of the case," said Mrs. Bradley, "and it certainly seems likely that the case of the murdered dairymaid will have to be taken separately from the rest, in certain respects."

"I should have thought it was the circus murder which was different from the rest," said Keith.

"Ah," said Mrs. Bradley, "now we come to the business which brought you here to-night: the garment . . . or rather, the portion of a garment . . . which you fished up out of the canal.

"First, I ought to tell you, the rag and bone man has been interviewed. He does not deny having thrown away the rag in question, and his story of how he came by it . . . or, rather, did not come by it . . . is interesting and may be true.

"He says that on the Saturday following the murder of the circus girl he went on his rounds as usual, and worked Pottery, Walnut Tree, Cressage, Kinley, Netley, George, Greet and Byford roads. He obtained a moderate haul of cast-off clothing, and, when he returned to the shed he rents from Mrs. Cockerton for the purpose, checked up his gleanings and sorted out the various kinds of rags in the usual way. It was then that he discovered the corset.

" Now, this is the point: he absolutely denies having received that particular piece of rag from any of his clients. You may think . . . as I did when I first heard it . . . that he would not know exactly what was in each bundle of rags that he bought, but this, it appears, was not so. The police have made exhaustive enquiries round and about the town, and it seems that his procedure never varied. He analysed every bundle of rags to see what it contained, because he gives more money for woollen goods than for cotton ones, and more still for silk. There seems to have been no possibility whatsoever that he could have over-looked the corset. Moreover, he does not buy old corsets. If any are included in a bundle he gives them back before weighing the rest of the rags. I may add, here, that he appears to be a perfectly honest man so far as his weighing is concerned. His scales are correct to a hair, and are open to inspection by govern-ment officials, just in the same way as are those used by more orthodox traders."

" He's mean to children, all the same," said Keith. Mrs. Bradley grinned, and continued:

" Now, when he discovered the corset, he saw at once that there was blood on it; so much blood, in fact, that he was seriously alarmed, because, of course, by Saturday everybody in the town, I suppose, had heard about the murders. He admits he lost his head. Fearful that the police might not believe his story of finding the corset among his stock when he knew . . . nobody better . . . that it had not been handed to him in the course of trade, he rashly decided to get rid of it. The canal occurred to him at once. It was fairly handy, it flowed past a locality in which he was not likely to be recognized . . . you said yourself, Holmes, if you remember, that the people of the Leys are a race apart from the ordinary townsfolk . . . and, best of all, to his muddled way of thinking, the water would wash away the bloodstains."

" So it had," said I. " We did not see any."

" There are ways and means of discovering the presence of human gore," said Mrs. Bradley. " Those tests have been applied to the garment in question, and there is no doubt that at some recent date it was considerably stained.

"Now, this is the crux of the matter: it seems reasonably certain that the corset belonged to the girl murdered on the circus ground. It is no ordinary corset, in fact, but a piece of a ballet-dress, being part of the tight-fitting bodice upon which the flounced ballet-skirt depends. As the girl in question was plump beyond the wishes of herself, her employers and her patrons, it had been stiffly and sturdily boned to minimize the generosity of her figure. It was, in fact, bodice and corset in one, and has been identified by several of her fellow-workers in the circus. Further to that, she was in the habit, according to them, of sewing her savings, in the form of pound notes, into the lining of this bodice or corset. No money was found upon the body."

"Ah, but was she wearing the ballet-frock?" asked Keith. Mrs. Bradley regarded him with approval.

"She was not wearing the ballet-*skirt*," she answered. "But that was detachable. She never left off the corset until she went to bed, and then she placed it under her pallet and slept on it. When she was found, she was wearing flannel trousers, a loose woollen jumper and an old raincoat."

"How did she keep her stockings up?" asked Keith. "Christina and June wear suspenders."

"I understand that she did not wear stockings when she wore trousers," Mrs. Bradley answered.

"How did the murderer get the corset if she still had jumper and trousers and a raincoat on?" I asked.

"We believe that the corset was slit down, and the shoulder-straps slashed through after the girl was dead."

"So the motive there was certainly robbery," said I. "And that brings us back to the circus people, and that takes us out of our depth."

"The circus people have alibis. Good ones," said Mrs. Bradley.

"You have to break alibis down," said Keith. "Oh, and what about the remarks we heard the circus people making? That girl—she might even have been the one who was afterwards murdered! Don't you remember? 'It don't

do to believe all you're told in a pub!' You remember,
Sim?"

"Interesting," said Mrs. Bradley. She made us detail the
circumstances. "It is thought that some of them went to the
Pigeons that night."

"All the same, though," Keith added to me, as we walked
home discussing the case, "if Mrs. Bradley says they had alibis,
and good ones, I'd take a bet that she's right. I'll tell you,
though, what I've thought of. Even if the circus people did
commit that one particular murder, it's most unlikely that they
committed the others. I'll tell you what I think we ought to do.
We ought to check up on Jack."

"But we know now that Jack is innocent. It was the *second*
knife which had the blood on it," I said.

"I know. But in checking up on Jack we might easily come
across something . . . a kind of pointer, you know. You *must*
begin with something definite, and that's the best think I can
think of. It may lead us to Danny Taylor for the rest of the
murders."

"It seems rather like sneaking," said I.

"All detective work is sneaking," said Keith. "That's why
only gentlemen and cads can do it."

As we went indoors by the back way he began to yodel. He
had a good voice and yodelled well, but it was a sound which
June particularly disliked.

"Be quiet, or go upstairs," said she. We took the wind out
of her sails by going upstairs at once.

"Notebook and pencil," said Keith. "You do the writing
and I'll talk."

"And I'll interrupt when you leave things out," said I. Our
efforts, when we had completed them, did not appear satis-
factory.

"Lots of gaps," said Keith critically, examining the finished
manuscript. "We shall have to get them filled in. Listen, and
see whether you can think of any more.

"Holy Thursday. We were in to tea by half-past four.
Jack had not come in from work. We visited Mr. Taylor's field
to arrange about the circus, and got home to an early supper.
Jack was then in. After supper Jack and June most probably

had a row about going to her mother's on Good Friday. Christina went to bed early. *When Jack has a row he usually goes out for a bit to get over it*. We broke out of the house to revisit the circus ground, so do not know whether Jack went out or not. *Memo*. Could ask him or June, but probably shall not. While we were out, we probably were within earshot of the murder. We believe we saw the murderer by the canal. We believe he crossed the ponds and went up to Mr. Taylor's field. The animals were disturbed. *We do not believe the man we saw was Jack*. We are sure we would have recognized him, even from a distance and by moonlight. *But* the murder did not take place for more than half an hour after we lost track of the man."

" Certainly nothing there," said I critically. " On balance, we've no reason to suppose that Jack was out of the house when we returned to it. As for the rest of the stuff, we've talked it over dozens of times withou' coming to any conclusion."

" All right. I'll go on, shall I ? . . .

" Good Friday. We heard about the murder from Mrs. Banks at the baker's. We helped Jack put in the potatoes. We were home to tea. Jack was not in. He came in at seven o'clock. He told Christina *he had a knife of the kind that the murderer was thought to have used*. *N.B.*: Would he have mentioned this if the murderer were either himself or his friend Danny Taylor ? "

" Of course," said I, " even if Danny *is* the murderer, Jack may not have known that at the time."

Keith nodded, added a footnote, and went on: " Jack was still in after we went to bed. We do not know whether he went out again that night or not, or, if he did, whether he went to the *Pigeons*, where the second murder was committed after closing time."

" There's nothing there," said I. " We were fools ever to think the murderer could have been Jack. As soon as you see the stuff down in black and white, you can see he must be innocent. I can't really see why we suspected him, even on the evidence of the knife, and that's all washed out now, because *it wasn't his knife that did the murders*."

" Well, I'll go on," said Keith. " It's all very well to keep harping on about Jack's innocence. What we're out to spot is somebody's guilt."

" Well, it doesn't exactly leap to the eye, you know, and I can't see anything at present which involves Danny Taylor," said I. Keith read on:

" Easter Saturday. We visited Mrs. Cockerton, and heard her curious story about the man under the canal bridge. She gave me my sabre and Keith his horse-pistol, and we are very grateful indeed for these favours. According to her reckoning, it must have been somewhere between ten and a quarter past that she heard the knife being sharpened on the stone."

" Tell you what ! " I interrupted in some excitement. " We could perhaps check that ! "

" Check what ? " asked Keith, looking up.

" Why, whether there's a stone there on which you could sharpen a knife, and, if so, whether a knife has been sharpened on it recently; and, thirdly, whether it's possible to sharpen a knife in the dark, because, personally, I shouldn't think it is."

" It was moonlight," Keith observed.

" It must have been pretty dark under the bridge," I pointed out. " Mrs Cockerton didn't *see* the fellow, remember. She said ' a person in the shadows.' We ought to go along there to-night while the moon's about the same, and find out what can be seen."

" What a beastly idea ! " said Keith. I thought so, too.

" But it's no good calling ourselves detectives if we don't take the rough with the smooth," I argued. " And, after all, we've got our weapons, you know."

" I'll go on," said Keith, without committing himself. " Mrs. Cockerton got back to the *Pigeons* at twenty-past ten, and did not go inside again."

" By the way, we don't *know* that," said I. " And I know for a fact she told Jack's fortune there once. I heard him telling Christina when June was out."

" *Right you are !* " Keith agreed; and he made a question mark in brackets at the end of the sentence, " Mind you,

I *think* we can take it for granted. She'd had her glass of sherry, and had simply gone for a stroll. Still, it's a point. We must try to check it, but, of course, without giving offence."

" Then it's your job, not mine," said I. He nodded, and went on reading:

" It was on this visit to Mrs. Cockerton that we *found the murderer's knife* in a chest full of odds and ends. *Query.* Why did Mrs. Cockerton think it was her late husband's pruning knife ? "

" We ought to find out who else, besides ourselves, had been in the shop that day," I said, and Keith smacked my knee in admiration.

" You're in great form," he said. " That's two jolly good suggestions. We're getting somewhere now."

" Of course, it's most likely it was the rag and bone man," I added. " I still think he's on the list of suspects, and higher, on the whole, than Danny Taylor."

" I think he heads it," said Keith. " Look, let's go on the assumption that he does. Start another clean page with his name."

I obliged, handed the notebook back to him, and lolled luxuriously on the bed. He did not continue to read aloud for a moment, but squinted down in a puzzled manner at our notes.

" Here's another thing," he announced. " When Mrs. Cockerton first saw the knife we had found, she said it was her husband's pruning knife, and she hadn't seen it for years. . . . We've noted that; but, do you know, Sim, I'm wondering whether the knife we *found* and the knife we *pinched* were one and the same knife. What do you say about that ? "

" A jolly good point," said I heartily. " I could have sworn they were, but, well, it makes one think. I mean, why *should* she think it was her husband's pruning knife ? "

" Very odd," he agreed. " Now, further to that, we noticed that Mrs. Cockerton looked extremely alarmed when we pointed out that it looked like the murderer's knife."

" Nothing in that," said I. " Any woman would look alarmed if you told her a thing like that."

"I suppose so," said Keith; and went on reading: "Jack and June went out together in the early afternoon. We went with Christina to the police station. We got home at just after five o'clock. Jack and June were in. We went with Christina as far as the Baths, where there was a dance. Then we went on to Mrs. Cockerton's and saw the knife in the window."

"We've called it *the* knife," said I. "Better put another question mark, perhaps." He did so, and then went on again:

"We went to bed at about half-past nine. Jack brought us some cocoa, so we know he was in then. We decided to take it in turns to be on watch. Tom got out of his cot and might have tumbled down the stairs. Jack was no longer at home. June did not know until then that he had gone out. He had not gone to bed when she did. She thought he was still downstairs. She sent Sim to fetch him from the Baths. He was not at the Baths. He had gone up the Manor Road. We met him near the station. His coat-sleeves were wet. He said he had fallen in some mud and had washed in the river. Sim had heard a mysterious whistle earlier in the evening."

"You know, I still think all that's jolly fishy," I said, "about him falling into the mud."

"I know," said Keith, "but it's the first time he was out at the time of the murders, as far as we know, and Mr. Seabrook thinks the murders were all done by the same person."

"Brings it back to Danny Taylor, that whistle. Anyway, that's the lot," I said, "until we come to this murder in Saint George's Court, and we know Jack wasn't out then."

CHAPTER THIRTEEN

The Break

"You KNOW," I went on, "before we do any more investigating on our own, I'm inclined to show Mrs. Bradley our notes."

"Why?" asked Keith.

"First, because you don't go out hunting lions without letting somebody know you've gone. Second, it may give her the hint to show us any stuff *she's* got."

" But we ought to do that canal business to-night, because of the moon. We'd better take our electric torches, in case it's very dark under the bridge, and our weapons in case of attack. Let's lie down on our beds for a bit without undressing."

" Supper."

" Oh, yes, we'd better go down for that now. Come on."

To our surprise, June was out. Christina gave us supper. Jack said he would have his later, but, rather to our discomfiture, Christina said she thought she would have hers with us and go straight to bed. Jack looked morose, and we looked at each other. For once, the very last thing we wanted was Christina on our landing and wide awake.

We had supper of bread and cheese and cocoa, and then we asked leave to finish our chapters, hoping that this would put Christina off. What we needed was for her and Jack to become involved in a long conversation while we went upstairs and planned our excursion of the night. The moon would not rise until after eleven o'clock. It was then only just on nine.

It seemed as though Christina really were tired, however, for she did not even wait while we finished our cocoa, but told us to put the cups away when we had washed them up, and to cut more bread if we wanted it.

" Isn't she well ? " asked Keith, when she had gone.

" She's gone up to pack," said Jack. " She's leaving on Friday."

" Leaving ? " We were stunned. We could not imagine the house without Christina. " Not . . . not finding somewhere else to live ? "

" Yes. I—I think she's changed her job." He was fiddling about with the lid of the cheese dish, and suddenly put it back as tenderly as though he were drawing the sheet over a dead face. " And June's gone, too," he added. " Oh, not for long. She had to go. She had a telegram. Her mother's ill. If she's away any length of time we shall have to get a woman in to do for us. It's all a confounded nuisance ! I believe that damned inspector's at the bottom of it."

" Oh, Jack ! " said Keith. He put his hand on Jack's arm.

I knew what he was thinking. If Mr. Seabrook had persuaded Christina to move, it must be because he was going to arrest Jack for the murders. Jack stared down at Keith's hand. It was brown and grubby, and still rather plump, for Keith was only eleven. Jack did not answer. He just sat there, staring at Keith's hand.

We waited for a minute or two, but he did not speak, so we looked at one another, and then went quietly upstairs.

" But *June* wouldn't leave him," I said. " Look what she was like when he was in trouble before. Seabrook might make Christina go, but not June."

" Oh, well," said Keith, " we've still got work to do. It may prove him innocent. Toss you who beds down first and who stays awake."

I won the toss, and said I would take first watch. It was agreed that when the clock in the hall chimed ten, Keith should take turn for three-quarters of an hour, and then we should escape from the house. This would be easier when the moon rose, but safer before it lighted up the houses.

Keith took off his jersey and tie, undid his shirt collar, took off shoes and socks, and lay on his bed covered only by the quilt. Then his feet felt cold, so he put on his socks again, settled down, and was soon asleep.

I felt miserable. It seemed horrible and unnecessary that at a time when life had become so full and interesting a particular crisis had to intervene between us and our pleasure; for, to us, the murders offered a field and a scope which nothing else had ever granted us. Now all this was to be lost because Jack was to be arrested for murders we were sure he had not done.

Of one thing I was certain. I would never, no matter what difficulties were placed in my way, lose touch with Christina. The most important thing was to find out her new address. That could be done at once. She would not be in bed. The inference was that she still would be packing, and to ask for her address would be legitimate, I thought. Besides, she might be able to tell me what the inspector had against Jack, and whether Mrs. Bradley had agreed to the arrest.

I sneaked out of our room and went to hers. I tapped on the door. She opened it. The gas was alight, and all sorts of

clothes were all over the bed and the armchair. A large suitcase
and a trunk were open on the floor and these contained clothes
and books.

" I . . . wondered whether I could help you, Christina," I
said.

" I'll have to finish the trunk to-morrow, Sim. I wish you'd
help finish this case. It's so late, and I've got to get down to
the *Pigeons* to-night."

" What on earth for, Christina ? "

" I'm going to stay the night there. I can't stay here, now
June has gone away."

" Why on earth not ? You don't have to go because *she*
goes ! "

" I do, Sim."

" Does Jack know you're going ? "

" I haven't said so, but, of course, he'd realize . . ."

" Has Seabrook made all this trouble ? "

She had knelt on the floor again to go on with her packing,
but, at my question, she stopped what she was doing, and looked
up.

" You couldn't possibly understand, Sim," she said. " It's
June, although, of course, Evan is pretty silly. He's jealous,
without any reason, and thinks ridiculous things, and so does
June. Oh, I don't blame her. I don't blame anybody. Things
happen like this. Give me those shoes, will you ? "

" Look here," I said, handing her the shoes, " you can't go
and sleep at the *Pigeons*. I won't have it. Think of that beastly
murder, and ask yourself." I understood everything now, and
my heart was considerably lighter.

" I know. But there's nowhere else to stay. It's such short
notice. June suddenly said she was going, and off she went,
with Tom. Oh, Sim, it's all so silly ! "

She was kneeling by the bedside, and she dropped her head
on to the cover, all among a pile of underclothes lovely with silk
and lace, and began to cry.

I did not know what to do, so I knelt beside her and put my
arm round her shoulders, aware, even then, of the scent of her
hair and the tender, heart-breaking smoothness of her skin.

" Oh, don't, Christina," I said. " Look here, I've got an

idea! Give me some money for the telephone. I'll see you put
up safely for to-night."

She flung me off, and got up and sat on the bed.

" Do what you like. There's my handbag. Take what you
want. Take it all. I don't care what happens. I didn't mean
anything wrong, and I didn't *do* anything wrong, and I've broken
off my engagement, and I'm terrified of the *Pigeons*. . . ."

" I'll get you some lodgings," said I. " You're not going to
stay at the *Pigeons*. That I do know. June's a mean vixen, and
I always thought Seabrook was an ass——"

" I'm not in love with Jack," Christina burst out. " I'm
not . . . not the least little bit. I never have been, and it's
abominable of people to stir up all this trouble."

She might not be in love with Jack, I thought, but there was
not much doubt that all three of us brothers were deeply in love
with her. But all I could think of for the moment was my joy
that Jack was not to be arrested.

" Shan't be a minute," I said. I rifled her handbag, and
took out some coppers and dashed to the telephone box which
was at the corner of the street next to ours. I rang up the police
station. Fortunately Mrs. Bradley had not left. She was
having supper with Inspector Seabrook and his mother.

" If you please, I *must* speak to her," I said. Then, when I
got Mrs. Bradley on the telephone, I told her what had happened.
I did not say that Jack and June had quarrelled, but only told
her the story Jack had told us about the telegram which had
called June away very suddenly, and added that Christina had
decided to spend the night at the *Pigeons*, and that I did not
think this advisable, owing to the murders. Mrs. Bradley was
good. She said she would come round at once, and come she
did. I do not know what she said to Christina, whom I had to
bring down into the drawing-room to talk to her, or what
Christina afterwards said to Jack, but the end of it all was better
than we could have hoped.

What happened was that Mrs. Bradley took Christina to her
hotel for the night, and invited us to go to tea there next day;
but, besides that, at the end of half an hour Mr. Seabrook arrived
to escort them. It appeared that he had insisted upon coming
with Mrs. Bradley, and had marched up and down our street

until he grew so impatient to see Christina that he wouldn't wait any longer.

Jack went to the door to let him in, and I was leaning over the banisters and heard him say, as the door of the drawing-room opened for him to go in:

" No more of this nonsense, Christina. We'd better get married, and then perhaps Jack can get things straightened out."

To this Christina replied:

" I meant what I said in my letter. Please behave like a gentleman, and not like the Moghul emperors."

I did not stay longer, but went quietly back to our room. My schemings and adventures had tired me. I was asleep within five minutes, and did not seem to have done more than close my eyes before Keith was waking me up again.

" Come on," he said. " I thought you must be dead. It's taken me more than three minutes to wake you up."

I was still abominably sleepy.

" Have you reconnoitred ? " I asked.

" Yes, I have, and it's going to be sticky. Jack hasn't come upstairs yet. I expect he's reading and smoking."

" I suppose the others have gone ? "

" Lord, yes. Twenty minutes ago. Snap into it, and for goodness' sake move like a cat, especially once we get on the scullery roof."

The night was black. There was, so far, no sign of the moon except for a faint glow far down behind the houses. We made no mistakes, listened hard at the bottom of the garden, heard nothing, and slipped along the alley. Keith's pistol was tied on round his neck and hung in the breast of his shirt. My sabre was suspended over my shoulders, slung rifle-fashion from its strap of pyjama cord. Once in the alley, we detached the weapons and carried them at the ready. One never knew, and I, for one, was nervous. My cock-a-hoop mood had left me. I was now a terrified boy trying to hold on to my courage and believe in my luck and set an example of steadfastness, grit and nonchalant ease of demeanour to my younger brother.

Keith broke the silence as soon as we crossed the road at the end of the alley.

" Hellish, isn't it ? " he said. The streets were as still as death, and of death we both thought as we made our way past the library and round the bend which had marked the boundary, once, of the Ancient British camp which guarded the ford that gave a name to our town.

" Do you think . . . the Butts ? " I asked.

" It will be much worse along by the canal," said Keith. We turned into the short, broad road, and remained in the centre of it, dreading even the lamp-lighted pavements because of the side entrances which marked off one detached house from another. In vain we looked for a friendly light in a window. Either the blinds fitted too well in that comfortable residential thoroughfare, or else the people were at the backs of their houses or in bed.

At the bottom of the Butts, when we reached the last house before the thoroughfare broadened out to the Bregant river at the bottom, and the yard of the *Lion* inn on the left, we saw a policeman standing under a lamp. In a moment he was joined by another, and they walked off together towards the market square.

The sight of them was a comfort in a way. It was clear that the town was patrolled. On the other hand, we did not want to be stopped and asked our business.

" You don't think," said Keith, when they had disappeared, and we were opposite the little bridge which used to belong to the miller before the mill was destroyed, " that if we were caught with these weapons they might think *we* did the murders ? "

It was a solemn thought, and did not appear to us ridiculous. Nor, from a purely physical and material point of view, was it ridiculous, either; two boys of our age and strength, armed with razor-keen knives or my little scimitar, would have been more than a match for the unfortunate girls on whom the murderer had laid his wicked hands. The psychology of the thing was another matter, but one which, at that time, was not within our knowledge.

" I'm glad to think that Christina's safe, and not at the *Pigeons*," said I, as we passed the iron bar-gate and came up the little street towards the market-place.

We did not want to go near the coaching entrance of the *Pigeons*, so we followed the narrow road, and, when we had to cross the market square, crossed it on the high street side and were soon past the now sinister building.

We could not forbear to take some curious glances at it. It was after closing time, and all was quiet. The sound of a late bus approaching along the high street was then, except for our footfalls, the only sound.

The moon had risen by the time we reached the bridge. We stood in the centre of the bridge and watched, in the oily canal, the murky, distorted reflections. Then, bracing ourselves, and with never another word, we walked to the farther side of the bridge, and dropped down the steep little slope to the towing-path.

The other bridge we sought was about half a mile further along. There were barges, three deep, drawn up by the side of the canal. We supposed that the barge people did not travel by night. We could hear the sounds of voices, and here and there could see lights from the tiny cabins. This was wonderfully cheering, but as soon as we had passed the anchorage, a terrible depression and a loneliness fell upon our spirits, and I, for one, would have given a good deal to be out of the business and safe in my bed at home.

Keith examined his torch to make sure that it worked. Mine had an almost new battery, but, following his example, I took it out of my pocket and switched it on.

" We shouldn't need them," I said, " with the moon like this."

" It was brighter than this for Mrs. Cockerton," Keith remarked. We put the torches away.

" What about single file along here ? " I suggested. The thought was timely. Apart from the fact that it might be much easier for the second boy to come to the rescue if one were attacked, to go in single file became almost necessary. The condition of the towing-path was good, but the path was constantly used, and in places the edge of the bank had crumbled into the water. Two people abreast could scarcely skirt these small landslides. I pushed Keith into the lead, proposing to leap upon anyone who attacked him.

A deep hedge marched beside the turgid water. I was greatly afraid of the hedge. Visions of not one but fifty murderers assailed me. I kept my eyes on the hedge, looked sometimes behind me, held my sabre at the ready, the strap round my wrist, and hoped that Keith could not hear the alarming thumping of my heart. I tried to listen as well as to look, but there was a drumming in my head which sounded as loud to me as the engine of a car, and through which, I felt sure, I should not be able to distinguish any other sound. So certain was I of this that the slight noise made by a fish jumping, or a water vole leaving the bank, quite startled me.

For all our fears, we reached the viaduct without adventure. We did not need our torches except for one spot along by the wall right under the middle of the bridge, and, except for a trickle of water which seeped through the brickwork from a spot some three feet up, in which greenish mould was growing, there was nothing unforeseen. There was certainly no stone on which a man could sharpen a knife.

I felt disappointed.

" There's nothing here," I said. Keith walked on, and I followed. At the further side of the bridge we switched on our torches again; but, except for the bricks of the bridge, some horse manure on the towing-path, the moon in the sky and the oily sheen of the water winding across our flattish countryside, the whispering reeds and the dark hedge stretching onwards alongside the water, there was nothing.

" The water does a big curve beyond this bridge," said Keith. " Let's go as far as the end of the bend. She might have heard the sound from a distance."

Unwilling, now that we had accomplished our task and gained our objective, to relinquish all hope of making some discovery of importance, I followed him round the bend. At the end of it there was a lock, and here there was plenty of stonework.

" Do you think she could possibly have ears sharp enough to detect a knife being sharpened from here, if she was on the other side of the bridge ? " asked Keith.

" I don't know. Sounds are funny over water. And it would almost be over water, if the sound came from here to the other side of the bridge, because of the bend," said I.

Almost immediately we had an excellent although frightening

example of how sound carries over water, for a girl's voice suddenly shouted from the lock-keeper's little house on the opposite side of the canal:

" Be off now, whoever you are ! I've got a gun ! " In proof of this, she poked one out of the lower window, and discharged it in our direction.

I should not think two boys have ever moved faster. We had turned, and were on the other side of the bridge, wiping sweat off our faces and trying to steady the trembling in our knees, before the echoes of the shot had died away in the fields and woods that bordered the canal.

" Well," said Keith, dropping into a walk, " that's that. I felt the bullet whizz past me. I think it must have singed my ear."

" One thing, if the murderer's about, I bet it scared him as much as it did us," said I. In this innocent belief, our progress back to the high street was robbed of much of its terror. The moon was now flooding the sky. Her image reflected in the water was no longer a thing of murky terror, for we were vainglorious; we were heroes. We had been under fire. We had been suspected of being murderers. We had filled some female heart with excessive terror. We felt we had been blooded, and were men.

I found myself thinking of Christina, and again congratulated myself on the stand I had made about the *Pigeons*.

" I will not have it, Christina ! I forbid you to sleep at the *Pigeons !* " Such, I began to persuade myself, had been the form and tenor of my words.

" I say, Keith," said I, halting as we were ascending the townward slope of the bridge, " don't let's go back the same way. What about the short cut over the lock-gates and round by the mill and the Boatmen's Institute ? "

" I don't mind," he said. " But I'm jolly well going to check up on Mrs. Cockerton to-morrow. What's she mean, telling us she heard a fellow sharpening a knife ? "

" We agreed that, over the water . . ."

" Oh, slosh ! I've been working it out. She *couldn't* have heard it that distance, not to be sure what it was."

" Then we'd certainly better question her," I said. " Now

we've worked over the ground, and under the same conditions, we'll be able to get a better idea from her evidence, very likely."

We left it at that, retraced our steps a little, and dropped down again to the canal-side. About thirty or forty yards along the towing-path were the lock-gates I had mentioned. We were trespassing once we had crossed them, but it made a short cut back to the bottom of the Butts.

" Hope there are no beastly dogs about," said Keith.

" Not very likely," I answered confidently. " Lots of the barge people come this way at night to the Boatmen's Institute."

" As late as this ? " asked Keith.

" Well, in winter, after dark, they come from the pubs."

This answer appeared to satisfy him, for he said no more, and we crossed the lock-gates, glad, for more than one reason, of the brilliance of the moonlight, and took a little path on the further side.

This path led towards the high street, and then came back on itself to the River Bregant, which it crossed by the little plank bridge by the disused mill.

Before we got to this bridge, however, Keith stopped. I was about to speak when he clutched my wrist. There was a light through the trees which bordered the path, and, in the moonlight we could see that another and even narrower path branched off towards this light. We followed the smaller path, and in about a minute, or even less, we found ourselves opposite a blank, uncurtained window. Between it and us stretched the small square courtyard of an inn.

" The *Pigeons*," breathed Keith. " And I can see into the room behind the bar. Isn't that where they're supposed to have kept the cash-box ? "

CHAPTER FOURTEEN

The Antique Shop

WE COULD see at once what ought to be done about this discovery. We also knew that it could not be done until morning.

"You think it's safe to write a note?" said Keith, when we reached the Butts and were past the worst of the journey.

"It will have to be. I can't miss my train, and you'd better not be late for school, either. As it is, you'll be cutting it very fine if you go to the police station with the letter."

"The letter's got to be written, too," said Keith. "Can you will yourself to wake up at six o'clock?"

"Yes, I expect so. What do you think I'd better say?"

"I should just say we would be glad to know whether the police know that you can see into the room at the back of the bar from the canal bushes. You see, they very likely do know, so we don't want to look mugs, giving them a lot of useless information."

"I'm glad *we* know, anyway," said I. "It makes that *Pigeons* murder a lot more interesting."

"It makes the possibilities very wide. The police will have their work cut out, I imagine, to check up on all the people who used that short cut on the night of the murder," said Keith, after a short pause during which we slackened our pace, for, once in the Manor Road, we did not want anyone to think that we were hurrying, "because I should think quite a dozen men coming out of the *Pigeons* may have used it."

"They probably wouldn't matter," I pointed out. "What the police want is somebody who was seen there well after closing time."

"Mrs. Cockerton may have spotted someone crossing the lock-gates when she walked along the towing-path," Keith suggested. "I know it was rather early, but somebody may have had reasons for getting into position to watch what went on in that room."

"We could ask her," I said, rather doubtfully, "but I'm wondering if she's very reliable. That story of hers about the knife being sharpened worries me."

"Women are nervous," said Keith. "They imagine all sorts of silly things. Look how June always thinks we're lost or killed if we happen to be out longer than we've said."

"That was only about twice. But I see what you mean. And we know she was nervous. She said so."

"What worries *me*," he went on, "is why, being nervous, she went for that walk at all."

"She told us she liked to have a stroll. Anybody would, after being in that shop all day long."

"Yes, but there are plenty of other walks. She could have gone up Clayponds."

"Courting couples," said I.

"An old woman wouldn't mind those."

"Old women are frightfully particular. They don't think courting couples are respectable."

We pondered upon this idiosyncrasy on the part of old women, and did not speak to one another again that night: What with the moonlight, the necessity for regaining admission to the house without waking Jack, and the uncontrollable desire to be safely in bed, we felt we had everything we could cope with. I was extremely thankful to be saying my prayers, which I had been saving up against our safe return (thus feeling that I had something in hand with which to bargain with God), and then to creep noiselessly into bed. Keith was already between the sheets. I could see his dark head as the moonlight streamed on to his pillow. The next moment I was asleep.

I had forgotten to will myself to wake up, with the consequence that the next thing I knew was that Jack was shaking my shoulder. It was a quarter-past seven. There was the letter to write, and I realized that, in June's absence, I would have to cut my own sandwiches for lunch at school.

Before I could begin to do this, however, Jack said, looking shame-faced:

"June thought of your dinner at school, Sim. She's made you a couple of meat pasties, one for to-day and the other for to-morrow. You can get them heated up at school, can't you ? "

I was very fond of June's pasties, and gladly relinquished the loaf to raid the larder.

" Better take an orange and a couple of bananas, too," said Jack.

I wrote the note after breakfast, having carried the ink to our bedroom.

> *Dear Mrs. Bradley*, I wrote, *this is to hope that you are not finding Christina any nuisance, and to ask whether the police know of the little path leading off from the miller's bridge and path by the Boatmen's Institute. We have discovered that the room behind the public bar at the* Pigeons *can be seen into from this path, and that there are no blinds to the window.*
>
> > *Yours faithfully and with compliments,*
> >
> > > *Simon Cathcart Innes*

Keith left the house a quarter of an hour earlier than usual in order to leave this note at the police station. We marked the envelope *Urgent. Re Murders*, and hoped that the sergeant or the inspector would see that Mrs. Bradley had it the moment she arrived.

I caught my train with five minutes to spare, but did not see Sparks that morning. It turned out that he had German measles, so it was quite some weeks before I saw him again.

When I returned from school, there were Mrs. Bradley and Keith at the station to meet me, so I guessed that the note had been delivered.

Mrs. Bradley looked benevolent and aunt-like. Her words were like her appearance, for, as soon as we met, she said:

" Your brother will outline our plans; then, if you approve, we can carry them out at once."

" Jack's taking to-morrow off," said Keith. " He's got a dead grandmother or something. Really he's going to June to tell her she's to come home and bring Tom, and her mother, too, if she likes. *We're* going on a visit. We're going to stay with Mrs. Bradley . . ."

" And Christina ? " said I; not, I hope, rudely, but my pleasure completely overwhelmed me and telescoped my good manners for the moment.

" And Christina," said Mrs. Bradley. " We have your night attire and a toothbrush. All else can follow to-morrow. We propose to have tea at Bridge End, and, immediately after tea, to repair to this extremely exciting path which you two discovered last night."

" Then . . . didn't the police know of it ? " I asked.

" The inspector and the sergeant did not. The detective-inspector returned to Scotland Yard this morning, and will be with us again in two days' time. He is still, in his own expression, checking up on the circus people. He thinks the answer lies in their evidence, and that the only mistake which the local police have made was to have arrested the wrong man in the beginning. This, he thinks, may have given the murderer some cover. He explains the other murders by saying that we shall find a local lunatic at the bottom of them, and that we ought to be better able to detect this person than he is."

" In other words, he hasn't found a thing," remarked Keith.

" It appears not," Mrs. Bradley agreed. She stopped a bus, and we bowled down Manor Road and along the high street to Bridge End, where there were some important shops and a restaurant which was too expensive for Jack unless there were only himself and June to be treated. We often looked at the cakes in the window. We were now going to eat them. This gave us a feeling of excitement.

The cakes were as good as they looked, and we were encouraged to eat as many as we could. Previously we had had egg and cress sandwiches, salmon sandwiches and chicken sandwiches. It was the best meal we had ever had out, and I hoped that Mrs. Bradley would have enough money to pay. She had, and she also gave the waitress a tip, so I imagine she must still have been rich in spite of giving Mrs. Cockerton all that money for the lace.

The thought of the lace made me remember to tell Mrs. Bradley about Mrs. Cockerton's mistake. She nodded solemnly, but agreed with Keith when he repeated his remark about women being nervous and imaginative.

It was half-past six by the time we got to the Boatmen's Institute, although we came back on the bus. As the *Pigeons* was open, Mrs. Bradley left us at the bottom of the Butts after we had shown her the path, and went into the public bar. When she came out she said she had had some sherry and a good look round, and that the room into which we had looked must certainly be the room behind the bar.

When that was settled, we went by bus back to the police station, and were allowed to stay in the room whilst Mrs. Bradley talked matters over with Mr. Seabrook.

He said he could not see that our discovery helped very much. We should never be able, he argued, after all that time, to trace the movements of anybody who had used the path that night.

Mrs. Bradley did not argue. To our great disappointment, she nodded. I racked my brains to see whether I could hit upon any means of finding out who had been along there on that night, but I was forced to admit to myself that there did not seem any way, after the lapse of a month, to find out anything more at all.

" What we want is an eye-witness," said Mr. Seabrook, " and that's just exactly what we haven't got, of course."

" There never are eye-witnesses to murder, are there ? " asked Keith.

" There are not often, no," said Mr. Seabrook.

At eight o'clock Mrs. Bradley took us to her home. We went by car, driven by George, her chauffeur. She lived in a tall house in Kensington. It was a long drive, and we enjoyed it. The house seemed very grand after our own, but we felt at home in it at once, especially with Christina there to welcome us.

We went to bed at nine in a high room containing a picture of a muddy lane with some leafless trees. The bathroom we used was enormous, and we were given a new cake of pink soap which smelt of geraniums, a huge sponge each, and towels so large that we used them as Roman togas.

Christina came to see us in bed, and looked more beautiful than ever in a new silk dressing-gown.

" I smell even nicer than you do," said Keith. So she smelt

him, and agreed that he did.   We told her our adventures, and she was very cheerful and said that Mrs. Bradley was a dear, and had promised to come to her wedding.

" Then are you engaged again ? " asked Keith.   She laughed and kissed him.

In the morning we had egg, bacon, kidneys, tomatoes, three kinds of bread and four kinds of marmalade for breakfast.   There were also kippers and haddock, but we did not require them. I had coffee, not tea, although I did not like coffee very much. However, I thought it looked better, from the butler's point of view.   He was a Frenchman, and told us that Madame had given him orders to see that we had enough to eat.

After breakfast Mrs. Bradley's chauffeur, George, drove us to school, dropping Keith first, and then taking me on.   It made Keith rather early, and only just got me there in time, but I *was* in time, and Kingston Major, Second Eleven captain, spoke to me at recess, and praised the make of car.

At lunch time I had the school cooked dinner instead of my usual sandwiches.   It was good, but not enough.   I did not worry, however.   I felt sure there would be plenty to eat in the evening, and, besides, I had June's second pasty in my desk, and ate it during French.

At half-past four George and the car reappeared, and we gave Kingston Major a lift as far as the station.

We picked Keith up at the library, and soon both of us were speeding towards London.   It was like the Arabian Nights, and so was our evening dinner, which we had at six o'clock. Mrs. Bradley had hers later because she said she had work to do until eight.   I was very glad we did not have to wait until then.

Christina came in at seven.   We were about half-way through, because we had the meal in several courses, as they do in books, and, I believe, at hotels: Altogether it was a wonderful time that we spent in Kensington.   It was better than the usual holiday.   Then Jack sent for us to go home, as June had returned and things had settled down.

It was on a Friday night that we returned, so the whole of Saturday was our own.   The moon was in her last quarter, and there had been no more murders.

"The town is too well patrolled, Mrs. Cockerton," said I, when we went to the antique shop next morning. "The policemen walk about in twos, and everything is under observation."

Mrs. Cockerton was getting ready her dinner. We peeled her potatoes for her. They were old potatoes and wormy.

"Time for new potatoes," said Keith. "Why don't you have some new ones, Mrs. Cockerton?"

"Because I've no time to go shopping," she replied. "Those are the last of the sack that my lodger brought me in for the winter. Don't do them if they're no use. I do not care whether I eat."

"What a thing to say!" said Keith. "Why, we've been living on the fat of the land just lately!" While she shredded some cabbage into a pot, peeled an onion or two for her soup, and got the dinner on, we told her of our holiday in Kensington.

"Ah," she said, "that lady who bought my lace. Does she always carry money about like that?"

"Well, she has a fair amount, I think," said Keith. He mentioned the bill at the restaurant. "I think she is very rich. Not a millionaire exactly, but what Mrs. Banks calls very comfortable."

"And that reminds me, speaking of Mrs. Banks," said Mrs. Cockerton, turning the gas down under the potatoes, "I need a loaf. I suppose you wouldn't . . . ?"

"Of course, Mrs. Cockerton," we said.

"I'll go," said Keith. "No need for both."

"Mrs. Cockerton," said I, on an inspiration, "would you care for winkles to your tea?"

"Whatever made you think of winkles, Mr. Innes?" she asked. I did not know what to say. The fact was that I could just afford to buy half a pint of winkles. "What I really fancy would be a couple of faggots and two pennyworth of pease pudding. I should put the lot in my soup and have a feast."

She gave me the money, and off I went to a little dark shop called Brevis's, further along the high street. To get to it I had to pass several public houses, and outside the *Wheelwright's Arms* was the handcart, with rabbit skins, of Mrs. Cockerton's lodger, the rag and bone man.

I got the faggots and pease pudding in the basin Mrs. Cockerton had supplied, but I had to wait a long time, as there was always a run on ready-cooked foods on a Saturday morning. When I came out the man and his barrow were gone.

" I saw your lodger, Mrs. Cockerton," I said. " At least, I saw his barrow outside the *Wheelwright's Arms*."

" No lodger of mine ! " said Mrs. Cockerton, stirring her soup. " Since Tuesday that dreadful fellow has been gone. I had to ask him to go. And it's my opinion," she added, mashing up the faggots with a fork and adding the mess to the soup, " that he knows more about those murders than the police have got out of him yet."

" Really ? " said I, much intrigued. " Is that why you had him go ? "

" Oh, no," she replied, scraping pease pudding from the basin into the pot, " that wouldn't worry me at all. It was the smell of human hair."

My flesh crept. I considered this horror in silence. But curiosity was stronger, in the end, than repugnance.

" The smell of human hair ? " I repeated. She stirred the pot. The smell of the faggots made me feel thoroughly sick.

" The smell of human hair," she insisted. " Ask no more, for no more can I tell. Besides, he'd been keeping late hours."

" Drinking, Mrs. Cockerton ? " I hazarded. She shook her head.

" Who can say ? When a man leaves his woodshed at seven, and is out until eleven; when he crawls from his bed like some beast from its lair while all Nature sleeps beneath the moon; when he washes himself, and washes himself, under the pump in the yard, I know what I think, and I think it is time I called a halt. So I gave him notice to leave, and leave he did, licking his chops like a dog that hopes you have not missed the beef-steak, the dirty . . ."

I do not know what names she called him. She went on for quite a long time. She stopped when Keith came back with the loaf of bread. I realized that she had been swearing, and was shocked and alarmed.

"Here's the bread, Mrs. Cockerton," said Keith. "I say, you remember telling us . . ."

I kicked him, very gently. He shut up.

"Telling you what, Mr. Keith?" asked Mrs. Cockerton, taking up a spoonful of the soup, sniffing at it with great delicacy and then tasting it. "That's good. That's very good soup."

"About port at threepence a dock glass," said Keith. "Well, Mrs. Bradley says it was fivepence." I could not help wondering what he had really been going to say.

"Threepence, fivepence or ninepence is all one," said Mrs. Cockerton. "It is all a fair price. It just depends upon the port, Mr. Keith."

"We ought to be going," said I. "We're going out with Christina this afternoon. We're going to the Zoo, and then to see her new lodgings."

Christina had found new lodgings in Manor Road. She was too independent (said Jack) to trespass on Mrs. Bradley's hospitality for more than the time it took to find a room. She was too independent by half, said Inspector Seabrook, with a scowl. He would have been glad for Christina to stay outside our town until the murderer was captured.

I myself was torn two ways. It was delightful to know that Christina was close at hand, and that we should be able to see her from time to time. On the other hand, the town, I felt, was not less dangerous, even though the murderer might have taken fright a little at the thorough precautions of the police. I realized, too, that, although the moon was down, the time would come when again it would light up our town.

CHAPTER FIFTEEN

The Circus

BUT WE did not go to the Zoo, after all, that Saturday. Dinner was over by a quarter-past twelve, and we were washed and dressed by one o'clock. Christina left work at twelve on Saturdays, and we were to meet her at Bridge End, so that no time need be lost. She had her lunch in Town, and, although we were first on the scene, we had less than ten minutes to wait. She was always as good as her word, and she had told us that she would meet us at half-past one. She was there by twenty-five past, and had expected, she said, to be first.

To our surprise, at exactly half-past one Mrs. Bradley's car drew in to the edge of the kerb, and George got out. He held the door open for Christina.

" Explain as we go," said she. We scrambled after her, George shut the door, climbed back, and we were off. " Mrs. Bradley wants you two to do a job for her," Christina continued. " She wants you to go to the circus."

We could make nothing of this.

" What circus ? " Keith enquired.

" Well, the circus which visited us and did not perform," said Christina. " She wants you two to see the show, and to keep your eyes open. If you recognize anybody, either in the audience or among the performers, you are to wave a handkerchief as though you are waving to somebody on the other side of the arena. Mr. Seabrook's men will take care of the rest of the incident."

" People behind us will complain," said Keith, " if we start waving handkerchiefs in the middle of the show. Are we to be given a hint ? "

" A hint ? " enquired Christina.

" We've been given the hint," said I. " I take it that Mrs. Bradley anticipates that there will be somebody there for us to recognize, and it doesn't leave a very wide field. It might be any one of about half a dozen people: that is all."

" Forget it," said Christina, " for the moment. There's something else. Mrs. Bradley has got a confession out of Jack which he ought to have made to the police. You know how worried Jack has been since that night he was supposed to be meeting me after the dance to bring me home ? "

" When he got his sleeves wet," said Keith. " We thought he was worried about you."

" So did June," said Christina sadly. " It was a nuisance. No, Jack's trouble was that he had helped Danny Taylor to move poor Marion Bridges from the roadway up to the farm buildings, to look as though she had been set on on her way up to the house. She had really been killed at the entrance to Danny's father's orchard, much nearer here, where she and Danny used to meet."

" So Jack met Danny that night ? " said I. " I thought he did."

" Yes. Danny has been arrested. It was that which made Jack confess. He didn't want to, of course. He didn't want to be involved in it at all, and he did not want to let Danny down. But when the police took Danny, Mrs. Bradley pressed Jack hard, and he admitted to meeting Danny that night and helping him."

" Does that mean that Jack can give Danny Taylor an alibi ? " demanded Keith.

" No. He wishes he could. But Danny, it seems, had already come upon the body, and whistled for Jack in order to get Jack's advice on what to do."

" Does Jack believe Danny murdered Marion Bridges ? "

" No, he does not, and neither does anyone else who knows Danny well."

" Mr. Seabrook ought to know him well enough. Do the police think Danny murdered the woman ? I suppose they do, if they've arrested him."

" Well, there's a good deal both for and against him. You'd better ask Mrs. Bradley," said Christina. " But don't say anything to June when you get home. Jack may not be there, you see."

" Arrested ? "   We were more excited than alarmed.

" It's possible.   But whether he's there or not, say nothing to June.   Let her tell you what she likes, and don't argue."

" Right," we said.   The car drove out into the country.   We must have gone forty miles before it drew up at the entrance to a town called Suttering where the circus was encamped in a field.

Except that this field was on the opposite side of the road, that is, on our right instead of our left as we entered the town, it might have been Mr. Taylor's all over again.   There were the three or four elm trees in line along the centre of the ground, there was the big marquee, the little paybox, the animals' cages on waggons, the brightly-painted caravans, and the even brighter roundabouts and swing-boats.   In fact, there was only one difference, but to us it made all the difference in the world. This time the circus was to be held, and we were to see the performance.

There were three prices.   Christina paid the medium price, which was a shilling.   We had excellent seats for this money, only about eight rows from the sawdust ring.   We were lucky, too, in having two little girls in front of us.   They giggled and talked a good deal, but, on the whole, they sat still, and both were shorter than Keith, so he had a good view.

".Don't forget we're here on business," he muttered, when we had settled down and Christina had given us some chocolate. I had not forgotten, and, as we ate, we looked round.   There was not much light on the audience and I thought we should be lucky to recognize anybody we knew unless we were very near them.

Then the performance began, and, while it lasted, we had eyes for nothing but the arena.   There were plenty of items, each one seeming better than the one which had gone before. There was even a tight-rope act.   Either there had been more than one tight-rope walker attached to the circus, or else they had found someone else to take the place of the woman who had been killed.

At the pay-booth we had been given handbills of the circus. They were as good as programmes, for, to our minds, they described the entertainment satisfactorily.

Circus   Circus   Circus

The Most Wonderful, Breath-Taking, Marvellous, Educational, Entertaining, Animated, Thrilling, Spectacular Show in the World.

Crowned Heads Have Seen It.

Unknown Multitudes Have Seen It.

Come and See for Yourself this Riotous Fantasy of Sublime Terror and Beauty.

See the Daring

See the Skill

See the Equestrian Feats of Superb Horsemanship.

See the Girl Rider of the Plunging Rodeo.

See the Cossack Hordes.

See the Red Indian Braves in their Attack on the Blazing Farm.

See Mazeppa's Terrible Ride.

See History in its Alivest Form of Wonderful Escapes and Daring.

See the Balance of Nature Brought to Nought.

See the Sunshade Spin. Dizzy and Terrifying Ordeal Two Hundred Feet Above the Ground.

See the Hoola-Lula Performed Without Nets on the Cobweb Trapeze.

See the Clown on the Clothes-Line. Twenty Laughs a Second.

See the Elephants.

See the Sea-Lions.

See the Most Intelligent Shetland Pony in the World.

See the Chimpanzees.

See the Lions.

See the Tiger.

See the Fat Lady.

See the Bearded Lady.

See the Living Skeleton.

See the Siamese Twins.

Do not miss this International Show.

Bring the Wife

Bring the Children

Clean and Refined.

Something for All.

Babies in Arms Not Admitted.
Admission 1/6   1/-   6d.
Children under Twelve half-price.
No money refunded.   Seats guaranteed.
Beauty   Comedy   Thrills.

It was as satisfying as it sounded. It was not until we were coming out that I gave another thought to our mission. Then, hesitating at first, I pulled out my handkerchief and waved it.

"What's that for?" asked Keith.

"Look to your left," said I. He did so. The next instant the quarry I had seen was lost in the crowd of people surging away from the fair-ground.

"Who was it, Sim?" asked Christina, as I put my handkerchief away.

"Over by that banana barrow," said I. "A fellow in a check cap. It was the rag and bone man."

"So it was," she answered. "I didn't recognize him. Wonder what *he's* doing here?"

We had rides on the roundabouts and swing-boats, tea in the town in some pretty tea-gardens, and were home by half-past eight. I saw two plain-clothes men tailing us.

"Keeping an eye on Christina for Mr. Seabrook," said Keith. "It's getting late for her to be out, and I don't suppose she'll let us go back with her to her lodgings."

He was correct in supposing that. Christina took us as far as the Baths, and waited until we got to our gate and waved. I was greatly relieved to know that Mr. Seabrook was looking after her so well, whether she liked him or not.

June asked whether we had enjoyed ourselves. I do not think she wanted to know. She still hated Christina, and had agreed most grudgingly to allow us to go out with her. Jack never mentioned her name, which I thought a bad sign. However, he was at home, and had not been arrested so far, although he seemed fidgety and looked worried.

"I'll tell you what," said Keith, when he was undressing for his Saturday bath and I was waiting for mine, "I shouldn't think your spotting the rag and bone man was very much good, should you?"

" No good at all," I answered. " It was somebody inside the marquee that we had to look out for. And, talking of the rag and bone man, you realize, don't you, that we didn't ask Mrs. Cockerton the things we ought to have asked her this morning."

" How do you mean ? " he enquired, turning off the hot tap and testing the water with his toe. " I think I'll have some cold in this, and make it really deep."

" Well, we ought to have found out more about that pruning knife she said belonged to her husband. You see, if the knife we pinched was *not* the pruning knife, her knife should still be about."

" I'm not keen on reopening the subject of knives," said he, getting into the bath and leaving the cold tap full on. " I'm afraid all the time it will come out in her presence that we stole one."

" That couldn't be helped, you know," said I. " By the way, the tiger isn't a boy. It's a tiger. I thought so all along, but to-day there was not the slightest doubt."

" Yes, so I noticed," he answered. " I suppose Mrs. Bradley hoped we should see one or both of those men at the circus."

" Which men ? . . . Oh, the one who lifted you off the railings and the shifty one ? "

" Yes. I looked for them before the show began, and when we came out. They weren't there, or else the crowd swallowed them."

" I wonder whether they *were* the ones she thought we might see ? She might have thought we'd see someone connected with Danny Taylor. You know, I can't see why Jack and Danny moved that woman's body, can you ? "

" I think Jack's a fool."

" *I* think Jack's a fool. Do you think he will be arrested ? I'm sure Christina thought he would be."

" I should think it makes him accessory after the fact, and in that case Mr. Seabrook must carry out his duties."

" How rotten for June ! "

" And us. It won't be nice at school. I shan't say anything to anybody if he *is* arrested, shall you ? "

" No, but everyone will know."

" Perhaps Jack and Danny will have the sense to plead that they thought the woman might be injured, not dead, and they were trying to get her to the house."

" Well, that might even be true."

" Hardly likely. The first rule about injured people, I thought, was not to move them."

" Jack may not know that, and Danny always acts first and thinks second. The Taylors are Irish."

" He's at work, and they even tell you that sort of thing at school about injured animals."

" Oh, I don't know. Even when people *are* told things, they don't always think."

" I shall ask Mrs. Bradley, when I see her, whether Jack will be arrested."

" She may not like to tell you. Wait and see."

" All right. Oh, curse ! I've made this water too cold."

" Well, you can't have any more hot," said I. " You've had more than your share already."

" Your turn for first bath next time, then you can pinch it all, if you let me turn it on now."

" All right. I'll let you have some, and get you clean and sweet-smelling," said I.

" Talking of sweet-smelling," said Keith, without resentment, " and also of cleanliness, what made Jack go down to the *river* to wash ? There's a pump at the end of the stables, at that farm."

" There's also still the question of the horses," said I.

" But the blood wasn't fresh by the time they got the body to the house. I wonder what time she died ? "

" All the inquests have been adjourned, so we shan't know yet. Which horse was your favourite at the circus ? "

" The little black one. An Arab, I should think, shouldn't you ? "

" Tell you what," said Keith, when we were both bathed and in bed, and Jack had brought us our cocoa and put out the light, " do you think we ought to have let Mrs. Cockerton know that Mrs. Bradley has money ? "

" Well, she knew it already. That thirty pounds for the lace."

" Oh, yes, I suppose so. Still, I rather wish we hadn't harped on it. Of course, Mrs. Cockerton's all right, but these things get about."

"Wonder who could have told the murderer about those pound notes in the trapeze girl's bodice?"

"Yes, I wonder that, too. Must have been someone from the circus who was getting tight at a pub."

"Must have been one of the women. A man wouldn't know about it, would he?"

"He might. A man had to catch her when she did that swinging jump. He might feel them, or hear them crackle."

"Yes, that's true enough, he might. By the way, was it rather queer that the rag and bone man should have been in that crowd outside the circus? It seems very suspicious to me that he should be following them up."

"Yes, I thought so, too. Mrs. Cockerton said she'd got rid of him, of course, but I must say I was surprised when he turned up there."

CHAPTER SIXTEEN

The Death of a Nursemaid

SUNDAY WAS dull without Christina. I would almost as soon have been at school. We went to Sunday school to get out of June's way. We had more than a suspicion that she was going to ask us to take Tom out for a walk, and that meant taking his push-chair, as she would not expect us back until one o'clock.

She could hardly, however, come between us and our spiritual exercises, so, sour-faced and cross, she gave us each a penny for the church collection, for our religious impulses rarely carried us as far as putting our own money into the offertory plate—at our church everybody could see, if they wanted to, what the other people in the pew had contributed: thus I remember being startled and impressed upon one occasion when Christina put in two shillings—and Tom howled to come along with us.

"Let's take him," said Keith, suddenly. "He can go in the

Primary. Rose Lanning can look after him there. He'll be all right with her."

"We'll be late if we do. He'll have to be washed and dressed, you know," said I.

"It won't take a minute," said June. She whisked away Tom, and in a quarter of an hour had him ready. He was delighted, and we went in during the hymn, and when Lefty Gillingham, who stamped the attendance cards, saw him, he gave us a sympathetic wink and stamped us with a red star instead of a blue one, as though we had been early.

Then I took Tom into the Primary whilst the notices were being read out, and Rose, a pleasant girl who was servant up at Mr. Hopkinson's house, made much of him and won his confidence immediately.

"I wonder *you* weren't the children's nurse, Rose," said I.

"Oh, but I am now, Simon," she replied. "I'm in behopes of living to see myself pensioned, too."

Mr. Hopkinson pensioned all his old servants. He had special quarters for them in a building at the end of the park. If they did not want to live there, but with their relations, he allowed them ten shillings a week. With that, and the Old Age Pension, June said they were well off, she thought.

It occurred to me that, as Rose liked Tom, it would be a good idea to turn the conversation, when we took him back, on to the murder of the other nursemaid, Bessie, and see what Rose had to say. Most likely she would know nothing, but one could never be sure about that. Many chance or innocent remarks have put the police on the track, and I thought I could remember all Rose's remarks, supposing that she were willing to make any, and pass them on to Mrs. Bradley and the inspector.

So when I went to fetch Tom, at the end of Sunday school, I said, as Rose put on his hat:

"I shouldn't have thought they could spare you, Rose, from the big house, if you are now minding the children."

"They've gone away for a week to the Isle of Wight," said Rose. "So I asked if I could come to Sunday school and church, and was allowed."

"Aren't you afraid of taking on Bessie's job?" I asked. Rose looked very wise. It was not easy for her to do this, for she was a simple girl with a good complexion and a heart of gold. She was managing it by squinting down her nose and then turning and looking at me sideways.

"There's them that knows what they knows about Bessie, cross my heart and speak no ill of the dead," she replied significantly, "and them that doesn't."

"She went to meet a policeman, didn't she?" I asked. Tom pulled at my hand. He wanted to go to church. He was taken sometimes by June, and always embarrassed us by singing very loudly, with no tune whatsoever, out of the hymn book held upside down. Keith had once reversed the hymn book for him, but Tom had responded to this with a howl of protest which brought all the congregation's eyes to our pew. Tom knew which was right way up, and preferred the other. Sometimes he would sing by himself in the middle of the minister's prayers. People enjoyed that, I think. Extempore prayers are often long.

"Half a sec, Tommy," said I. Keith came to find us, and I gave Tom over to him, and walked over to church with Rose when I had helped her collect up the pictures the Primary played with, and their bricks with the twelve Apostles on them. As we collected and stacked, and as we walked over to the vestry entrance—for Rose was in the choir—she told me more about Bessie.

Bessie, it seemed, was really no better than a thief, although no one had found it out until after her death.

"Have you told the police?" I asked.

"Oh, no, of course not!" said Rose, looking thoroughly shocked. "You don't say things like that when people are dead!"

"Why, what did she take, then?" I asked.

"The housekeeper says she took clothes and trinkets and such."

"But surely they would be missed?"

"Well, you see," said Rose, "they belonged to the children's grandmother, and she's been dead some years. Bessie might have gone on, and never been found out at all, only it so happened that the housekeeper had orders to turn out some of the stuff for a jumble sale down at Saint Anthony's. So, of course, in going through, and her having been at the house such a number of years, and having a pretty good memory, she found that half of the clothes and a lot of other things, too, had disappeared."

" Jewellery and watches ? " I ventured.

" No, nothing so valuable, I don't believe," replied Rose. " Oddments from foreign travel, and the like of that, I think. The Colonel, the old lady's son, had been all over the place, I believe, and the old gentleman, Mr. Hopkinson himself, had been at foreign courts."

" Yes, he had been in the Foreign Office," I interpolated.

" Ah, that's what I was told. Well, he'd given little things to his wife, and forgot all about 'em, like enough. He's an absentminded gentleman, the master, and getting very old. Mrs. Green says he's older than her, and she's over seventy now. He offered to give her her pension, but she says she shall last out his time."

Rose went into the vestry, and I went round to the west side of the church to catch up Keith and Tom. I did not catch them, but Keith had saved a place for me in our usual pew in the gallery. Tom approved of the gallery, and spat on a lady's hat, so we had to threaten to take him home. The lady, fortunately, did not know what he had done. She had just come in, and was praying.

Tom behaved after that, and sang a good deal, but otherwise was no nuisance. We did not stay for the sermon, but went out after the collection. We would like to have missed it, but knew that Tom would tell June, not intending to do any harm. He was too young to be trusted.

We went for a walk up Manor Road, my mind leading me unconsciously in the direction of Mr. Hopkinson's park. As we went, I told Keith all that Rose had said. He was interested, but not particularly impressed.

" I don't see how it helps us," he said. " She may have been no end of a thief, but thieves are not usually murdered."

" Thieves don't usually have policemen for their sweethearts," I pointed out, " and, so far as we know, she was in Saint George's Court to meet a policeman."

" I don't see why she had to meet him there. It almost looks as though there was something fishy."

" It was on his beat, and she took him something to eat, I expect. He's quite above board. It's Bill Kelsey."

" I know it's Bill Kelsey. All the same, he's been transferred."

" Not for anything except the shock of his girl being murdered, though. There was nothing against Bill at all. Bob Cammond told me, and Bob knows everything, because his mother cleans for Mrs. Seabrook."

" Well, I can't see what her thieving had to do with her murder," said Keith. " Now, if she had murdered someone who might have given her away to Mr. Hopkinson or his housekeeper, there might have been something in it."

" Anyway, I shall tell Mrs. Bradley," said I.

" Oh, of course. I agree about that. But I can't see she'll make much out of it. I wonder what Bessie did with the things she stole ? "

" Sold them to someone, I suppose. The rag and bone man, perhaps."

" Oh, she wouldn't get enough from *him*," said Keith. " He's mean. He only gave John Wilkins a paper windmill for a dozen perfectly good jam-jars and his mother's old coat. And Arthur Bates only got one goldfish . . . . and it died the next day . . . for his father's old shoes and two wheels off a baby's pram."

" Yes, but his father's shoes had gone right through the soles. He showed them to Jack, and Jack said he wouldn't care to mend them. And the pram wheels came out of the canal. I saw Fred and Arthur fishing for them myself. And they thought the goldfish ate grass, although I *told* them ants' eggs . . . the owls ! "

" Still, it shouldn't have died the next day," persisted Keith.

I went to the police station directly afternoon Sunday school was over. June and Jack had gone to her mother's with Tom, so we were left to get our own tea, and were under oath not to be out of the house after half-past eight in the evening if nobody had returned home.

Inspector Seabrook was in, but his mother was not. He was not very pleased to see me, but allowed me to use his telephone.

I knew Mrs. Bradley's number because we had stayed at the house. She answered the telephone herself, and greeted me kindly. She called my news about the dead girl, Bessie, contributory and corroborative evidence, and thanked me warmly for it.

" Is it really any good ? " I enquired. She assured me that it was, and added that she had been fairly certain, for some time, of the murderer's identity, but, so far, there was not enough evidence on which to risk making an arrest.

" And you mean this helps ? " I almost shouted.

" Who is there with you ? " she asked.

" Only Mr. Seabrook. And he's in the kitchen," I replied.

" Well," she said, " don't ask me whom I suspect. I can't tell you yet. It would not be right. But this piece of information helps as much as anything else I know about the murders, and that is absolutely true."

I expressed my gratification, and rang off. Next morning there was a letter for me. It came by the eight o'clock post, before I set out for school. It was from Mrs. Bradley, and said that if I wanted to continue my excellent detective work, all I had to do was to meet her at the entrance to Mr. Hopkinson's park, at the wrought-iron gates, immediately after tea.

I worked well at school, in deadly fear of being kept behind if I did badly, and raced to the station immediately we were set free. I then had to wait for the train, and was in a fever for it to come in. When it did I thought we should never get away from the station, for fellows kept drifting along and the guard kept waiting for them. When I got home June was out, and Keith was laying the tea. This was a great advantage. We cut thick bread, put butter and jam on it, drank cold milk and water mixed, and by five o'clock I was in the bathroom washing my face and hands.

Keith came with me as far as the bend in the Manor Road where the line of elm trees with their enormous trunks and thick underbrush marked the outskirts of Mr. Hopkinson's park, and then I went forward alone and he went home.

Mrs. Bradley arrived at five-thirty. I heard it strike at the farm. She was accompanied by Mr. Seabrook. He wore uniform, and looked very smart. Mrs. Bradley looked smart, too, in bright colours and a hat I had not seen before. I was glad I had washed and had put on a clean collar. I almost wished I had worn my Sunday suit.

There was a great bell which one had to pull. Mr. Seabrook pulled it, and an old man came out from behind the stables and opened the gate. There was a broad lawn flanked by rhododendrons and laurels, and as we rounded a bend in the drive, for Mr. Seabrook had left his car at the roadside in charge of a constable-driver, we came in sight of the house.

It was a truly magnificent mansion, built in the reign of King James the First, so Mr. Seabrook informed me. The old man, having relocked the wrought-iron gates, had gone back to wherever he had come from, so we were left to make our own way.

The front door had a square porch, and the windows of the house had been altered to fit in with modern conditions. As soon as the front door was opened, I could see that all round the ceiling of the hall were arranged small, brightly-coloured shields.

A maid let us in. I knew her. She was Teddy Ransom's sister Bella. I thought, however, that she would prefer us to meet as strangers, so I nodded distantly, as though I did not really know her. She would have none of this, however, but giggled, and gave me a kiss on the ear, before she showed us into a room to wait.

Mr. Seabrook was amused, but I felt somewhat embarrassed. I thought servants had to be trained not to behave familiarly inside their employers' houses. No wonder, I thought, that Bessie had gone to the bad in so loose and informal an atmosphere.

"You are moralizing, my dear Simon," said Mrs. Bradley, when we were seated. "Do you disapprove of kissing among friends?"

"Well, when on duty, yes, ma'am," I replied. She cackled and wagged her head and Mr. Seabrook said:

"Quite right, quite right."

He had no time to say more, for the housekeeper came just then. I had never seen her before. She was certainly an old lady. She looked well-nourished and prim. I thought that perhaps the girls in her charge were on too tight, and not too loose, a rein. I have noticed the same sort of things with very strict masters at school.

"Good afternoon, Mrs. Green," said Mr. Seabrook. "Here I am, back again, you see, with my witnesses." He presented Mrs. Bradley and myself.

"Not that *child?*" said the housekeeper.

"I am afraid his presence is absolutely necessary, ma'am. His evidence is material to my case, as no doubt you will agree when you have heard what he has to say."

"And what *has* he to say?" she enquired. I took a dislike to her. She sounded extremely disagreeable, and evidently took me to be younger than I was. I glanced at Mrs. Bradley. She directed my glance to Mr. Seabrook. Mrs. Green sat down, thus allowing the inspector and myself to sit, too, which we did at her invitation.

"Now, Simon," said the inspector, "you have often been in Mrs. Cockerton's antique shop?"

"Oh, yes, very often," said I.

"You've turned over most of her stock?"

"All of it, sir, I believe."

"Can you remember what you've seen?"

"Oh, yes, I think so. Most of it, anyway."

"Right. Now, leaving aside all such things as furniture, and any other stuff too big to be easily transportable, give Mrs. Green an idea of what's there."

"Well," said I, "in the window there are paperweights, made like the Buddha, some ivory elephants, some beads, a ship in a bottle, a pair of bellows ornamented with brass, small framed pictures, lockets, paperweights in brass, glass, stone and bronze, small statuettes in bronze and plaster, some Japanese lacquer, some nests of boxes, a death-mask, several brooches, rings, bracelets, necklets of shells, a box ornamented with shells and upholstered in crimson plush and embellished with a photograph of Tunbridge Wells, some gold crosses, one or two silver cigarette cases, a brass bell made like a lady in the costume of Queen Elizabeth's time, a pair of duelling pistols, a dagger in a sheath of sharkskin, another in a velvet scabbard, two others in brown leather sheaths, a model of a ram in gold . . ."

"Enough, boy," said Mrs. Green. She looked at the inspector. " I will get my bonnet and come with you. *Some*, at least, of the objects mentioned, might well have come from this house."

" One moment," said Mrs. Bradley. She took from her skirt pocket an oilskin package and weighted it in her hand. " I may be able to save you a journey, Mrs. Green. I see that your rheumatism is very troublesome to-day."

She handed the oilskin packet to the housekeeper.

" I need not tell you how extremely important it is that you do not mention the object of our visit," said Mr. Seabrook before she could open the package. " And I need not emphasize the fact that if you have any doubt whatsoever . . ."

But the old lady did not wait to hear the end of the cautionary sentence. Her gnarled fingers were hastily but carefully unrolling the oilskin covering, and when she saw what was inside she stood up in astonishment and fury.

" That wicked girl ! That child of Satan ! " she said. " How dared she sell such a thing ! How dared she do it ! "

Inside the oilskin package was the strange, striped goddess which Mrs. Cockerton had given to Mrs. Bradley.

" I thought it came from a private collection," said Mrs. Bradley complacently. " All the same, inspector, I think perhaps Mr. Hopkinson himself should identify it for us."

" Mrs. Bradley is right," said Mr. Seabrook. " If you would kindly inform Mr. Hopkinson that we should be glad to see him . . ."

" Mr. Hopkinson," said the housekeeper, " is having his nap before he dresses for dinner."

" Madam," said Mr. Seabrook, to my great admiration, " I am here on duty to investigate a series of cases of murder. Will you, therefore, have the goodness . . ."

The housekeeper went out. In about ten minutes' time Mr. Hopkinson came in. He was a tall and stooping old gentleman with the profile of an eagle and the manners of a dove. He greeted us vaguely and kindly, and seemed to have no idea whatsoever of the purpose of our visit. He even told me that he thought I should find his grandchildren in the garden.

Mr. Seabrook politely called him to order, and Mrs. Bradley, who had taken it back from Mrs. Green, showed him the archæological specimen, and asked him whether he had ever seen it before.

" God bless my soul ! Athens in 1890 ! " he observed, turning it over in his hands. " Presented to me personally by the finder. But how do you come to have it ? It was among my wife's treasures in the little cabinet she always kept in her sitting-room. I have not seen it since she died. All her things are still there. I don't understand . . . the room was kept locked. Ah, no doubt our excellent Mrs. Green . . ."

" I know my place better than that, sir, I hope and trust," said the housekeeper.

" We shall have to trouble either Mr. Hopkinson or Mrs. Green again," said Mrs. Bradley. " What about this, Mr. Hopkinson ? "

She held out her hand to the inspector, who, after some fumbling, drew from his tunic the length of old lace which Mrs. Bradley had purchased for thirty pounds.

Mr. Hopkinson touched the lace, and shook his head, but Mrs. Green, with an exclamation, identified it at once, and described the gown from which it had been filched. The inspector put the lace away, and explained to Mr. Hopkinson that the goods which Bessie had stolen had been taken to an antique shop down in the town, and that it would be useful if other missing articles could be identified.

" But not to-night, my dear fellow. It's almost time I dressed for dinner. That reminds me. Have some sherry," said Mr. Hopkinson. He rang the bell, but the inspector and Mrs. Bradley said that they could not stay.

" To-morrow, at about ten-thirty, if you will be so good, sir," said the inspector, on taking his leave. Mr. Hopkinson promised, and Mr. Seabrook said to me when we were walking down the drive towards the gate, " And you'll have to come as well, Simon. I'll telephone your headmaster."

On Tuesdays we had mathematics, so it was with considerable pleasure that I assented to this proposal. I had been put back on homework, and maths. homework followed the Tuesday lesson, and so I should miss that as well. I blessed Mr. Hopkinson, his wife, all his works, and, I am afraid, the murdered Bessie, at the thought of this blessed relief from the worst of my earthly toil.   There was only one thing which perturbed me.   Common honesty demanded that I should bring my beloved scimitar, and, if he agreed (and I knew that he would) Keith's horse-pistol to the old gentleman's notice, only hoping that he would disclaim all knowledge of either.   However, I was immediately ashamed of this hope.   If Mrs. Bradley could give up thirty pounds' worth of lace and her valuable goddess, I ought to be willing to part with my scimitar, I felt.   But the parting would almost break my heart.   We had few possessions, and this was my favourite of all.

CHAPTER SEVENTEEN

The Temporary Disappearance of a Husband

MRS. COCKERTON was aghast.

" I had no idea ! " she said.   " Really, Mr. Inspector, you must believe me.   No idea at all."

" That's as may be, ma'am," said Mr. Seabrook, not, I thought, too kindly, " but you will understand we must check up pretty thoroughly on your shop.   You're in the position, at the moment, of a receiver of stolen goods."

" But surely not ! " said Mrs. Cockerton.   " I had no *intention*, inspector."

" That's as may be again," said Mr. Seabrook.   " Do you mind showing us upstairs ? "

" Well, Mr. Simon Innes," said Mrs. Cockerton, seizing upon me as soon as she had shown the others into her top-floor room, " and do I owe this invasion to you ? "

" Indeed no, Mrs. Cockerton," said I.   " At least . . ."   I paused, wondering whether the denial was absolutely true.   To my confusion, I did not think it was.

" No matter, no matter," said she.   " It is best for it all to come out, if wrong has been done.   There is nothing dark enough to remain undiscovered for ever."

" Even the murderer has been discovered," said I ; and, of

course, could have bitten my tongue out on the words. She looked at me in a startled and interested fashion, and put her hands on her hips.

" They really know ? "

I nodded. I could do no less, having let the cat out of the bag.

" But it's no use asking me to name him," I continued, " for his name has not been mentioned, and won't be, until the evidence is complete."

" They have evidence, then ? " she asked.

" Oh, yes, they have evidence," I answered. We gazed at one another for some time. I could feel that she was trying to read my thoughts. I laughed, to break the spell of her gipsy eyes. " It's no use, Mrs. Cockerton," I said. " I don't know anything more."

" But what has my shop got to do with it ? " she enquired. " Really, I could have swooned with surprise when these people turned up this morning. Was it the Point d'Alençon ? "

I thought there would be no harm in answering that.

" I believe, ma'am, it was the Greek goddess," said I. She nodded, as though she were satisfied.

" I knew it was unlucky," she said. " For this visitation, you know, Mr. Simon Innes, is very unlucky for me."

" How so, Mrs. Cockerton ? " I asked.

" If some of my things, for which I have paid the fair price, are stolen goods, I suppose I shall have to yield them up," she said. " I cannot afford to be out of pocket, Mr. Innes."

" Oh, dear ! " I exclaimed. I had not realized that she would suffer a dead loss on the stolen property. " And the trouble is that you won't be able to claim on the thief or have her punished."

" I would not wish either," said Mrs. Cockerton, with dignity. " It is no part of my policy to grind my fellow-beings back into that mud from which, it is only too obvious, far too many of them have climbed."

" That's very handsome, Mrs. Cockerton," I remarked. She smiled.

" I was not brought up to it, Mr. Innes. Now let us see what they're about."

There was a collection of odds and ends, chiefly of clothing, on the big wooden chest near the door.   The inspector was looking down at it.

"All that I had from my lodger," said Mrs. Cockerton, turning it over with a strong and bony hand.   "And I am sure the poor fellow did not steal it.   For his honesty I would go bail as readily as for my own.   What he sold to me he first paid for; possibly in kind, as his old-world custom is, but steal it . . . never ! "

I thought it rather surprising of her thus to stand up for her absent, disreputable lodger, considering how she had referred to him the last time I had been in the shop, but I made no comment.

"Show us what you have in the back room on this floor," said Mr. Seabrook curtly.   She led the way, and all of us followed behind.   In this room old Mr. Hopkinson identified a considerable number of objects.   It seemed as though the wretched girl who had been murdered had made a search of the locked rooms once occupied by old Mrs. Hopkinson and had sold the whole of her gleanings.   Even a rug from the bedroom floor and the coverlet of a bed had been brought to the shop to be disposed of.

"Shocking ! " said Mrs. Cockerton.   "Really shocking ! Well, and what happens now ? "

"I propose," said Mr. Hopkinson, "to give you the money you paid for these articles, provided you will get somebody to bring them back to my house."

Mrs. Cockerton neither argued nor thanked him.   She brought out an old brown book and looked up various pages.

"Four pounds sixteen shillings and ninepence," she announced at last, looking up, it seemed to me, warily.   Mr. Seabrook put out his hand and took the brown book from her.

"By your leave," he said, "and not quite so fast, Mr. Hopkinson, if you please.   Now, ma'am, conduct us to the woodshed where your lodger, I believe, has his haunts."

"I don't think you'll get in there," said Mrs. Cockerton. "The poor fellow keeps it locked."

"Keeps it locked, does he ? " said Mr. Seabrook.   "Why should he want to do that ? "

"It's his own.   He pays rent, albeit but little," Mrs. Cockerton replied with a smile.   "Why shouldn't he lock up his lodgings ? To him it is all the home he has."

"Until he sees the inside of a prison," said Mr. Seabrook nastily. But he did not press the point about the woodshed. Mrs. Cockerton, offended, said no more. She did not receive her four pounds sixteen and ninepence, but Mr. Hopkinson raised his hat to her in parting, and patted his breast-pocket in a reassuring manner which must have gratified and soothed her.

"That woman is no thief!" said Mr. Hopkinson, as soon as we got back to his car which he could not park in the high street because the road was too narrow. Mr. Seabrook shook his head.

"Most probably not, sir. But we cannot proceed without proper precautions," he said. "The girl who sold those goods to the rag and bone man, who, after all, lodges at the back of that shop and admittedly sold the stolen goods to that woman, was foully and brutally murdered. *That's* what I have to face. Your stolen property comes second."

"Well, inspector, I am making no fuss about my stolen property," said Mr. Hopkinson mildly.

"Another thing," said Mr. Seabrook. "How does it come that your housekeeper did not know that the goods were missing? Doesn't she live up to her title?"

"Apparently not," said Mr. Hopkinson, still in the same mild voice. "Poor Emma is getting old. She does not get about as she used to do. And the rooms are never used. I don't suppose, except for the routine dusting and cleaning, they are entered from year's end to year's end. My wife has been dead these twenty years, inspector."

His chauffeur drove him home, and Mrs. Bradley and I walked westward along the high street as Inspector Seabrook crossed the road to the police station.

"Poor Mr. Seabrook," said Mrs. Bradley, grinning. "Nothing will satisfy him but the rag and bone man's carcase, rotting on the end of a string."

I pondered upon the picture thus described, and did not find it pleasant. Keith and I had once, with enormous labour, made a Guy Fawkes and stuffed the figure with straw. We left our finished work in the garden and during the night of November the fourth it rained. The sodden, half-human wreck that the morning disclosed provided me with nightmare for several weeks after that. Our Guy Fawkes had become an obscenity. The thought of the rag and bone man dangling on a rope made me sick. Mrs. Bradley glanced at me and took my sleeve in her grip.

"These bestial realities must sometimes be faced," she said. "Life is inclined to be sordid. Our friends are not always what they seem."

"The rag and bone man is no friend of Keith's or mine," said I. She shook her head sadly, let go my sleeve and took me into Cowell's to buy some sweets. By the time we reached the Half Acre it was after half-past eleven. June had told me to get home by twelve if I could, as she wanted dinner over early because she had to go out. She was taking Tom with her, and I suppose I should have gone to school after dinner, for a train left in plenty of time; however, it seemed flying in the face of Providence not to take the holiday that offered, and I reflected, also, that by going to school in the afternoon I could not so easily get out of doing my homework. So when dinner was over I offered to wash up the plates, and, June accepting the offer, I was soon alone in the house.

When I had done the washing up I cleaned the sink and polished the taps as a sop to my conscience for not returning to school, and then wondered what I should do with the three golden hours that remained before June came home and we had tea.

To assist thought I cut myself a piece of bread and jam, and, munching this, went thoughtfully down the road. It was deserted. Our dinner had been so early that the neighbours were only just settling down to their meal.

I decided to take a short stroll and see what adventure Fate provided. It was seldom I took a walk round the town alone. I went down the Butts to the *Pigeons*, crossed the high street, and dropped down Church Alley and so to the Leys. There was much for a boy to enjoy. I stood for some time on the grassy verge of the canal where the Leys turns sharply away from the little street leading from the town, and watched the people on the barges. Then a woman came up and said:

"Are you one of my children?"

I raised my school cap.

"I don't think so, madam," I replied. She smiled and said: "Not off the boats?"

"Oh, no," I replied. "I'm on holiday."

"Wouldn't you like to come to school?"

I had forgotten that there was a school provided down by the Boatmen's Institute where children off the barges could learn to read and write while the barges were idle in the town.

"I am only in town for the day," I politely replied. She looked regretful. "And the only subjects in which I am backward are mathematics and physics," I continued. This choked her off. She smiled again feebly, and said:

"I *must* find some children from somewhere."

She then wandered rather disconsolately back towards the high street, where I imagine she descended to the towing-path beside which, near the bridge, some more of the barges were moored.

I passed along up the Leys, feeling that no one was safe if, without warning, he could be set on by teachers who wanted to form a class. The only road across the Leys soon petered out, and I found myself faced by alternatives. One was a narrow path which led to the village of disused barges and hoppers which now housed the regular inhabitants of the Leys, and I had been told that it was silly and dangerous to venture along this path if one were a stranger. In the evening, or during darkness, I should not have gone. But at half-past two in the afternoon it seemed fantastic to be afraid of anything, and the whole place was peaceful and quiet.

Picking up a stone in case I met savage dogs, I strolled along the path and looked at the jumble of craft in the almost dry basin of what was in reality one of the mouths of our little river, the Bregant.

No one interfered with or even addressed me. The one or two people I saw looked up with indifference as I passed. The women looked somewhat slatternly and ill-dressed; the men were sullen. I did not see any children except a number of babies and tiny toddling girls. The others, I daresay, were out of sight in case they were called on to go to the barge people's school.

The path, however, was a cul-de-sac. It ended abruptly at a

narrow plank placed across a hopper.   I would have given a good
deal for the pluck to walk over this plank, and might have found
it, I think, but for the advent of a thin and aggressive dog, which,
from the stern of a decrepit boat on the farther side of the
hopper, planted its forelegs, bristled, and proceeded to bark and
to snarl.

It seemed to me that I might be on private land, so, whistling
to show that I did not mind the dog, I turned and began to walk
back.   It was at this moment that I saw the rag and bone man,
and it was at the same moment that I knew in my own mind
that it was he, and none other, whom Keith and I had seen in
the moonlight, knife in hand, on Dead Man's Bridge on the
night of the circus girl's murder.

He was again on a bridge.   This time the bridge was that
which carried the alternative path—for the path I had selected
branched off from another at about a hundred yards from the
village of boats—over the canal to a path which was not part of
the towing-path but had been made for the convenience, I suppose, of the men who used the small dock at the mouth of our
river.   The bridge was narrow and high.   A stone ramp led
steeply up to it, and on other side of this ramp there was a
handrail which was continued up to and over the bridge.
On the broad end of this handrail the rag and bone man was
seated.

I was afraid.   I was more afraid than I have ever been in my
life except during nightmares, than which no terror is more
awful.   As soon as I saw him I dived in among some alder
bushes which grew on the rough land traversed by my path, and
lay there on my stomach watching the man as he took from his
pocket some various odds and ends of gloves and silk scarves and
conned them over.   One, apparently, had a maker's tab or the
owner's name on it, for all in a moment out came a glittering
sheath knife and the offending label was ripped out.

I could make very little of the knife.   It could have been a
leather-knife, it is true, but I did not think it was one.   It looked,
in the daylight of a sunny afternoon, more like a sailor's or a
scout's knife.   It told me nothing, for it was likely that the man,
having lost the knife with which, I was certain now, he had cut
the throats of his victims, had purchased another which would

equally well serve his purpose. On the other hand, the knife
I now saw in his hand might just as easily be the very same knife
as the one which had glinted, by moonlight on Dead Man's
Bridge on the night of the first of the murders.

There was, in fact, no proof that the man on Dead Man's
Bridge was the murderer. In fact, if the knife we had stolen
from Mrs. Cockerton's shop was the knife with which the
murders had been committed, and the knife in the possession of
the rag and bone man was the knife he had had on the bridge,
it seemed unlikely that he was the murderer.

I worked this out as I lay in my bush, but it brought me no
relief. I reflected that, after all, the later murders could not
have been committed with the knife which we had stolen and
which the police had finally impounded. Besides, there was
something so furtive and yet so triumphant in the demeanour of
the rag and bone man as he sat out there in the sunshine, that
my blood ran cold as I watched him. I would have taken my
oath, evidence or no evidence, that the Ripper was under my
eye.

He soon got up and walked on. I debated whether I should
follow him, and soon made up my mind, for he crossed the
bridge and began to walk towards the old lock from which he
had thrown the corset into the canal.

It was impossible, for the first part of the trail, to keep under
cover. Once I had left my hiding place and had taken the path
for the bridge, crossed it and followed him along the canal-side
path, I should be in his line of vision if it occurred to him to look
round.

At first I decided to risk it, but then another plan came into
my head. If only I could cross the plank which formed a narrow
bridge across the hopper, I could cut him off at the end of
Catherine Wheel Yard, down by the Brewery Tap, without being
seen at all.

I weighed up the risks, and had to do this quickly, for fear I
should lose him altogether. The one path held the dog; the
other a man who, as far as I could make out, was a more dangerous killer than any man-eating tiger. The dog would probably
bite me, and the bite might turn septic and I might die of it.
The man might not kill me there and then, but, if he suspected

that I was a menace to his safety, sooner or later I should be knifed and my body found like those of his other victims.

I plumped for this latter consummation. The man, after all, might not see me. The dog most certainly would. With a trembling in my legs, I marched boldly towards the bridge and mounted the steep, stone ramp.

The man was already some distance along the path. I stood at the end of the bridge, and, affecting to look at the water, watched to see whether he crossed by the lock or went on. There was no way out that I knew, unless one had a boat, without crossing the lock or returning to cross by the bridge, so I felt fairly certain that he would cross by the lock.

He did not. He walked along past the old lock gates, and disappeared where the canal made a bend and reached the broad waters of the Wyden.

I stayed where I was on the bridge. He had not seen me. I had plenty of time on my hands. It was true that the moment he returned he must see me, but I had hopes that he would not notice a boy who was doing no harm. If he crossed by the lock, I would follow. If he came back over the bridge I felt I should leave it before he set foot on it. I could not endure the thought of his squeezing past me.

I suppose I waited ten minutes, for the clock on the church at the top of Church Alley chimed the quarter, but had not chimed again when he reappeared. To my enormous relief and thankfulness, this time he crossed the lock. As soon as he was gone I ran down the ramp on the other side of the bridge and then hastened along the path that he had trodden.

I picked him up again opposite the Brewery Tap after we had both crossed the two little bridges which led over the lasher and the dry basin, and after that I had no need of any concealment, for, although I kept close to the side, ready to efface myself in doorways or gates, of which there were a sufficiency in the alley to afford cover for a dozen boys, he walked doggedly, although not rapidly, onwards, head down, and his old bulging sack upon his back.

He turned to the right at the high street, and I followed him to the alley which led to the back of Mrs. Cockerton's shop. I loitered for a quarter of an hour, by the clock in the jeweller's window, and then sped back to the canal. I lost no time, but plunged to the left when I had crossed the old lock, and went down the path towards the mouth of the river.

Here there were often men working, shoring up the edges of the river which had been strengthened with sacks of concrete, or dredging the channel which soon got silted up; but this afternoon nobody was about.

Greatly desirous of discovering what the rag and bone man had been doing, I made my way to the edge of the bank until I was facing the Wyden. Below me the bank fell away to a stretch of soft mud and some gravel. Beyond, and away to the right, was the edge of the dock where the branch railway came to the river. I could see cranes, and the steep concrete edge of a pier. On the pier were great heaps of coal. Lying off the pier were a couple of squat, dirty tugs of the kind which draw the barges up the river.

Knowing that any men working on the dock would probably take no notice of a boy poking round at the river entrance, and that they were, in any case, unable to interfere except by shouting at him, I turned my back on the Wyden and began a close survey of all the ground between the confluence of the rivers and the lock. Alas! I was no true detective; at any rate, I seemed to have lacked the basic training necessary to my task. In vain I went over the ground. There was nothing that I could find. The only discovery that I made, that of a flight of steps which led up to the railway approach at the top of the bank, seemed trivial at the time, and unexciting.

Dejected and disappointed, I returned to the high street and directed my steps towards Mrs. Cockerton's shop. I did not, in this locality, entertain the slightest fear of the rag and bone man or of anyone else. I was on my own ground, and had a right to stare at her shop-window if I chose.

I did choose, and with good reason; for the window was almost empty, and when I peered in at the doorway, in place of the usual setting out of her goods, there were sacks and bundles and a melancholy array of collections of smaller articles all tied together with string. She must have worked hard since the morning.

As I gazed, Mrs. Cockerton herself appeared in the doorway. " Spring-cleaning, Mrs. Cockerton ? " I enquired.

" Moving out of the neighbourhood, Mr. Innes," she replied with great dignity. " I do not choose to remain in a town which now knows me as a receiver of stolen goods."

" But it doesn't ! I mean, nobody would think of you like that ! "

" Would they not ? The world is not as charitable as your young heart, my dear Mr. Simon."

" And you're really going ? " I said. This was very bad news. " I am."

" I'll help you pack up, then," I said dispiritedly. She shook her head.

" It would take me longer to tell you what to do than to do it myself," she replied. " Away to your tea, my dear soul. I shall manage. I must run my poor lodger to earth, and tell him the news. I've had him back, you know."

" Run him to earth ? " said I. " But . . ." I was about to tell her that I knew he had returned to the back of the house not more than an hour before, when I caught back the information. It would never do to allow that murderer to know that I had been spying on his movements. " But he'll be upset," I finished lamely. She nodded.

" He'll be upset. We were married, you know, last week. I shall take him with me, of course, unless he prefers to stay here. I shall not attempt to persuade him, either way. People should be left to themselves, to make their own decisions. Do you not think so, Mr. Innes ? "

" Certainly," I said, accepting the news of the marriage without showing surprise. Jack had married June, Christina proposed to marry the unemotional although handsome Inspector Seabrook, and Mrs. Benson, down our road, had married a Chinese shopkeeper. Marriages were made in heaven, a realm I believed in vaguely but had no desire to visit or understand, but that Mrs. Cockerton should marry the loathsome murderer was past all understanding.

" There's one thing you could do for me," she said. " I have to get the copper on for some cooking. We must have something for the journey. I should think some haunches of venison and a large Christmas pudding would do. After all, we are only two people."

I was accustomed to her conversational oddities. I thought the probability was that she had some garments to wash.

" When do you go ? " I asked. " And what do I use to light the fire ? "

" As soon as the vanmen can come. Perhaps on Saturday. Use the kindlings beside the woodshed door. Do not go into the woodshed. The police explored it thoroughly this morning, although I pointed out to them that it was my husband's property and premises whether he was present or not. I hope you agree ? "

" Oh, yes," I answered, my stomach becoming unpleasantly empty at the thought of approaching the domain of the horrible and sinister rag and bone man. There was no fear that I should go inside the woodshed. I would sooner have entered the tiger's cage at the circus. I was certain that he was in there, and I remembered, shuddering, her remark about the smell of human hair.

" Where is the copper ? " I asked.

" Through to the right. You will see it on your way to the shed. And you might put some water in the copper before you begin. It ill becomes an empty vessel to sustain the heat of a fire."

I went out as she had directed, and found a remarkably clean and tidy scullery, with a pail beneath the sink. I filled and refilled the pail until the copper was half full. Then I ventured out to the woodshed. The stout padlock was still on the door, so that I could not have entered, however much I had tried. The pile of kindlings was ready, and a billhook lay beside them. I gathered them up and lighted the copper fire.

There was no sign whatever of the rag and bone man. He had certainly come in, and, it seemed, as certainly gone again; but I said nothing to Mrs. Cockerton on the subject. If she and the rag and bone man were husband and wife, it would be worse than foolish to confide in her that I had spied upon his movements after having seen him out on the Leys.

" Well, good-bye, Mrs. Cockerton," I said. " I shall see you again before you go ? "

" Of course, Mr. Innes," she answered. " We must bid our

old friends farewell. Perhaps you will take a stoup with me. Who knows ? I must send my rascal out for a bottle of port. It is like the lazy wretch to make off when I am so busy. But there ! Saving your presence, Mr. Innes, most men are lazy and all are wretches. You agree ? "

" Oh, yes, within limits, ma'am," said I. It was fair enough criticism, I thought.

CHAPTER EIGHTEEN

The Gleaning

I HAD MUCH to confide to Keith that evening, and something to tell Mrs. Bradley. We went together to the police station at six o'clock, passing Mrs. Cockerton's on the way. She was in the shop and saw us. She came to the door.

" The copper goes well," she said.

" And Mr. Cock. . . . your husband ? " I enquired. She shook her head.

" No news, no news. And no news is good news," said she.

" You know, I think she gets more peculiar," said Keith, when we were well past the shop and mounting the rise towards Drum Lane.

" She *is* peculiar, but how much we shall miss her ! " said I. " More than anyone else except Christina, I think."

" That's true," said he. " I wonder where she will go ? You didn't ask, I suppose ? "

" I hardly liked to. She seems very sensitive at present."

" Perhaps she will tell us to-morrow. Where do you think the rag and bone man went, after you saw him go round to the back of the shop ? "

" I've been wondering whether he went to the woodshed at all. I saw him go into the alley, and I waited a quarter of an hour, but I've no reason to be certain that he ever went to Mrs. Cockerton's, you know."

" No, I suppose not. But, if not there, where *did* he go ? I'd very much like to find out."

" We might look along there on our way back home, I suppose," I conceded doubtfully.

" Good heavens, no ! " said Keith. " Not with a murderer like that ! Oh, goodness, no ! "

" I wonder whether Mrs. Cockerton knows he's a murderer ? " I asked, struck by a dreadful thought. " I say, you don't think *that's* why they're going away ? Before he gets caught, you know."

" I don't see why she married him, then," said Keith. " If she *did !* You know what very queer things she says. She was probably having you on."

" Do you really think so ? " I asked doubtfully; for, although it would have been completely in character for our old friend to amuse herself by testing my credulity and good manners, I felt, in my own mind, that she had told me the truth. " It would be very awkward for them both if I let it out to people, and it turned out to be untrue."

" It wouldn't matter, if they're going away," said Keith.

There was news at the police station. The Scotland Yard detective had been withdrawn temporarily from the case in order to operate against some dope smugglers in the West End. We had seen almost nothing of this man, and his preoccupation with the idea that the circus people had the first murderer among their number, and that the other murders had been committed by a local man had been interesting, but, in our view, utterly illogical. Presumably he had received from Mr. Seabrook the information that the corset thrown away by the rag and bone man had, at one time, contained money, but this news to him could have meant very little, it seemed.

" But he's coming back," said Mr. Seabrook gloomily.

" Not until after you've made your arrest," said Mrs. Bradley. " And now," she added, fixing us with an evil smile and poking Keith in the ribs, " what fell enchantments under yon green moon ? "

I told her all, not omitting the marriage between Mrs. Cockerton and the rag and bone man.

" A case for the police indeed ! " said Mrs. Bradley, when I had done. " Mr. Seabrook, you and I must be together in this."

" At your orders, ma'am," said he, not, I thought, with any great enthusiasm.

" First, every inch, if necessary, of that bank and path by the mouth of the River Bregant must be searched and excavated. Second, we must discover at once whether the rag and bone man has returned to Mrs. Cockerton's woodshed. That investigation must be secret. Third, we must interview young Mr. Taylor again, and, fourth, we must send these boys on holiday."

" On holiday ? " said we, seizing upon, to us, the material point.

" But we're not afraid of the rag and bone man," said I.

" Besides," said Keith, " our education . . ." He looked at me anxiously. The last thing we wanted was to be banished at the climax of all our adventures.

Mrs. Bradley cackled.

" Poor children," she said. " Inspector, what proof have we that these boys are not themselves the murderers ? "

" I have none whatever," said Mr. Seabrook, with a very sour smile.

" And my notebook scarcely whitewashes them," said Mrs. Bradley, producing it. She took from it folded papers. I could see that they were very thin sheets of typescript. " Here is the history of our case. Only, of course, in jottings. But your wits will fill in the gaps. Take the results of my labour; compare them with your own. Bring me your conclusions to-morrow at seven o'clock. Avoid lonely places. Avoid everybody with whom you are acquainted, saving only your own relations and Christina, and, possibly, myself and the inspector. Be watchful and suspicious. Trust no one. Do not loiter. Do not go or remain out of the house after seven o'clock in the evening. Do you promise ? "

" No, we can't promise," said I, " but we'll do our best. Please don't send us away. Really, we're not afraid."

Mrs. Bradley regarded us thoughtfully, but did not say any more. She did not, however, give us the papers, but put them back in her pocket.

" We'll have to close the communicating channels before we go over the ground on the Leys," said Inspector Seabrook. " We can open the old lock.   That will fix things from that side, and the other thing will be to bar off the little bridge over the canal.   It had better be early in the morning.   Would seven o'clock suit you, Mrs. Bradley ? "

" Oh, please, Mr. Seabrook ! " said I.   He looked at me, shrugged, and turned to her.   She cackled, and said something about being all boys together.   Keith and I gripped hands.   To be in with the police on a real piece of work such as that involved in an official search and digging up of the foreshore of a river was, to us, more than meat and drink.   I decided to get up at four, to be certain of being there in time.

We went home at the double up Drum Lane and through Braemar Road.   We did not want to pass the mouth of Saint George's Court or Mrs. Cockerton's shop, and avoided this by our change of route.   As soon as we were indoors we told June that we were needed very early in the morning to assist the police.   I do not think she believed us, but she could hardly contradict what we said, so she told us we would have to get our own breakfast if we wanted it earlier than usual, and left it at that.

We went to bed without being told that night, and, what was more, went to sleep.   I had willed myself to wake at four o'clock, and woke at half-past, which was not bad.   I woke Keith, and we crept downstairs with our boots in our hands and washed under the tap in the scullery and dried on the roller towel.

We used no plates for breakfast to save the washing up, and had cups without saucers, and one knife and one teaspoon between us.   By five we were out of the house and on the road.

" Which way ? " asked Keith.

" The long way, through Church Alley," I replied.   I was not going to run any risk of being seen by the rag and bone man before he saw us.   So along the Butts we went, and across the market square, and past the *Pigeons* to the narrow passage on to the Leys.

The police were not to be seen, and the place was quiet.   The morning was clear and cool.

" We ought to have brought a spade, perhaps," said Keith.

I had thought of this before we left home, but I knew we should be coming the long way round, and it seemed too far to carry it.

" We shan't need one," I said. " We can use theirs, perhaps, to give them a rest."

We hung about for more than half an hour, and heard the church clock strike six. We began to wonder why we had come out so early. Then Keith said:

" What about a swim ? "

" We can't, just here."

" Too dirty, anyway. Let's cross the high street bridge, and walk along beyond the railway viaduct. No one will see us there."

" They'd better not ! We haven't got any costumes."

" Nor towels."

" Dry on our shirts. We can come back in our shorts, and the shirts will dry over our arms.

" June will know they're rough-dry."

" It doesn't matter. She's better since Christina left the house."

" I say, Sim," said Keith, as we walked back towards the high street along Church Alley, " I wish we could have Christina back. Do you think we'll see much of her, once she's married ? "

" No, I don't," said I.

" Not even if *she* wanted to ? "

" No. Seabrook's a bossy fool."

" *I* think Seabrook's a bossy fool. So what ? "

" So we don't see Christina," said I. We crossed the high street, dropped down on the other side of the bridge, and followed the towing-path as we had followed it on the night we had taken the path Mrs. Cockerton had taken on the night of the murder at the *Pigeons*.

Just beyond the bend the canal ran deep and clean. We stripped behind the hedge, and were soon in the water. It was cold at that time in the morning. We swam fast, and enjoyed it, but did not go far from our clothes. A barge came along, and we came in under the bank to let it go by, the tow-rope passing over our heads. We could hear the clop-clop of the old horse long after it had gone round the bend, for, except for a lark which was soaring somewhere out of sight, and the roar of one train which thundered over the viaduct near at hand, there was no sound to be heard.

" Better be dressing," said I. So we dried ourselves on our shirts and put on our shorts, and, naked to the waist, trotted back to the high street and across it, and were at the spot near the old lock just as the police and Mrs. Bradley turned up.

" Good morning. Well met," she said.

" Do you mind us without our shirts ? " I enquired politely.

" Such handsome torsos merit display," she replied. " Allow me to congratulate you on the development of your biceps and the three-inch expansion of which I note your lungs are capable."

I should have thought that anyone else was teasing us, but she looked both calm and serious, and her congratulations, I felt, were not ill-founded. I thanked her for her remarks, laid the shirts over a bush in the hope that no puff of wind would blow them into the canal, and, dancing about—for the morning was still rather chilly—came to the edge of the water to see what the procedure was to be.

It was very simple. There were two policemen, one of them the sergeant, besides the inspector and Mrs. Bradley. Between the old lock and the river's ending they quartered the ground, and searched and hunted and probed. Keith kept near the sergeant; I stuck to Mrs. Bradley. If there were anything hidden in that ground I knew that among the four of them it would be discovered, but I wagered privately that Mrs. Bradley would find it. It was not she and I, however, but the sergeant and Keith who made the great discovery. The sergeant had a park-keeper's stick with which he prodded the ground. I was absorbed in Mrs. Bradley's removal of a dandelion root which looked as though it might have been moved before, and did not see the consummation of all our efforts. An excited shout from Keith, the grunt of rewarded effort from the sergeant, and all of us had swung round upon them to see what they had found.

Almost at the end of the Bregant, where the Wyden flowed with it at its mouth, were the wide, uneven, clumsily-made, cinders-covered steps which I had discovered on a previous visit. There had been men at the top of the steps in a kind of signal-box from which, I think, they directed the work of the cranes, and checked the lorries in and out along the private road.

The sergeant, poking at the steps, had dislodged a square piece of tin. It was rusty and stained, and unworthy, one would have thought, of regard or scrutiny. But the sergeant, an observant man, had seen that the ground underneath it was wet. Immediately he had got to work again with his useful stick. The object he contrived to uncover sufficiently to be able to pull it out of the ground was something of which I had heard before . . . some time before, but since the beginning of our murders.

"That, sir, is a pruning knife," said the sergeant, holding it up with a handkerchief wrapped delicately about his thumb and finger. "And should still yield prints, sir, subject to careful coaxing."

"Now what do you know about that?" said Mr. Seabrook, extremely pleased. He meant it as a rhetorical question merely, but, as one man, Keith and I told him. His face changed.

"This hangs the pernicious brute," he said. "He must have lifted it out of the old lady's possession after the first knife was lost. We'll go along there at once and nab him before the birds fly away." He gave me a clout across the shoulders. "You're a good fellow, Simon," he said. "This is all we needed. Just this."

"I suppose that's really all there was?" said I. "He was rather a long time just to be sticking a very sharp knife in the ground."

The sergeant, a painstaking man, ignoring Mr. Seabrook's snort of amusement, returned to the hole which he had made at the foot of the steps, and dug down deeper with a trowel which he had produced from his clothing.

"By George, sir, the boy's right," he said. We all crowded round him, as, with large and tender hands, he excavated an old mackintosh.

"That's Donald Kenley's mackintosh," said Keith. "His mother gave it to the rag and bone man on Saturday, just a week ago."

"Did she? Then I'd say that settles it," said Mr. Seabrook, as he and the sergeant unwrapped the mackintosh parcel. "Look here at this!"

The brown-paper parcel inside the mackintosh contained a hundred and sixty-five pounds in Treasury notes.

" He didn't dare try to bank them or spend them," Mr. Seabrook grimly observed. " Afraid we might trace the serial numbers."

" A nice morning's work, sir," said the sergeant.

" Thanks to our young friend," said Mrs. Bradley, putting her claw-like hand on my naked shoulder. Mr. Seabrook grunted. He was not the most generous of men.

It was not until we reached the Butts on our homeward way that recollection burst upon me with such suddenness that I stopped dead in my tracks.

" What's up ? " asked Keith.

" Up ? We forgot to ask Mrs. Bradley for her notes ! They're still in her pocket from yesterday."

" Golly ! Go get 'em, quick. We'll have time to skim them over before breakfast."

" That we shan't," said I. " By the time we've had another wash and changed our clothes, we'll be lucky to be early to school."

" You *are* a fool ! It's Saturday," said Keith. I was unspeakably thankful. In the excitement of other matters I had forgotten at which day of the week we had arrived. I remembered now that Keith had mentioned Saturday in speaking of Donald Kenley's mackintosh. I turned, and tore back to the high street, and was lucky enough to catch Mrs. Bradley before she drove off. Then I went straight home.

" Had a good time ? " asked Jack. He had become, as the days had passed and the police had left him alone, a good deal more cheerful, although I think he missed Christina as much as we did.

" Yes," I replied. " Quite good."

" Police find what they wanted ? "

" Yes, they think so."

" What ? "

" We are not at liberty to say," put in Keith, before I could answer. Jack cuffed his head good-humouredly, but did not ask the question again. After breakfast we lolled on my bed with Mrs. Bradley's notes. They were typewritten, I was thankful to see. I could scarcely ever read grown-up people's writing and Keith could not read it at all except that of his teacher, a lady, who writes at the bottom of nearly every exercise, " Come and see me about this." Rude boys call her Mae West, but Keith calls her Lucy, after William Wordsworth, because she is a maid whom there are few to praise and very few to love. She made his class learn the poem. That was how he came to know it.

The notes were simple to understand, and very good. We appreciated, too, the fact that we were given, in them, full credit for all we had done. Mrs. Bradley was, in that, as well as in many other ways, unlike some other people we had known. *Facts* (it began). On Friday, April 3rd, body of Coralie Bellinger, circus performer (murdered by having her throat cut), discovered at six o'clock in the morning by Vasco Castries, circus performer, on an enclosed field (property of Daniel O'Shea Taylor), hired as a fair ground.

Inferences. First possibility is that Bellinger murdered by another of circus performers. Suspicion falls on Castries. He found the body (at a very early hour) and was known to be jealous. Of Southern blood, and owned a knife which could have inflicted the injuries.

Sidelights. Field closed on side facing road, but open (hedge intervening) on side facing canal. Two local boys, S. and K. Innes, brothers, aged thirteen and eleven years, saw man with knife on canal-side on night of murder. No direct evidence that this man was involved in murder, but circumstantial evidence includes possession of knife and report that he left canal-side opposite circus ground.

N.B.—This man later identified (?) as James Fisher, alias Joseph Smith, second-hand clothes dealer (known locally as rag and bone man) by these boys. This man seen by the same boys to rid himself of part of a garment, later identified as corsage of a ballet dress, by throwing it into the canal. Corsage known to have contained savings in Treasury notes, and to have been property of Bellinger.

Addenda. Castries arrested. Later released on evidence given by circus performer Veralie Simmonds with whom Castries spent night from 11 p.m. until 6 a.m. Upon leaving her caravan he discovered body of Bellinger. Evidence corroborated by Joan

Ticknell and her son Bert, who shared caravan with Bellinger. All circus personnel questioned. Results negative.

Queries. Could any person or persons apart from circus personnel have known of savings sewn into corsage? Could murder have been primary object, and theft of money secondary consideration, or even accidental corollary of murder? Could mention of money in corsage have been made, (at public house in the town for example), and overheard by murderer?

N.B.—Town contains over forty licensed houses.

Later. House to house enquiries of landlords, barmaids and potmen made by police. Results inconclusive. Nevertheless, possibility remains. Circus personnel, including Castries and Bellinger, known to have walked round town. No evidence public house visited, because drinking strictly forbidden to circus performers on night before show, but strong presumption Bellinger visited *Pigeons* licensed house.

Facts. On Friday, April 3rd, at 11 p.m., Ruby Machree, barmaid, murdered outside back door of *Pigeons* licensed house. Body discovered at twelve midnight by George Travers, barman, upon leaving the *Pigeons*. Subsequently discovered that contents of tin box representing takings in public bar, exact amount not known, had been stolen.

Inferences. Probable motive of murder was robbery of the barmaid who had previously transferred cash from tin box to her own possession.

N.B.—No direct evidence that she had stolen contents of cash-box, but police convinced no forced entry on to back premises.

Further facts. Complete alibis for hotel servants. Murder committed by throat-cutting. Various other wounds. Weapon probably similar to one used in murder of Bellinger. Landlord and his wife cleaning up at time of murder, barman assisting. No other person on premises, except for two servants, both upstairs and in one another's company.

Addendum. The room in which the cash-box was kept can be seen from an overgrown and almost unused path leading from the River Bregant, hereabouts known as the old mill stream. Fact discovered by S. and K. Innes.

Facts. On Sunday, April 5th, body of Marion Bridges,

dairymaid, found outside the cowsheds of Manor Farm house at
5 a.m. by Ezekial Viccary, farmer, out on his usual rounds.
Throat cut, and wounds and lacerations similar to, but more
pronounced than, those upon body of Bellinger.   Body had been
moved.   Bridges was not killed where body found.

Inferences.   Bridges killed by murderer of other two victims.
Against this, fact that body had been moved.   Robbery probable
motive.   Deceased had had purse and handbag, gold wristlet
watch, necklace of cultured pearls, brooch with seed pearls,
diamond hair-clip and ring set with rubies.   All were missing.

Addenda.   Confession by Diarmid Daniel Taylor, son of Daniel
O'Shea Taylor.   Had found Bridges' body lower down Manor
Road.   Confession by John Carpenter McCallum Innes that he
had assisted Taylor to carry body to place where it was discovered.   Police investigations proved Bridges murdered at
entrance to orchard, as stated by witnesses Taylor and Innes.
Bridges discovered to be pregnant.   Taylor said to be secretly
affianced to her, but a rumour that he was in love with Anna
Viccary, farmer's daughter.   Further inference that Taylor may
have murdered Bridges because she was importuning him to
marry her.   Some suspicion also attaches to Jack Innes, as his
knife found just inside farm gates when police arrived on scene
of crime.   Whole question of Innes' knife extremely complicated,
owing to extraordinary substitution of the missing knife for one
used by the murderer (?) and bearing distinct traces of dried
blood proved by analysis to belong to same blood group as that
of Ruby Machree.   This blood-encrusted knife may have come
from antique shop kept by Septima Cockerton.

Facts.   On Wednesday, April 29th, servant from Manor
House murdered at about 11 p.m. in cul-de-sac known as Saint
George's Court.   Further evidence suggests that girl in the
habit of meeting second-hand clothes dealer, Joseph Smith, *alias*
James Fisher, for purpose of selling to him goods filched from
the house of her employer.   These goods conveyed and sold to
aforesaid Septima Cockerton, antique dealer.

Inferences.   Girl may have become dangerous to Fisher by
attempting to blackmail him.   She may, on the other hand,
have been awaiting him, as usual, and so offered herself as
unwitting victim.   The first inference would indicate Fisher as

the murderer. The second would tend to exculpate him.
Fisher of low intellect, cunning but stupid.

Sidelights. Goods stolen from Mr. Hopkinson at Manor House
and sold to Fisher have been discovered among stock of antique
shop kept by Cockerton. This woman drank regularly at the
Pigeons, where Machree was murdered; was, on her own
showing, along canal towing-path on night of Machree's death;
could have been in *Pigeons* on evening of Thursday, April 2nd,
and conversed with members of circus troup, including Bellinger
and Castries, *if they were present*. No known motive for any of
the murders except possibly that of servant, Bessie Gillett, in
collusion with James Fisher or alone. Bloodstained knife found
among her stock could have been placed there by Fisher or
herself, *or could have been handed to Simon or Keith Innes by Jack Innes
to be ' planted ' and then ' discovered.'* Jack Innes by no means free
from suspicion. He is friend to Inspector Seabrook, and could
have been cognisant of fact that a young constable often met
Bessie Gillett in Saint George's Court. Suspicion also strong in
case of Diarmid Daniel Taylor, but only for murder of Marion
Bridges.

Possibility that Fisher might turn King's Evidence (?) pre-
supposes Fisher not more than an accessory to the crimes.

" *Well !* " said I to Keith. " What do you think of all
that ? "

" Pretty good," said he, judicially. " But they'll never prove
a thing against Danny Taylor."

" Unless Marion Bridges was blackmailing him about the
baby she was expecting," I reminded him. " After all, Danny
had the wind up all right that night, or he wouldn't have whistled
for Jack. I don't like the look of things at all ! I wonder why
she's given us these notes ? "

CHAPTER NINETEEN

The Rising of the Moon

THE NEXT event to which I had to look forward was my half-term holiday, which, during the summer term, was included in the short break at Whitsun. Keith and I laid plans to spend the Whitsun Bank Holiday with Christina, and, to that end, went to her new lodgings, taking Mrs. Bradley's *dossier* along with us.

We found her at home, for we knew enough of her habits to waylay her on the doorstep, so that she could do no less than ask us in.

" I have dinner with the family at seven," she said, " so you'll have to go before that."

" I wish you were back with us," said Keith. " It's no fun at home without you."

She smiled at him, but did not say whether she would like to return. In any case, both she and we knew quite well that the desire on either side was not likely to be realized. June would not have her in our house any more. We had already advertised for another lodger, and June had specified that it must be a man.

Christina looked well, I thought, and very pretty. She had on a summer frock which we had not seen before, and did her hair a new way. I liked it.

She took us up to her bed-sitting-room. It was very comfortably furnished, and, although it was at the back of the house, it was a good-sized room and had large windows overlooking a garden which had a lawn and fruit trees. She had some chocolate in the sideboard cupboard, and shared it with us.

" Well, and what have you come for ? " she asked.

" To ask what you're doing on Whit Monday."

" Whit Monday ? Nothing at all, and I've got the day off, of course. Let's go to the Zoo—and we really *will* go, this time ! "

We acclaimed the idea, and fixed a time and a meeting-place.

" And now," said Christina, " I have something important to

tell you. Something you will be very glad to hear. Danny Taylor is cleared of suspicion."

We were indeed glad to hear this, and begged her to tell us how it had come about.

"Well, it seems to have been Mrs. Bradley's doing," she said, "although Evan won't bring himself to admit it. I'm afraid he's not very generous. But there is no doubt that Mrs. Bradley has worked very hard to establish Danny's innocence, in which she has always believed, and most of her work has been done upon Anna Viccary."

"Anna Viccary?" said Keith. Christina nodded.

"How she has managed it no one knows, for Anna is desperately afraid of her father and very much in awe of the Taylors, but Mrs. Bradley concluded, it seems, that Danny was pretending to be in love with Marion Bridges in order to cloak his real affection for Anna, and Marion acted as go-between, and took letters and presents and flowers. Then Marion grew greedy and wicked, and began to blackmail both of them.

"She threatened Danny into promising her a hundred pounds in Treasury notes, which he was to pay out on that very night when she was murdered. Well, Danny paid over the money which he got out of his father by pretending it was for some debts he had incurred and might be sued for, and there is no doubt that Marion received the money, because Danny took along a witness, and that witness was Jack. The money was handed over in a brown-paper packet at the *Pigeons*, where all three met before Jack came in from work."

"He *was* a bit late that day," said Keith.

"Yes, I remember. Danny also met Anna that evening. She had made the excuse that she was going to choir practice and then would go to the home of one of the girls to sleep, so as not to have to return up Manor Road by moonlight. Instead, she was going to spend the evening with Danny at the pictures at Bridge End, and then go to this girl's house.

"On the way back from leaving Anna with her friend, Danny found Marion's body at the gate entering into the orchard from Manor Road, and went to fetch Jack. There is no doubt, from the doctor's report on the time of Marion's death, that Danny's alibi is perfect. Anna told all about it—her father was dreadfully angry—and the cinema attendant and a bus conductor have confirmed what she said."

"And Danny never gave her away?" We were staggered by Danny's Irish chivalry.

"He said he would sooner have been hanged," replied Christina. We digested this, and then turned to ordinary conversation and gossip. Christina said that one of the high street shops was to be let.

"You know, that little antique shop not far from Drum Lane," she said. We said we knew, and a sadness fell upon the party. We had been down once or twice to stare mournfully in at the empty window and to try to see in through the top of the curtained door.

"She was our great friend," said Keith. "I wonder whether her husband ever turned up? I shouldn't think he'd dare, after what was found!"

"The rag and bone man," I explained.

"Evan told me he had been reported missing," said Christina. Abruptly she changed the subject to one in which, as she knew, we had only the very faintest interest. "And how are you both getting on at school?" she enquired. Keith and I exchanged glances. It was altogether too transparent. For some reason she did not propose to discuss the rag and bone man.

"We know he's the murderer," said I, "so you need not be afraid of giving away Inspector Seabrook's secrets."

"I don't know his secrets," she said, soberly, "except that he suspects the rag and bone man. What makes *you* think that poor wretched creature was the murderer? Evan had a look in the woodshed, by the way, and was annoyed to find nothing incriminating."

I produced Mrs. Bradley's notes, and then wondered whether they were intended for any eyes but ours. As Christina put out her hand for the papers, I drew mine back. "Perhaps, on second thoughts . . ." said I. I put them away. She laughed again, and pretended to be disappointed, but I was not to be drawn. I laughed, too, and then explained what the papers were.

"I see," she said gravely. "I am sure you are right not to show them." She was always good like that, and most unlike

June, who, if she thought we were concealing anything from her, would give herself and us no peace until she had satisfied herself that she knew all about it.

We stayed with Christina while she washed, changed into another dress for dinner and tidied her hair, but at a quarter to seven we left. She kissed us both and rumpled Keith's hair and put my tie straight, and then kissed us again.

" Don't get into mischief," she said, when we had said good-bye for the last time, and were half-way down the stairs. We did not promise. " And don't forget nine o'clock sharp on Monday morning."

We did promise not to forget nine o'clock sharp on Monday morning. It is difficult to see how we *could* have forgotten anything so important and delightful as a Whitsuntide visit to the Zoo.

We felt flat when we turned the corner of the street, and, without a word to one another, we turned southwards to the high street and walked to the empty shop. With melancholy hearts we gazed once more at the vacant windows. There was nothing to be seen but a few bits of discarded paper, a broken hand-mirror and some dirty shavings.

" Seems queer, all that stuff to have gone," said Keith. " I suppose she *did* take it all away ? "

" Sure to have done," said I. " People always do."

But even as I made this answer, a faint expectation was born in me; something not as strong as a hope. But a gleam of interest came, as I remembered that a friend of ours had gone into a new home and had found, in an upstairs cupboard, two valuable old books in leather bindings which his father had sold for two and ninepence and three and sixpence respectively.

" We could get in round the back," said Keith tentatively. " The way the rag and bone man used to come out with his barrow."

" I don't want to meet him," said I.

Keith agreed.

" Not a murderer like *him*," he said. " But there isn't the slightest chance we shall run into him. The police are on his track, and may have found him by now."

I was almost convinced that we were in no danger, but we

both slowed down as we approached the end of the alley. Double gates opened into it from Mrs. Cockerton's backyard, but these gates were closed. We pushed them, but they did not budge. We thrust harder, but they did not give at all.

"Locked!" said Keith, in disgust. "Oh, blow! Let's get over."

"Reconnoitre first," said I. He stole to the end of the alley, and I gazed along the backs of the houses that, jumbled with no thought of lines or planning, formed this part of the high street. There was nothing to be seen or heard. Keith came back in a minute and reported all clear from the front, so, without losing further time, I helped him up and he mounted the gate, gave a glance round from his perch, said that all was well, and dropped down on the other side. It took me rather longer. It was not an easy gate to scale without assistance.

The yard behind the shop was very small. It was almost square, and was half-filled with rubbish of various kinds. There was a dustbin in the corner near the house, but it was empty. Apparently the dustmen had called after Mrs. Cockerton had left.

The woodshed was built on to the side of the scullery. We approached it cautiously, knowing it as the rag and bone man's base.

"Toss up to see who opens the door," said Keith. But it seemed to me that, as the elder, my duty was clear.

"No. Stand by," said I. I took my small scimitar from my neck. I carried it slung from its strap across my breast inside my shirt in a long slant across my body, so that the hilt was almost up on my shoulder and the point dangled coldly on my hip. Keith took his horse-pistol out of his belt, and held it by the barrel, ready to use it as a cosh. Then I advanced to the woodshed door, pushed it open and stepped hastily back again.

All these bold preparations were to no purpose. There was nothing in the woodshed except some evil-smelling boxes which proved to be empty except for a lot of large white maggots of the kind that bred once in some meat that June put back on a shelf in the larder one summer holiday and forgot.

"That's that," said Keith, disappointed. "Let's wash under the pump."

He pumped for me, and I for him. The pump was beside the woodshed wall. We dried our hands sufficiently by wiping them down our shorts. Our handkerchiefs were covered with some coal-dust they had collected at the bottom of Ferry Lane earlier in the afternoon, just before we went to waylay Christina on her front doorstep.

"Now to explore the shop and house," said Keith, advancing towards the back door. I hesitated. I had an overwhelming sense of repugnance at the thought of entering that house, but Keith looked round at me in such immense surprise that I was pricked to shame, and advanced too.

"I thought that's what we *came* for," he said.

"Yes, it was," I answered; and, to my own chagrin and his astonishment, my throat was dry, and I could only manage a thick and heavy whisper.

"You don't think he's in there, do you?" asked Keith, catching a little of my unrest. I shook my head. I did not think this for an instant. Not only was it most unlikely that the rag and bone man would haunt a place where he was so close to the police who wanted him so badly, but the idea of his bodily presence was not at the root of my fear.

"And you don't think we'll find one of his victims in there, do you?" Keith went on, but this time with a lightening of his tone. I shook my head again. I did not know what I dreaded. My fear was of the empty house itself, but I could put no name to it. I think the bravest action that ever I performed was to lift the latch of the door.

It had not occurred to either of us that we should be able to march straight into an unoccupied house, and yet I was not much astonished when the door opened and we almost fell in over the threshold.

The next things of which I was aware were that the scullery smelt of cooking, and that the house was not unoccupied. Before I had the chance of remarking to Keith that the copper fire, after all the days that had gone by since I had lighted it at Mrs. Cockerton's request, was still burning, and could request his observations on this phenomenon, there was the sound of a door opening, and, coming into the scullery from the kitchen, Mrs. Cockerton herself stood before us.

She stood facing us for a full minute without speaking. She wore her usual hat and had her hands on her hips. She wore an apron over a plain black dress, and her feet were astride in an attitude to which we were accustomed. She fixed us with her faded, cornflower eyes.

" Well ! " she said. " I had half a mind to come at you hatchet in hand, Mr. Innes, and Mr. Keith. What say you to that, sirs ? "

Keith laughed and flourished his horse-pistol.

" I have this, Mrs. Cockerton," said he, " and Sim has the sabre you gave him."

I made her a mock salute with the sabre, or, as I preferred it, scimitar, and she responded with a curtsey, a gesture which had grace as well as irony in it. Keith sniffed the air.

" Cooking, Mrs. Cockerton ? " he asked. He jerked his head at the copper.

" Not I, Mr. Keith. The devil, mayhap," she replied. " Ask me no more. I cannot speak of it. Tell me why you have come."

" Sentimental reasons," said I. " We wanted to see the place again."

" And so you shall," said she. " And before you leave I think we must confer together, just a little, as of old. What say you, gentlemen ? "

" Anything you like, Mrs. Cockerton," said I. I slung my sabre round my neck again, but, this time, left it outside, in case she should think I did not fully appreciate it. Keith put the horse-pistol back in his belt, but left the butt sticking out so that she could see it.

" Armed and well prepared, I see," she said, leading the way along the passage. " And are you versed in the management of your weapons ? "

" I could cleave you from neck to knees with a single stroke, Mrs. Cockerton," said I.

" And I," said Keith, " could stretch you senseless, whether my bullet should find its billet or not. But, of course, I wouldn't do it," he added.

We did not go into the shop, but, as I peered from behind Mrs. Cockerton's elbow—for she continued to lead and we to

follow—I could see that it was empty. She took us into the
room upstairs which was not yet entirely clear of rubbish.

" Explore, excavate, disclose," she said, waving her hand.
" I leave you for half an hour. At the end of that time I must
go. My lease of this house is concluded at moonrise to-night."

" At moonrise ? What a funny time," said Keith.

" I have a morbid and fanciful mind, Mr. Keith," said Mrs.
Cockerton grandly. " I give up the keys to-morrow, but at
moonrise my tenancy closes."

She left us with her blessing, bestowed with papal unction,
and we commenced to root among her discarded treasures.
These consisted of bits and pieces too battered and broken to be
worth the cost and the trouble of transport. We did not know
how she had managed the removal of her stock to its new home.
For all we knew, she might have made the requisite number of
journeys with the stuff piled high on the rag and bone man's
barrow.

She came back once or twice to watch us at work. The
redolence of her cooking followed her through the open doorway
into the room. Keith looked up at her the second time, and
said :

" Not your supper, Mrs. Cockerton ? "

She smiled. She looked secretive, sly and pleased.

" I keep my meat good," said she, " by boiling it up every
day. Every day, Mr. Keith. Every single day. But what is
it ? It is goat, Mr. Keith. Goat."

" She *is* more peculiar than she was," said Keith, when she
had gone. " There's not much here, Sim. Nothing good
seems to have been left. I've got two bits of wood and a piece
of paper that we can draw on, and a stick that I think will make
a mast for my boat, and that's all. How are you getting on ? "

" A quite decent bit of muslin curtain to make a new top for
my fishing-net; a piece of string two yards long—can't see how
she came to overlook that !—a bit of thick wire, the spring out
of an armchair, a bit of binding that has come off a rug,
two trouser buttons (but I don't think I want them) and
the spar of a chair. Might be able to carve it into a knob-
kerrie. It's mahogany, I think. That's all. Still, it's been fun
looking."

" It's getting very late," said he, looking out of the window. " Think we'd better be getting back ? "

" I suppose so. Nobody will worry, though. They'll think we're still with Christina."

He agreed, but we decided, all the same, to go home. We cleared up the mess we had made, and went down to show Mrs. Cockerton our trove and to ask whether we might keep it. She assented graciously, praised Keith's industry and intelligence when he explained that he and Jack were making a model yacht, complimented me on my foresight in mending my fishing-net and in deciding to manufacture what she called an elegant and instructive weapon, and then showed us out through the scullery.

We had reached the gate, and were about to scramble over when Keith said suddenly.

" She never showed us the copper."

" She didn't intend to. She was joking when she said it was goat." He looked obstinate, and said he must see it.

" You don't want to see the copper now," I objected. It was almost dark. The moon would rise within an hour. June would be worried and Jack annoyed.

" But I do," he insisted. " Nothing would console me if I didn't see the copper. The copper, Sim, is mysterious and improbable. I mean, its contents are. Sim, we *must* see it. It's the only thing worth seeing in the house."

I could not agree, but he seemed so much set on it that it would have been unkind to have gainsaid him.

" O.K.," said I. " Let's go back."

So we returned to the scullery door. Mrs. Cockerton was upstairs. We could hear her singing.

" No time to lose," said Keith. I made no response to this, but whipped the wooden lid off the copper.

" And now," said I, laughing, " to see Bluebeard's eighth wife."

We peered in. I ceased to laugh. The contents of the copper were indescribable. Even after this considerable lapse of time I cannot bring myself to speak of them in detail.

" And now," said Keith, with his teeth chattering, " do you still think we didn't need to look ? "

" All I want is to be sick," I said. Keith *was* sick. His stomach was always far more delicate than mine. He went outside to the drain, and got there just in time. " But what does it mean ? " I demanded, following him out.

" It means we've got to get out of here quick," he replied.

We were not quick enough, however. There was a slight noise in the doorway connecting the scullery with the kitchen, and there stood Mrs. Cockerton.

What she saw in our faces I do not know, but she came forward and said at once:

" So, gentlemen, you halt upon the order of your going ? "

" No," gasped Keith. He seized my arm. " We're just off. Coming, Sim ? "

" Stay a moment, gentlemen," said Mrs. Cockerton. Keith shrank against me as she stepped towards us. I put my arm round his shoulders, and stood my ground.

" You can talk to me," I said. " I'm sorry we didn't go when we said we would, but——"

" But *I* am not sorry, Mr. Innes," said she; and nothing, I think, had ever horrified and fascinated me quite so much as the fact that her face and her tone and voice were the same as we had always known them. " You have seen what you have seen. We will not particularize. Yet, gentlemen, there is only to-night if you are to have the benefit of my advice and experience. We must lay this Attila by the heels. I know where he works, and we must apprehend him. Gentlemen, I depend upon your co-operation and support. Are you with me ? "

" I don't understand," said I.

" It is simple. To-night, without benefit of clergy or police, you and I will rid this town of its scourge." To my amazement, Keith, rallying, and putting away my arm from his neck, said loudly:

" Very well, Mrs. Cockerton. We're on."

" Spoken like a prince," said she. She looked at me. I could do nothing but nod my head. What idea Keith had in his I did not know, but he had given a lead which I felt compelled to follow. " By moonlight, then," she added.

" By moonlight, then," said I. " And where, by moonlight, Mrs. Cockerton ? "

"At the end of Drum Lane. We shall adventure from the *Royal Horseguardsman*, unless you prefer the *Lamb*, the *Marquess of Granby*, the *Barge Aground*, the *Half Moon and Seven Stars*, the *Black Boy and Still*, the *Magpie and Stump* or the *Duke of Cambridge*."

"What's the matter with the *Pigeons*?" asked Keith.

"Vulgarized since the murder behind the public bar," said Mrs. Cockerton blandly; and I have never been so much afraid of anyone in my whole life as I was at that moment of this odd but respectable old creature in her wide gown and rusty black hat; yet, so normal was her manner, and so much in keeping with all we knew of her was her conversation, that I began to feel within my breast a twinge of doubt which refused, at the moment, to be stifled.

"The *Horseguardsman*, then," said I. She bowed, conducted us through the house to the front door, and watched us go. As we walked briskly homeward, for it was now getting late, and was, in any case, far past the time that June liked us to be out in the evening since the murders had made everybody nervous, I was wondering how we should make certain of leaving the house when the moon rose. Keith's mind, it seemed, was similarly occupied, for, as we passed the Butts, he asked:

"How shall we manage it, I wonder?"

"As usual," said I. "Fairly early to bed, and slip out. Nothing else to be done. I wonder who it was in the copper?"

"I don't mean that," said Keith. "How shall we lay her by the heels?"

We were home by nine, but June and Jack were very angry. We could not incriminate Christina by pretending that she had kept us out until that hour, so we made no particular response to Jack's demands to be told where we had been and what we had been doing, and were sent to bed without supper.

"Good enough," said Keith. "I could not have eaten a thing, and shan't be able to for days."

"What do you think Mrs. Cockerton knows?" I asked. "And how much hand did she have in it?" He shook his head, and began to take off his pull-over, looking in the dressing-table mirror as he did so.

"It doesn't seem to show," he said, "but I have aged ten

years since tea-time. I don't know what she knows, Sim, but we'll have to find out to-night."

We washed well, as we were going to meet Mrs. Cockerton again, but were soon in bed. We had thought it best to undress completely, in case Jack or June should decide to come upstairs and make sure, as we had been sent to bed in disgrace, that we were not in mischief. It was a sensible precaution, for June came soon after half-past nine, and found us blamelessly in bed, our clothes folded on chairs, our faces clean, and our breasts rising and falling in innocent, boyish slumber.

" Suspicious cat," said Keith, when she had gone. He sat up. " How soon, Sim, do you think ? "

" Give it another half hour, but don't go to sleep if you can help it."

" I shan't, don't worry. I keep thinking——"

" That's enough. Let's forget it," said I, for I did not want him to enlarge upon what we had seen. I had contrived to get my stomach and my visual imagination more or less under control, and I did not want this precarious triumph undone. Keith was silent. We lay in the darkness and listened. Jack and June came upstairs soon after ten. Impatient though we were to be gone, we felt impelled to wait until we could be fairly sure that our brother and his wife were in bed. At twenty-past ten it seemed safe to make a move. We got up and dressed, and left the house by what had become our usual nocturnal route.

" I wonder what she really wants with us ? " said Keith, as we caught our first sight of the rising moon where, large, round and orange, she lay low down in the sky, apparently on the other side of the canal.

" It's too late, anyway. I expect she thought we'd be here much earlier than this," said I. " The *Royal Horseguardsman* will be closed by the time we get there. I really believe, you know, she's crazy. I hope she's not there, and I'll tell you what. I'm not going inside that shop of hers again for anything she offers."

I was wondering, in fact, as we walked soberly along towards the *rendezvous*, what had induced us to obey her command (for it had amounted to that) and come at all. The more I thought of it, as we trudged along Drum Lane and down to the high street end of it, the less I could see any sense in what we were doing.

"I suppose," said Keith, as though he were reading my thoughts, "we are committed to this adventure? We promised, didn't we? I don't feel as keen on finding out about her as I did."

"Well, as a gentleman of honour," said I, as I felt my sabre flap against my thigh, "I don't see how we can disappoint a lady."

"Um!" said Keith. "I suppose she *is* a lady? You don't think she'd lead us into a trap, and cut our throats for us?"

"If she tries, we must sell our lives dearly," I responded. "The thing that worries me about *that*, though, is whether we ought to set about her with these weapons which, after all, she gave us."

"We're fools to come," said Keith.

I stopped short outside the *Horseguardsman*, and looked at him.

"We'll be all right," said I. "There are plenty of people about. We must meet her, and refuse to go anywhere with her, that's all. I always thought she was to be trusted until she married the rag and bone man, but now, to tell the truth, I don't know what to think. I wish you hadn't agreed to meet her to-night. Why did you?"

"I don't know now," said he. "Would it hurt to step across the road and let Mr. Seabrook know what she told us this evening?"

"That she could lead us to the murderer? Well, it's difficult. One would think, if she wanted the police to know, she would have told them."

"Yes," said he, doubtfully. "I was a fool to let you in for this. I thought it might be a scheme to go with her and find out what she was up to, but I'd give a lot to be out of it now."

"What do you think she felt when she knew we'd seen what was in the copper?" I enquired.

"We ought to let somebody know about that, at any rate," said Keith, "and here comes a policeman."

"Tell Mr. Seabrook to look in the antique copper," he said to the man. "He'll understand."

The man was about to reply when all conversation was

arrested, for there beside us was Mrs. Cockerton herself, having just been turned out of the *Horseguardsman* private bar. The policeman had moved away, and I do not think Mrs. Cockerton had noticed him.

" Ah, nice of you," she said. " You have elegant manners in the keeping of appointments, gentlemen. Shall we go immediately to the lair, or shall we break our journey for bite and sup at my house ? "

" I thought your lease expired when the moon rose, Mrs. Cockerton ? " said Keith. She looked up at the round orb.

" I have left matters full late, full late," she admitted. " Come, then, to Dead Man's Bridge."

" Where we saw the murderer," said Keith. She looked at him with curious intentness, then turned and began to lead the way along the high street.

Our high street is narrow and long; so long that in the year 1748 the inhabitants at one end of it insisted that the parish church at the other end was too far from their homes, and demanded a Chapel of Ease. From where we were it was a mile and a quarter to walk to the canal, and another mile and a half to Dead Man's Bridge. By the time we arrived at the Bridge, the moon, I deduced, would be high enough in the gentle summer sky to give almost a daylight visibility. What we could expect to see by its waxing radiance I had not the faintest idea. I felt nervous and excited, and found myself to be filled with the greatest reluctance to embark upon this extraordinary night stroll with an old woman, who, whatever her value as a friend and companion, was, according to our standards, as mad as a hatter, and almost certainly a murderess.

Keith, it seemed, had similar feelings. No sooner had we passed the mouth of Saint George's Court, beside which nobody now lingered even by daylight, than he touched my arm, and, as the pavement narrowed at the beginning of the long and gradual descent to the Half Acre, he fell in behind Mrs. Cockerton and I behind him.

She turned her head, but, finding us to be meekly following, lengthened her stride and took us at a pace which kept us alternately striding and trotting at her heels. We passed her shop almost at the double, and neither she nor we so much as hesitated. On we went, to see the now risen moon reflected in the empty windows of shops, and crossed the Half Acre and went into the oldest part of the town. We passed the mouth of Catherine Wheel Yard, but were on the opposite side of the high street, went past our oldest inn, the *Castle*, whose foundations were said to date from the time of King Henry the Fourth, arrived at the market square and passed it, and so came up the round slope to the high street bridge over the canal.

As we began to mount, Keith stumbled and I cannoned into him. He clasped me as though to hold me up, muttered, " Bunk for it when I say. We've done enough to keep our promise," and set off again after Mrs. Cockerton, who had halted for a moment to allow us to catch up.

We were accustomed, both of us, to following a plan made suddenly by the other. My nebulous fears had crystallized. I now felt certain that I did not want to go to Dead Man's Bridge, along the towing-path or by any other route, with Mrs. Cockerton, and I now feared her almost as much as the rag and bone man himself.

We crossed the bridge and dropped down the soft earthy slope to the towing-path and the lock. There were people about, and men still awake on the barges. We heard a baby crying, and a man's harsh voice bidding the woman in charge of it to hush it and let him have his sleep. Somewhere a dog barked, and from the old tower of Saint Anthony's the clock began to chime.

The moon grew smaller and more luminous. She was gibbous. The effect was of a fairy tale, unreal, dreamlike and pretty. The summer weeds by the canal bank were long and lush. Summer grasses grew in the hedge. The hawthorn flowers were long past, and the leaves were thick and close-set. On the opposite bank tall trees stood black against the moonlight, and before us we saw the heavy lines and thick, silhouetted girders of the railway bridge across the water.

It was quite light under the bridge except in the one shadowed patch against the wall. I walked on behind my younger brother, feeling settled, serene and almost happy. I knew he had a plan in his head, and there was no sense in having two plans. I was prepared to act upon his nod, and to act at once.

We lagged a little upon approaching the bridge, allowed our guide to come out on the other side of it, and then trotted through. She turned her head and laughed.

" You do not like the bridge, gentlemen ? " she asked us, over her shoulder. We laughed, too, politely, and did not answer. Beyond the bridge the towing-path made a long bend to the lock, and beyond the lock was a footbridge which took the towing-path over the canal and alongside those fields, among which was Mr. Taylor's field, which bordered the Manor Road.

Beneath our feet the towing-path had turned soft and loose, like Rotten Row in Hyde Park, where people can gallop their horses. Our footsteps made no sound.

" Are you there ? " Mrs. Cockerton asked.

" Oh, yes," said Keith, almost on her heels. On the words he added, " But my bootlace is coming undone."

He stopped, and I stopped. He faced round. Our guide strode on like a Scotswoman walking over heather. We took to our heels, and ran as we had never run in our lives. The long bend was in our favour. Almost at once she lost sight of us.

" Let me get in front," gasped Keith. " I must make the pace. I can't keep up with your stride. Let's hope that policeman's got some sense ! "

He shot past me on the hedge side, and we did not slacken until we gained the bridge.

We had reckoned without our host. Mrs. Cockerton, running like a miler, came into sight round the bend.

" The Leys, when we get into the high street," said I. " She'll never catch up with us there."

We were hard pressed, however. One would have supposed that two boys would readily lose contact with an old lady cluttered up by petticoats, but this was not the case. Mrs. Cockerton ran like a Spartan, and was going strongly, and even gaining on us a little, as we scrambled up the slope and on to the road.

CHAPTER TWENTY

The Old Woman

THE HIGH STREET, fortunately, was deserted. A last dash took us down Church Alley and on to the Leys. We turned the corner by the first row of cottages, and dropped into a walk, straining our ears for the sounds of pursuit. There was nothing to be heard except our own echoing footsteps past the blank and lifeless houses.

Then we heard her, but not until we were on the grass verge of the path which led to the village of barges. Terror had lent me wits. It seemed to me that by far our best chance of eluding Mrs. Cockerton was to cross the plank bridge which was laid from side to side of the hopper, and then jump from boat to boat until we gained Catherine Wheel Yard, up which we could dart to the high street so long as she did not see which way we went.

I did not communicate this scheme to Keith. There was no need. By virtue of longer legs and deeper lungs, I was in command now. It was later, very much later, that I remembered the dog. He gave tongue as soon as we approached, and we heard Mrs. Cockerton beginning to run again, for now she knew where we were.

" Quick! " said Keith. " Get on quick! " I had always supposed him to have much stronger nerves than I had, but it was evident that, on this occasion, at any rate, his nerve had failed him. Risking an attack from the dog, which was off the chain, and stood, a silhouette of bristling rage, on the half-deck of one of the mudbound boats, I took the lead and unerringly found my plank bridge. Somebody growled at the dog, but nobody tried to stop us. We crossed the hollow hopper and jumped from gunwale to gunwale of four boats which lay between us and the concrete bank of the further side of the basin, and jumped for the bank.

Here, once ashore, we dropped down in the shadow of some barrels, and listened to our pounding hearts and for Mrs. Cockerton's footsteps.   We did not hear them.

" She must have kept to the path and crossed the bridge," said I.   " If so, we've gained a little."

" Better stay here," whispered Keith.   " Once she knows she's lost our trail she'll cast about to pick it up again.   She daren't let us escape her, now we've seen what we saw in the copper. Then, when she's trying to get on our track, we must get the police to secure her."

This made nonsense to me.

" We want to get home," said I.   " We don't want to bother any more to-night."

" You ass ! " said Keith.   " She'll follow us !   She'll lie in wait and get us !   It's to-night or never with her.   *That was the rag and bone man in the copper.*   I knew I'd seen that black tooth somewhere before.   He grinned when I told him Arthur Bates' goldfish had died, and I noticed it then.   I suppose she had her reasons for killing him, but she's knocked away her last prop now that we know he's dead.   The police might have put the murders on him, but I don't think they will, after this."

" Do you think Mrs. Bradley knew ? " I asked.

" Mrs. Bradley knew, of course," said Keith.   " I've been wondering all along why she gave us those notes of hers to read. I understand now why she did.   It was to lay the seeds of misgivings in our minds, so that when the truth came out we should not, perhaps, mind quite so much.   She's a very kind old woman, Mrs. Bradley."

We lay where we were for more than a quarter of an hour, but heard no more of Mrs. Cockerton.   We deduced from this that she had not crossed the old lock, but, guessing that we should escape from her on the Leys, had hurried back by the way she had come, to cut us off as we approached our home.

Our way lay up the Half Acre, and it occurred to me that we could avoid her altogether on our way to the police station by using the flight of cinders-covered steps built neatly on their wooden foundation, and leading to the railway yard, which I had discovered on a previous occasion.   The railway ended at the quay-side, and these steps came out on a well-constructed road along which lorries and vans could get from the high street to the goods yard.

On the occasion of my effecting this discovery, several railway-men had been talking together at the top of the steps, and, fearing lest they should take umbrage at my unauthorized and probably illegal presence on railway territory, I had effaced myself as soon as I could, and had not walked along the road.

Memory, and sense of topography had informed me, however, that this road must come out between the Half Acre and Mrs. Cockerton's shop. If, therefore, our deductions were correct, and Mrs. Cockerton were lying in wait for us on our homeward route, this way to the police station would prove both safe and speedy.

We took it, trotting gently, in the moonlight, along the cobbled private road, and emerging, after forty or fifty yards, into the high street. The hour was not yet late. At this part of the high street there were people about. We walked at a moderate pace to the police station, went in through the great gates, and rang Mr. Seabrook's bell. He came to the door himself, and let us in.

Explanations were short. The inspector, to our surprise, accepted all that we said without question. All he said was:

" Sit down a minute while the car comes round. Thanks for the tip about the copper. We've seen all we want to see there. I suppose he pinched the money from her and she laid for him, having already got his finger-prints on that knife."

" Are you going to ring up Mrs. Bradley ? " asked Keith.

" No, no," said Mr. Seabrook, with a frown. " No need. We don't require her presence to make an arrest." His frown disappeared. He laughed, most unconvincingly.

" Are *we* coming with you ? " asked Keith. The inspector grunted, and then decided to reply:

" We shall need you. You have an important part to play."

" You know what it is," said I, when he had left us. " ' The bleating of the lamb excites the tiger.' Remember ? "

" We're to be the decoy ducks, in fact," said Keith. " I wonder why he doesn't want Mrs. Bradley ? "

" Wants all the credit himself, mean swine," said I. " I've a good mind to ring her up myself, although she won't get here in time to do *us* any good, I'm afraid."

"He's gone into the yard for the car," said Keith, "and his mother won't know it isn't his voice on the 'phone if you keep yours low."

I stepped over to the 'phone and dialled Mrs. Bradley's number, and told her very quickly what had happened. I had finished long before the inspector came back. With him was the sergeant.

"Ah," said Mr. Seabrook, to us. "So you're still here? Thought you might have cut and run for it. You know what we want you for, I suppose?"

"Oh, yes," said Keith, cheekily. "To get your evidence for you."

The sergeant regarded us, and then scrutinized Keith in particular.

"And what do you mean by that, young man?" asked Mr. Seabrook sternly.

"Well, I see now that you've all known it was Mrs. Cockerton from the beginning, but you just couldn't pin enough on her to satisfy a jury," said Keith. "Whereas, now you know that this time we are her predestined victims, you propose to nab her in the act. I can't say I like the part we're cast for, but our lives are your responsibility, I suppose."

"This boy," said the sergeant, grinning, "would make a policeman, Mr. Seabrook."

"I shall make an Assistant Commissioner," said Keith.

A constable also came with us, and sat between us two boys on the back seat.

"If she's who we think she is," I heard the sergeant say to the inspector, who was driving, "I reckon we've got the Deptford murderer, Mr. Seabrook. The deaths in Creek Road, and down those cuts by the river, were the very spit of these, so Mr. Cosgrove from the Yard was saying the other day. We never thought of a woman. It took Mrs. Bradley to do that."

"Well, she did point out that these deaths were not the work of a Ripper," said Mr. Seabrook. "That is, they were not the work of an ordinary sex maniac. And that idea of spoiling the victims' looks—she saw the significance of that long before I did, I believe."

" Or me. By the way, Mr. Seabrook, beg pardon, but isn't it risky to bring these boys along to-night ? "

" There she is," said Mr. Seabrook suddenly, taking care not to answer the question.

" I see her," said I, for I was on his side of the car, and could see her out of my window. To my surprise, we flashed past her, making no attempt to slow down. She was just turning out of the Butts. We continued up Manor Road, and then took the slant to Orchard Road, a small thoroughfare connecting Manor Road with Field Lane. Back along Field Lane crept the car, and turned into the entrance to Layton Road, another long narrow street which led to Drum Lane.

Half-way along it was a footbridge leading over a branch line of the railway. Opposite this bridge the car drew up.

" Now, you boys," said Mr. Seabrook, " if you've got the pluck—and I hope you have—I want you to cross the footbridge, go along Hammer Alley, and so get into your own road by what our good lady will think is the route from Drum Lane. You'll be coming face to face with her, and she'll stop and talk to you— any old blarney will serve her purpose now. Don't be afraid, and don't worry. Just answer her, and go with her, and—well, we shall know what to do. Now, wait for a minute. I've timed this."

" Here, half a minute, Mr. Seabrook," protested the sergeant. He got out with us. The inspector, with the constable still in the back, turned the car, and, without a word, went back by the way we had come. We three stood at the foot of the steps, and, as the car turned the corner, the sergeant gave us a slight push, and up we went.

" Don't worry, boys," said the sergeant. " I don't like this, any more than you do, but I can see his point, and he's a fellow that'll make his way. Don't worry. I'll keep close. You've got nothing to worry about."

" Says you ! " said Keith, under his breath. It was the only indication he gave of his feelings. Having given vent to it, he stepped out boldly. I quickened my steps to keep up with him, my head singing as though someone had clouted it, my stomach turning over, and a strange and disconcerting weakness in my knees.

They had timed it well. We could see Mrs. Cockerton turning into our road by the Baths. It was extraordinary, this walking towards the woman who intended, we thought, to kill us. She had nothing in her hand, however, and, as we approached, we could hear her, in the deathly stillness of our sleeping street, singing softly to herself to the sound of her own hollow footfalls.

Keith slowed, and so did I. She saw us, stopped her singing, and hastened towards us.

" What made you leave me ? " she said. " I thought we were comrades, gentlemen."

" Got scared," said Keith, " along there. Didn't want to see the murderer, after all."

" No ? Ah, well, each to his taste. But, Mr. Innes, and Mr. Keith, we cannot stand talking in the middle of the road at this time of night. Perhaps you would be good enough to escort me to my lodging ? I have a little house, you know, not very far from the water. I am winding up my affairs before leaving this town."

She walked back by the way she had come. We walked beside her, one on either side, and chose the middle of the road on which to walk. Out of the corner of my eye I could see Mr. Seabrook's car drawn up in Field Lane to our right as we rounded the library bend.

I began to be assailed by doubts. She was offering us no harm. This might be her cunning, and probably was, but we had known her in her capacity as antique dealer for more than two years, and in her capacity as vile and iniquitous murderess for not more than a few brief hours. We had no proof whatever that she intended to kill us. I was still in a state of suspended panic, but the fairy-gold logic of childhood was reasserting itself, with ultimate hope of victory, in my mind.

We came to the Butts, and passed, still three abreast, down the moonlit centre of that wide and awful thoroughfare, the scene, in former times, of archery contests, election riots, at least one pitched battle of the Civil War and, it was said, of the burning of Protestant martyrs. At the bottom was the Boatmen's Institute, and, flanking it, the old millhouse, the miller's bridge, the backwater of the Bregant, and, beyond, the canal lock opposite the high street bridge. Forking from the path which carried the trespasser from the miller's bridge to the canal bank, was, as we knew, the narrow, bush-entangled path which led to the back of the *Pigeons*.

We came to the bottom of the Butts.

"Now, Mr. Keith," said Mrs. Cockerton. I strained my ears, but did not dare to look round. I thought I could hear the sound of footsteps in Bregant Close, a short lane connecting the Butts with Somerset Road. Help was at hand, and I took courage. "You first, Mr. Keith," said Mrs. Cockerton. "Then you, Mr. Simon Innes, and then I shall come in the rear under your protection."

"No," said Keith loudly. "Ladies first." He knew, as I did, that the victims were believed to have been caught from behind, a hand across their mouths and their heads pulled back to expose the throat for slitting.

I heard the footsteps coming closer. Mrs. Cockerton seemed to hear nothing.

"But, gentlemen," she began, "pray do fall in with my wishes. Surely any danger lies ahead. We cannot stand arguing here while the murderer escapes."

"I thought we were taking you home to your lodgings," said Keith.

Suddenly there was the sound of a car in the market square. It came up to the iron bar which divided the sidestreet of the market from the lower end of the Butts. The car door opened. Mrs. Cockerton had not answered Keith. She was listening. Two figures came running from the market. Something in me suddenly came to life. I forgot my fears. My knees took strength. My heart settled down in its place. I came to myself, remembered that I was a man and not the cheese in a trap, drew breath in my lungs, and shouted:

"Get out, Mrs. Cockerton, quick! Police! They're here!"

"Mr. Innes, you're a gentleman," said she.

From the shadows around the tall houses which enclosed the little street and its barrier ran policemen. From the opposite side came the inspector. Mrs. Cockerton picked up her skirts, and fled, like some discordant ghost at cockcrow, across the miller's bridge to the no-man's-land of the canal-side. Then there was a great splash as the policemen closed in on the bridge.

No one took any further notice of us. Mr. Seabrook and his men were attempting, in a body, to cross the bridge which was wide enough to take only one at a time.

Keith seized my arm.

"Come this way, Sim!" He led the way past the bar-gate into the market, and we darted between the *Anchor* public house and the back of the magistrates' courts. The coach entrance into the *Pigeons* inn was open. We ran across the cobbles under the archway, and went straight across the yard to the fence at the back.

I had understood the plan as soon as Keith formed it. By scaling the *Pigeons*' back fence and taking the hidden path between the bushes, we should reach the canal before the police could get there.

Nothing was of any use, however. Mrs. Cockerton was drowned. A policeman took us home. The inspector would not have us stay while they got her out of the water, and I am glad of it now.

Mr. Seabrook received some credit, but asked very soon to be transferred. It was thought wrong that he should have risked our lives in order to catch a murderer. Christina agreed, but our opinion was not canvassed.

Danny Taylor ran away with the Viccary girl, and is doing very well in Australia.

Christina is still unmarried. We found her at our house, with Mrs. Bradley, when we arrived in charge of the policeman. Mrs. Bradley looked yellower than ever, and Jack said, when she had gone, that he would not care to be in Mr. Seabrook's place when she told him what she thought of him. He added that, policeman or no policeman, he was going round in the morning to punch Mr. Seabrook on the nose, but Mr. Seabrook disarmed him by coming round, wet as he was, and very tired, to apologize. He said that he had taken all precautions, and was certain we could have come to no harm. He tried also to make it up with Christina, but she had her arm round Keith, and would not listen to a word.

I spent some time in trying to work out why Mrs. Cockerton had murdered the rag and bone man. It did not seem to me it was only the money. I had to ask Mrs. Bradley in the end. She said there was not much doubt that the rag and bone man's disappearance was necessary to Mrs. Cockerton's safety. She added that she had been unable to convince the police that Mrs. Cockerton had been the instigator of the murders, and had certainly committed some, if not all, of them. The police had fixed on Danny Taylor and the rag and bone man as the culprits until Danny produced his alibi for the murder of Marion Bridges, the stolen goods were found in Mrs. Cockerton's shop, and the rag and bone man was found in the copper.

The police took the view that Mrs. Cockerton had acted primarily as a receiver of stolen goods, but there seemed little doubt that she had picked up a good deal of information at the *Pigeons* over her glass of port or sherry, about the tight-rope walker's savings and the hush-money paid to Marion Bridges.

The antique shop sells ham and beef at a snack-bar counter now.

" The classic touch of Fritz Haarmaan of Hanover," said Mrs. Bradley, when she heard of it; but I have not the slightest idea what she meant by this, and perhaps it is just as well.

Virago now offers an exciting range of quality titles by both established and new authors. All of the books in this series are available from:

Little, Brown and Company (UK),
P.O. Box 11,
Falmouth,
Cornwall TR10 9EN.

Alternatively you may fax your order to the above address. Fax No. 01326 317444.

Payments can be made as follows: cheque, postal order (payable to Little, Brown and Company) or by credit cards, Visa/Access. Do not send cash or currency. UK customers and B.F.P.O.: please send a cheque or postal order (no currency) and allow £1.00 for postage and packing for the first book, plus 50p for the second book, plus 30p for each additional book up to a maximum charge of £3.00 (7 books plus).

Overseas customers including Ireland please allow £2.00 for postage and packing for the first book, plus £1.00 for the second book, plus 50p for each additional book.

NAME (Block Letters) ....

....

ADDRESS ....

....

....

☐ I enclose my remittance for ....

Number ⬚⬚⬚⬚⬚⬚⬚⬚⬚⬚⬚⬚⬚⬚⬚⬚

Card Expiry Date ⬚⬚⬚⬚